I'll Tell My Story

Sinmisola Ogúnyinka

DEDICATED to YOU.

Me?

Yes, you. Your struggles, your life, your faith. This is your story, and it's time for you to pick yourself up wherever you are now and start to fulfil God's purpose for your life.

Chapter 1

"Let's make love!"

Chloe jerked up from her lounging on her couch and flung her upper half body over to see why seven-year-old Irene would say that. She closed her eyes and breathed easy when she saw her twins were making shapes with plasticine on the carpeted floor of her living room beside her couch. Serena, the slower of the two mumbled her consent, and Chloe lay back. The doorbell rang, and she sighed. It should be the new physiotherapist expected to work with Yọde. She was tired of her husband's arrogance in the face of pain. It was no one's fault he had weak bones, fell down the stairs and now had to learn again how to walk at almost seventy.

Dara, her twins' nanny's voice interrupted her thoughts. "Madam, the doctor is here."

"Show him to the gym." Chloe sighed again. She ought to meet him in case she'd have to intercede in the nearest future but nothing in her body moved.

"He had a parcel for you," Dara said.

Chloe raised herself up. "A parcel? What sort of parcel?" Just as she asked, her eyes went to Dara's hands. The servant had a wrapped box in her hand. "That?"

"Yes, madam."

Chloe flared. She had enough of stupidity in her life. "Why will you take a parcel from a total stranger? Are you mad, Dara?"

"It's from DHL, ma. I think." Dara turned the box and stared at it too as though to confirm her words. "The doctor collected it. He came almost at the same time the delivery..."

"Return it to him! Since when did a guest start collecting our deliveries?" Chloe snapped. "Now! Idiot."

"Yes, ma. Thank you, ma." Dara curtseyed and briskly walked out of the living room.

Irene yelled. "You can't make love! Serena. Idiot!"

Chloe rolled her eyes. She could see Serena's face crumble in her mind's eye, followed by more of Irene's bullying, and then crying. She stood and followed Dara to the anteroom.

The man waiting was tall and had his back to Chloe. He had a presence she couldn't resist immediately.

Dara curtseyed. "Excuse me, sir. Madam said…"

"I'll take it from here, Dara," Chloe announced. "Good morning. I'm Chloe." She stretched her hand even before the man fully turned to her.

He hurriedly took her hand. Hers disappeared in it, warm huge rough, like a shield.

"I'm Dr. Elijah. Pleased to meet you, Chloe."

She liked his voice too. Deep, soothing. A warm feeling ran through her body. The aged sick man she was married to had better keep this one.

"Elijah. May I call you Elijah?" She arched an eyebrow and without waiting for him to respond, continued. "You are the third therapist we're getting. He's sick, I know but disgustingly annoying and rude."

Elijah smiled. "I'm sure I can handle that."

Chloe's stomach dropped. Cute, cute smile. Goodness, who would have imagined a physiotherapist would be so good-looking. Tall, not too dark, just right, with a big warm handshake and a sexy smile.

"You don't understand. Until you meet him. I just want to warn you ahead." She stole a glance at Dara and with that one, hard look, the servant knew to disappear. She left, holding on to the parcel. "Shall we sit for a minute?"

"Of course."

Chloe took one of the two high-backed fancy white chairs with the huge mirror in-between, facing the hallway to the front door. Her anteroom was super inadequately furnished but Chloe loved it so. When you walk into her house, you see this big room with nothing but the mirror and the two imposing seats.

"You definitely have his file and know the history of the accident?"

Elijah nodded. "I do."

"He was banging a teenage girl when he had the penile fracture." Chloe looked at him, he stared back. It made people uncomfortable when she did that. But she liked to. And this handsome man didn't seem to mind unless he was good at the gazing game too. "Penile fracture. I never heard of it before. He's sixty-eight, Elijah."

"I know."

Chloe stared into his eyes to his soul. "The stupid girl drove, trying to get him to the hospital. You know she's as good as dead? Head on collusion. If you see the Bentley. Gone."

"I didn't get details of this event." Elijah held her gaze. His eyes were not dark, but light, as though he had albino traits, but they were the most beautiful eyes Chloe had ever seen. Maybe he wore contacts. "Just that he was in an auto accident."

"His legs may never work again, but he is bent on using them. He was lucky. He comes home, discharged though his doctor was against it, and falls from the stairs. Stubborn cow." She giggled out of nowhere. "Penile fracture. God's judgement."

Elijah chuckled. "I hear it's one of the most painful injuries ever."

"I'll never know, Elijah." She stood. "Come. Let's meet my darling husband."

After dinner, and alone in her bedroom, ready to sleep, Chloe remembered the parcel Elijah supposedly brought. Seeing him, she'd totally forgotten about it. Gracious professional funny Elijah. *Hawt!* His meeting with Chief Yọde Pedro had gone as smoothly as ever.

The first thing her husband said to the therapist was, "Did she tell you I was f*cking a teenager when my cock broke? Stupid, she would have told you."

Elijah had laughed. "Pleased to meet you, Chief Pedro. Your legs look ready to run."

Ha! As though that should have snapped the dirty old man from his madness, but Elijah handled him well, like he said he could. She hoped he could. She was done and tired of this man and marriage, and his sickening sickness.

"Dara!"

"Yes, Madam." Dara near-screeched. She knocked and entered. "Ma?"

"The parcel you said the doctor brought with him; did you give him back when he was leaving?"

Dara curtseyed. "No, ma. I wanted to but I was with the twins outside when I saw his car zoom off."

"Dunce. Bring it."

"Yes, ma." Dara hurried off. She returned within minutes with the parcel.

Chloe sat at her dresser and applied her night cream on her face. "I wonder what it is. Does it say where it is from?"

"The sender's address is Lagos, ma. Somewhere on the mainland. Festac."

"Festac? I don't know anyone from Festac. And the doctor gave you. He didn't mention it to me." She sighed. "And look at me, I just forgot to mention it to him."

"He said the courier man brought it, and he only helped to bring it in," Dara said.

Chloe gasped. "Do you know you're very stupid, Dara. Why didn't you say that since morning? Open it, jare!" *Of course, Dara had said something about DHL*, Chloe thought.

"Yes, ma."

Dara carefully found the seal and tore the edges of the courier company's cardboard envelope. The content was in a thick brown envelope. Chloe stared hard at every move.

"It's a binder file, ma."

Chloe stood. "Binder file." She walked over and took the hard file and stared at the first loose sheet. "I'll tell my story...Bettina Jaja... Mum!" She frowned at Dara. "You can go."

"Yes, ma." Dara curtseyed and left.

Chloe marched to her bed and sat at the edge. The hard file contained several typed pages, a story. Her mother's. She closed it with a snap and pushed it aside and massaged her temples as she could feel a headache coming.

"I can't believe it." She lay on her back. Closed her eyes. "I can't believe you, Mum!"

Chapter 2

I MET MY HUSBAND *the night I think I might have gotten engaged to John.*

John and I had been "friends" for a while. I had a feeling he would propose soon, and it would be that night. We prayed and fasted for the day as we normally did once every week, and then he took me to a nice restaurant after which he wanted us to attend a program in one of the "happening" churches in town.

"A very anointed man of God is coming. I have been looking forward to when he will come to Oṣogbo!" John said excitedly. "He is so gifted. Blessed!"

I ~~know~~ knew John. When he was like that, nothing could stop him. I shrugged and accepted, though I was a bit tired and still had a night vigil for executive members as I was the sisters' coordinator at my campus fellowship. Afterall, it was a program, I loved programs, and serving God, and doing things for God, and I'd likely be wearing John's ring on my finger at the end of the day, and so I was ready to go with him.

We talked about everything over dinner as we usually did. I could talk to John about anything. I liked him as a person; diligent in his work as a federal civil service accountant, neat, tall, handsome man, soft-spoken, determined lover of God. I was just about to graduate from the university. The timing for a courtship for me was perfect.

But John did not propose. In fact, he talked so much about this anointed man of God, that I didn't think I wanted him to propose in such a gingered spiritual mood.

The program had started by the time we got to the venue. It was jam-packed. In my mind, I thought we would stand at the back, but John had made some arrangements earlier so we could sit close to the front where ministers from other churches sat. This was a youth meeting and I know John was friends with the youth pastor of the church.

Anyway, to cut out the boring stuff, the meeting went so well. The guest minister from Lagos, was a dashing young man named Pastor Love Jaja. He was of medium height, wore a very nice dark suit, and carried the crowd on eagle wings.

Several times, John jumped to his feet and with his face squeezed in concentration clasped his hands and lips, soaking in the word. And the word was strong. I had never heard anyone divide scriptures like Love Jaja.

After the message, Love Jaja walked back to his seat. The host minister hugged him and led him through a door out the front of the altar. To the office.

"I want to try and see him," John whispered in my ears. "I need this grace."

"No problem. I can wait outside for you."

John chuckled. "Of course not. Let's see him together."

I shrugged. "Hmm, okay."

"Just to let you know, I want to submit to him. I know he doesn't have a church, but I've been following him in the news for some time." John squeezed my hand. "Thank you, for coming with me."

I smiled. "Of course."

I loved this guy. He was just the perfect one for me. I had known for a while I would be with him. We had met through a mutual friend about six months earlier and ever since, we talked every day. John was just it for me.

Contrary to what I expected, we didn't have long to wait. It was very late already, about ten in the night before the meeting ended. A few people were in the waiting area in the pastor's office to see Love Jaja. John and me I joined them to wait. And then we were called in. If Love Jaja was older than John, it couldn't be more than a year in my thinking, I would later find out they were the same age, John older by a couple of months. But out of respect, John squatted.

Love Jaja chuckled. "Great man of God, please stand up. I'm only a youth." He pointed to a seat. "Sit down, please." He turned to look at me, and out of respect, I believe, I looked down. It was just an involuntary act. "Beautiful woman of God, please sit. Are you together?"

John nodded. "Yes, sir. She's. My friend."

Love leaned forward towards us. "What's your name, dear?"

I think John realized he couldn't be referring to him as "dear", so he answered for me. "Her name is Bettina."

"Beautiful. Beautiful." Love nodded. "And yours, sir."

"I am John. I have been listening to your tapes and CDs for so long. I'm sure I have heard them all." John shifted to the edge of his seat. "I am so blessed you have finally come to Oṣogbo."

Love nodded. "We thank God. We thank God."

"Huh, I just have a little seed for you, sir." John took out an envelope from his pocket and stretched it towards Love.

"Um, I'm sorry, but by principle, I don't take money or an offering, or honorarium," Love Jaja said. "But I want you to be blessed. Is this your church?"

John's mouth dropped open. "No. Sir."

"You can do one of two things. Give this offering to this church? Or give it to your church or pastor, either way, but don't take it back for yourself."

John nodded vigorously. "Yes, sir."

"Let's pray."

We all stood, and Love prayed. When he was done, he walked us to the door.

"Say, can you both come tomorrow to my hotel? I am holding an exclusive meeting with some young men and women in this city. I do this everywhere I go. Just to encourage and to share fellowship."

John nodded hard. "Yes, Pastor Love. Anytime."

Love shook John's hand. "Twelve noon. I'm at Sheraton. We'll be in the lobby." He looked at me. "Bettina."

I had never heard anyone call my name so softly, breathily, intimately. It's hard to describe. My throat went dry, I felt sweat cover my face, in between my thighs. His voice scratched the most sensitive parts of my body. Shame enveloped me. Nothing registered from then, and all I know was that we were in John's car, driving back to my campus, and he was speaking excitedly about Love, and the ministry and being a part of anything the man did, and how his principle of not taking money was the reason why God would bless him. It was endless. I heard it all, and I heard nothing. Only the wetness between my legs and my racing heart. I didn't remember my expectation for John's proposal, only the voice.

Love Jaja saying, "Bettina."

The meeting at Sheraton, Oṣogbo the following afternoon was indeed exclusive. I was determined to control my reactions and refused to look at Pastor Love. He ordered lunch for us, and another couple and shared his vision for the world. It was a great vision indeed. He said God had shown him the world, and that his voice would be heard, but he needed men and women. Scriptures punctuated every word he said, every phrase. I avoided his face, refused to contribute, or even murmur. After almost two hours, he invited us to Lagos. John of course, accepted eagerly.

"I'll be starting weekly night vigil meetings," Love said. "I will take care of your transportation and accommodation, feeding, everything."

"No, sir. In fact, as you mentioned the meeting, the Lord spoke to my mind to bankroll it," John said.

I couldn't believe my ears. Bankroll what? John was a civil servant. His monthly stipend hardly catered to his needs. But I knew my darling John was a giver and a man of faith. I wanted to challenge it but kept quiet. John would not appreciate such a confrontation.

Since I was close to graduating, my position in the campus fellowship was going to be filled, and my commitment would be reduced. And so, the following Friday after John closed from work, all four of us travelled in John's Nissan Sunny to Lagos from Oṣogbo. We lodged in a hotel in Ikeja. Two rooms, girls in one and the men in the other. I formed a friendship then, with the girl, Sunbọ. She was already engaged to her partner, Jide, and even planning their wedding at the time.

Every week, we travelled to Lagos. I don't know how John managed to pay our way and for everything else, but the night vigils were very powerful. I had never seen the raw power of God like that. When Love Jaja held the microphone to preach or teach, it was as though the spirit of God oozed off his mouth, and body. He carried such an anointing and a grace that made him super. We all respected him like our mini-god.

I didn't feel the emotion of that first day again, so I relaxed a bit. I blamed the devil for making me feel such a repulsive thing. It had never happened to me before. Such spontaneity of sexual energy! Not even with John.

Three weeks into our Lagos trips, Love said he wanted to talk to us, John, me, Sunbọ and Jide. He asked us to come to his house after the night vigil, so we didn't book a hotel because we could sleep before and after the vigil and then drive back. He lived in a three-bedroom apartment all by himself, though there were several people in the house when we got there, praying, preparing, you know, brethren stuff. John and Jide joined in the activity, but Sunbọ and I slept in the guest room.

I don't know how long I had slept but there was a knock on the door. It woke me. And I was alone on the double bed.

I called out. "Yes? Who is it?"

"It's me, Love."

I scrambled off the bed. "Come in, sir."

He entered and his gaze was fixed on me. "Sorry, if I woke you. John said you sing. And you cook. He told me you led sisters in your fellowship too. You're a natural leader." He smiled and walked to sit on the bed. "Come." He patted the space beside him. "Sit down. I have a favour to ask. If you don't mind."

My heart was beating so fast, I didn't know what had come over me. I glared at him, wondering why I was having this reaction again. He took my hand and pulled me to sit beside him.

"You're very pretty, you know that." He stared at my lips, and then caught my gaze. "Why has John not married you?"

"Huh. I."

"He's not as smart as he looks." He smiled. "I have guests coming over and they will spend the night. I've told John I'll get you back to Oṣogbo latest by Sunday evening."

I wanted to beat John. Why would he offer me up like that without my permission? I didn't even know what to believe any more. Did he love me? Ever since we met Love Jaja, John had talked about nothing but ministry. Of course, I knew he had passion and would one day become a pastor, and I wanted to be a pastor's wife. Pastor John's wife. But it never crossed my mind John would become that now.

I saw myself first, now as an accountant's wife. I'd finish my degree in estate management and get a job. We'd live quietly in Oṣogbo, continue to be committed in our church, him as a Sunday School teacher and me in the choir. I knew he listened to Love Jaja's messages, had them supplied to him by one of his friends who was also addicted but I never expected this kind of sold-out attitude.

"You're not saying anything," Love said softly.

I shrugged. "I guess I have to stay back."

"You don't want to." He searched my face. "Hmm?"

I looked away. "I'm just not prepared. I. I didn't prepare."

"Thank you." He stood. "I have a ministration tomorrow night and Sunday morning. I'd like you to sing for me when I come up on the altar."

"Huh! I. I. Can't. I'm. I."

Love chuckled. "John said you do the same for your pastor in your church. Why won't you do it for me?"

"I'm sorry sir. I don't even have anything to wear. I didn't know..."

"Don't worry. We'll go and buy you clothes tomorrow." He walked to the door and blew me a kiss. "Thank you."

Did he just blow me a kiss? Or was I seeing double?

The following morning, John, Sunbọ and Jide left. In the evening, Love's guests arrived. A couple he introduced as his spiritual mentors. I cooked dinner of jollof rice and fried fish with coleslaw, and then we took them to their hotel in Love's Benz. It meant I was going to spend the night alone with Love Jaja at his house. After that blown kiss, and the deceit of having guests stay overnight, I didn't even know what to do.

There was a ministration he had to attend. It gave me a little assurance he would not dare touch me and then go on the altar. I was one of those people who believed so much in the fear of God. That men of God feared God. With all the anointing on Love Jaja, he would not try to do anything. He would not sin. Fornicate. Make me fornicate.

We stopped at a shop in Ikeja and got two dresses for me and a pair of shoes. Then we returned to his house to prepare for the program.

It went well.

Everything turned out as I expected. As I prayed. Hoped. Begged God. The program was very powerful. People trooped out to give their lives to Christ and rededicate themselves, souls were saved with conviction and tears, demons shouted and left people, sicknesses disappeared, and he never once touched anybody. He just spoke the word. My fears for the night vanished. God ~~can~~ could not use a man this much and the man would do anything silly with me, or anyone for that matter.

The night was quiet. We got back and he went into his room. I slept like a baby in the guest room. The following morning, we went to church. The host pastor invited us to lunch. We returned to his house.

"I'll take you to Oṣogbo myself," Love said.

"I can take public transport, sir. I don't want to stress you."

He smiled. "I just need you to do one thing for me. I need a massage."

My mouth dropped open. I had never touched a man's body in my life. And vice versa. The highest with John was to hold my hands when we prayed prayer of agreement. A massage. We just got back from church and such a powerful meeting…I sang before he ministered, and many thanked me for it. A massage.

I glared at him, and he started to unbutton his shirt, right there in his parlour. I thought I should scream for him to stop! A massage. Never! I cannot give you a massage. I am a woman; you are a man. My Scripture Union background already had me thinking I was a sinner to have even agreed to sleep in his house, just two of us. A massage.

He groaned. "I feel so stiff."

Does he not know this is wrong? He didn't even look at me. Or he'd see the horror on my face. It was a sin to undress in front of a woman you were not married to. Even the one you are married to. He dropped his shirt on a chair and lay on his back on the couch. That was when he looked at me.

"Bettina?"

All through the ride to Oṣogbo, I could only feel the texture of his hard-hairy chest under my soft palm. He had moaned all through the ten or so minutes I massaged his chest and shoulders.

Chapter 3

"Mummy!"

Chloe opened first one eye, and then the other. Serena knelt in the bed beside her, tears streaming down her face. She wore a torn nightgown, drenched in sweat.

"Go back to bed. Or go to Dara." Chloe groaned. "Come on." She rolled on to her stomach.

Serena raised her voice and wept louder. Chloe, without turning or opening her eyes, lifted her hand high enough in the direction of the girl and pushed hard. Serena tumbled and hit the soft rug on the floor with a thud. Her wailing stopped abruptly but Chloe didn't stand to check if she was alright.

Chapter 4

Ọlayọde Pedro Jr, called OPJ by everyone, had his every meal in the massive white dining room Chief Yọde Pedro, his father, liked to entertain important guests in. It happened to be OPJ's favourite room in the house. He liked to use the huge white screen to watch movies, seated in one of the fancy dining chairs, eating freshly made popcorn. The chairs were not convenient for movie-watching and each time he watched a movie on the screen, he had to connect a cord to the multimedia processor, and then use an extension to the USB for his phone, still he liked it. His Mac Pro never worked with it. The screen itself, was placed there for business only because OPJ's father believed during dinner was the best time to showcase business.

However, OPJ liked this room for reasons best known to himself only, although the Pedro mansion had a mini theatre with state-of-the-art equipment for movie-watching.

Chloe walked into the white dining room, a maid in uniform called Alice with her, to prepare it for two expected guests coming in for dinner, and found OPJ in his pyjama, eating popcorn from a giant bowl, both his booted feet on the uncovered table. Chloe had good reason to take her expensive tableware with her each time the room was not in use by guests to avoid a scene like this, a grown man in pyjamas and boots at close to three in the afternoon.

She strolled to OPJ. "You need to go watch your movie somewhere else. Alice is setting the table."

OPJ arched one shaped eyebrow. "For who?"

Chloe shrugged. "Ask your father. They are his guests."

OPJ batted his eyes, but his response was intersected by a loud crash from his movie. "Boom!" He screamed. "D*mn! I knew they would blow it up. S*it!"

Chloe threw his feet off the table in one sudden sweep. "Get out. When I come back, this room should be ready." She turned to leave.

OPJ flew to his feet and grabbed her by the waist exchanging it for his popcorn bowl. Dozens of white puffs flew all over the marble floor. Chloe giggled hysterically and slapped off his hand.

"You like looking for my trouble." He bit her ear and she shrieked.

"Leave me, jọ! OPJ!" She wriggled but not with enough energy to get out of his hold.

"I'll get a broom," Alice hurried off before either could stop her.

The two players stepped on popcorn and slid. OPJ put himself between Chloe and the floor and she fell on him, both laughing so loud they couldn't have heard anyone enter the room.

"Ma!" Dara ran in with tears streaming down her face, screaming at the top of her voice. "Mummy! Please come!" She hopped on the balls of her feet as though the floor was on fire.

Chloe raised herself a bit and OPJ turned in the lady's direction. "What?" OPJ snapped.

"Serena, ma! She broke bottle. On Irene's head."

Chloe folded her hands in her laps, her lips tightly pressed together as she waited alone in the luxury lounge of Mildred Memorial Children's Hospital. Intermittently the ice machine released freshly frozen cubes with a chuckle-like sound that jolted her every time the sound was made. Once every ten seconds or so she thought.

Calli walked in carrying her two-year-old son, Victor, who was fast asleep in her arms. "I came as soon as I heard. How's she?" She laid the toddler on a small bed in the corner, designed exactly for that.

Chloe grunted at her younger sister. "Couldn't Idong take him for just a bit. Must you carry this boy everywhere you go?"

Calli hugged Chloe's neck and sat next to her. "Idong is with Daddy." As though that simple statement explained everything. And it did.

"She's in surgery. They said a few stitches would not do." Chloe threw her head back on the couch and stared at the suspended ceiling. "It shouldn't take long though."

"Pẹlẹ." Calli patted Chloe's cheek. "Goodness! Where did Serena learn that from?"

Chloe shrugged, her gaze fixed. "Does Idong know?"

"No."

"Good. He'll just tell Daddy. And I'm not ready for that now."

Calli rubbed the back of her head. "She'll be fine. Before anyone notices. That's the good thing about children."

Chloe dragged in a shuddering breath. "They said they had to scrape off all her hair."

Calli's hand flew to her mouth. "Oh! All that beautiful hair. Anyway, it will grow back."

The beautiful hair Chloe and Calli had, came from their mother, and Chloe's girls had inherited it too. Otherwise, the Jaja sisters looked different. Chloe had Mummy's sleek darker skin, beautiful big eyes, and shapely figure. Calli was more of Daddy's lighter brown skin, harder features, and a slender stature.

Calli smoothed back Chloe's hair from her face, natural wig with bangs covering all her forehead. "She'll be fine." She sighed. "And Serena?"

"I don't want to hear her name."

Calli shook her head. "Dara was hysterical when I got to your house, but she managed to say Serena broke the bottle and hit Irene more than once!"

Chloe shrugged. "Yeah. Four times actually. Each tore Irene's skin."

Calli gasped. "Lord Jesus!"

A middle-aged man in full scrubs and looking fresh from the theatre walked in. The two sisters stood.

He nodded. "She'll be fine."

Chloe slumped against Calli. "Ah!"

"Thank God!" Calli let out a huge breath. "Thank you, Doctor."

"I suggest you go home, get some rest, and come back later. She won't wake up for another four to five hours," the doctor said.

"Okay. Thanks." Chloe dropped back into her seat. "Thank you, Doctor."

"You're welcome. I'll see you later." He left.

"Can you get me a cup of strong coffee?" Chloe closed her eyes. "What time is it?"

"Sure." Calli walked to the coffee percolator. "It's almost seven o'clock."

"I'm not going anywhere." Chloe slid to her side on the couch. "I have to be here when she wakes up."

"I'll be here with you, Sis." Calli returned to the couch with a mug of coffee. "You have to sit up."

Chloe did. "Thank you." She took the coffee and sipped. "I hope this works."

"You need to rest." Calli sat beside her. "Meanwhile, guess who called me yesterday? Bettina Jaja, your mother."

"She's not your mother anymore, I reckon."

Calli smirked. "I let her talk. And when she was done, I hung up."

"What did she say?"

"Ask me if I know. I muted my end and was listening to music."

"She wasn't at your wedding." Chloe smirked. "That can never be forgiven."

"Do you want more coffee?" Calli looked at Chloe's half-full mug.

"I'm sorry. I know you don't like to talk about it." Chloe smiled. "No. The coffee makes me feel nausea."

"Let me take it to the sink then."

It gave Calli something to do and avoid the awkwardness brought on by the mention of her wedding. Chloe remembered her mother's book for the first time in days. She had no plans to read it, anyway, so why tell Calli about it.

"I wish her luck," Chloe mumbled.

Victor whimpered, and Calli went to attend to him.

Chapter 5

I WENT HOME ABOUT *thirty minutes journey from the outskirts of Oṣogbo city, to restock from my mother's pantry, something Maami and I both enjoyed. It was just two weeks to final exams, and I was very excited to be so close to graduating.*

As the first child in my family of three children - we had a set of twin boys but lost them to cholera when they were three years old - my mother and I were very close, like sisters. The twins were after me, and Maami used to say she feared I would die too. Then she had my two younger sisters one after the other: consolation for losing her twins.

Maami opened her pantry, which she locked with a padlock. "Because this our neighbourhood full of thief," she always said.

I grinned, as I did each time she brought it up. "A thief who goes into your pantry is hungry."

"I just buy this garri yesterday. It is very dry and sour. And I ask the butcher who live down the road to bring me some extra meat." She entered the small store. "Or you will not fry meat this time."

"I will. Ehh, Maami!" I laughed. "Do you have fufu?"

She giggled. "Trust me. I make it just last week. I wanted this Shaki girl, Baba Elero's daughter, to come turn it for you, but the girl na thief, and she allow hoodlum enter the house when she's around."

I wet my lips. "Please ask her to come, I don't have energy to pound fufu."

Maami shrugged. "No problem. Skola is so lazy! When you dey her age, you pound yam, fufu, turn amala, everything. She can do no more than fry egg!"

We chit-chatted as we measured dry foods into polythene bags. Intermittently, Maami would ask if I wanted more or not – rice, beans, and garri.

"Skola will fry the meat for you." Maami tucked in the last bag into a big raffia bag.

I gasped. "This looks too much o. I have less than a month left in school."

"Don't you have friend? That your boy who follow you around like a dog, will he not eat?" Maami slapped my shoulder. *"Hmm?"*

"Huh! Maami! Leave me."

"What's his name? John, abi?"

Skola, my sixteen-year-old sister walked in. *"The butcher is here, Maami! Ah Sister, I didn't know you were around."* She hugged me.

"I just came, Skola. And I'm even going back today."

"I can't wait to go into university too. And leave home," Skola said.

"Olodo!" Maami cursed. *"You think university is easy than pounding fufu. Lazy goat!"*

I laughed. *"Maami, leave her jare. You know how to harass someone."*

John picked me from home later in the evening after work and we returned to my campus together.

"I'm not coming to Lagos for a while," I told him in the car. *"Because of exam."*

He scoffed. *"Since when did exam become an excuse to not serve God?"*

"This is finals, shey you know. I want to read, and the travel time alone to Lagos is a lot."

"You cannot read in the car? Or are you the one driving?"

I shot him a surprise look. *"Read in the car? Heh! I can't believe you said that."*

"I can't believe you want to use exam as an excuse," he said. *"Especially now Pastor Love depends on you every weekend for praise and worship."*

"Which I find ridiculous. That sister who led praise worship before you and Pastor Love turned your attention to me, is still there. Redundant! Probably upset with me too," I said, already getting angry at him, which rarely happened. *"God forbid, if I fall sick, will the night vigils not continue?"*

"Why are you shouting at me, Bettina? What's wrong with you?"

In the past two months, John had been even more invested in Pastor Love's ministry, and I knew he would not be happy with my decision to step back during my exams. But I was not ready for the ups and downs of going to Lagos in the middle of my final exams, and sometimes having to sleep over. Giving Pastor Love a massage of his biceps. Could I tell John, and would he believe me?

A local dog ran across the road as we approached the busy part of town, and John pressed on the break, screeching!

I yelped. *"Ah, don't kill me o!"*

"Kill you? Why will you say that? Because I'm questioning your commitment?" He stole a quick glance at me. *"I don't understand you anymore, Tina!"*

He only called me Tina when he was confused or serious.

"I don't understand you too. When you wrote your final exams, didn't you take time off fellowship to concentrate?"

"I did not."

"Well, that's you."

He inhaled noisily. "Do you know how this will affect Pastor Love? He'll not be happy."

I snapped. "I don't care."

"Bettina Silas! You don't care about the things of God?" He drove into my campus. "I can't believe you just said that. You don't care about the move of God? Are you backsliding or what?"

Me? I was a church girl. My parents became born again when I was in secondary school and since then my whole family worshipped God in spirit and truth. I had been so invested in God. Backsliding because I didn't want to attend a night vigil in a particular ministry? I found John's words quite offensive.

John went into a long tale about how God had been using Pastor Love to heal people, as though I was not aware. When he got to the front of my hostel, I picked my bag and foodstuff, refused his help, and walked off though he called me back a few times.

How could I explain what I was going through to anyone?

For the next four weeks, John religiously showed up to take me to Lagos with him for the night vigil, and I promptly declined. To my amazement, he didn't want to discuss anything else. We had never had such a quarrel or disagreement about anything so serious. At this stage, I was weary of waiting for him to propose and guilt filled me each time I think about what went on between Pastor Love and I when no one was there. I had never had second thoughts about sharing anything happening in my life with John.

Exams finally ended and I was a graduate. John didn't even come to visit or help me pack from the hostel. The next time I saw him, two days after I returned home, was Friday afternoon, with Jide and Sunbọ in his car, ready to go to Lagos.

He honked, as he had done in the last four weeks. This time, I had an overnight bag.

"Oh, you're joining us today," John said.

I ignored him; my heart pained. "Good afternoon, Bro. Jide. Sister Sunbọ, hello."

The couple responded, and I got into the back seat with Sunbọ.

"How was your exam? I'm so happy you can join us again," Sunbọ said.

"Best exam of my life," I said. "I'm a graduate!"

"Congratulations." Jide smiled at me. He nudged John. "Bro. John, smile now! Are you not happy she can join us again? I will let out your secret now, how you miss her the last four weeks."

I waited for my "boyfriend" to respond but he only snickered, and we went on to talk about other things. It hurt that John was so cold to me just because of this. I couldn't even fathom it.

On this particular trip, Pastor Love was so excited to see me, and it was only then John became lively and joked with me. The ice at least was broken, and we had another powerful vigil. Instead of going to our hotel afterward, Pastor Love invited me to his house and asked the rest to pick me up on their way out later in the day. I struggled with the decision to refuse, but under the circumstances, I imagined John would get angry again. I told myself however, that if I was asked to give a massage, I was going to decline, and this time, I would confide this intimate act to John. His super-power Pastor Love had emotional issues, definitely.

When we got to Love's house, it was full. Brethren from the night vigil were everywhere, brothers and sisters milled about, talking, getting comfortable, reading the Bible, chatting. It was like a party. Previously, I knew after the vigil, some of the young men and women who worked closely with him came home to sleep or do meetings, but I'd never seen it so busy. There were people in his two extra rooms, and even his bedroom.

"Let's just sit somewhere and talk," he said. "No privacy."

I sighed inwardly. At least, he could never take his shirt off and ask me to massage him in the presence of all these people.

We sat at his six-sitter dining table, though three sisters sat there and seemed to be planning a feeding outreach.

"I wanted to talk to you." He stared at my face; his eyes intense. "How was your exam?"

"It went well, thank God." I couldn't help but smile. "I'm a graduate."

"You're so beautiful. Especially when you smile." He smiled. "Congratulations my dear."

"Thank you, sir."

"I really missed you. It's as if my air was taken from my nose." He sighed. "Each week, I stood outside waiting, hoping you'd be in John's car."

"I'm sorry, sir."

"I totally understand. Exams can be very demanding and confusing." He patted my cheek. "I'm just glad you're back."

The contact made me cringe. At least ten people were in this room and could have seen the gesture. I couldn't take my eyes away from the wall behind him, afraid everyone saw him touch me. Were there no boundaries?

"God is doing so much for us. Do you see the number of people coming? More people want to be trained and they just want to drink from this well. It's exciting," he said though I couldn't feel the energy in his words or demeanour. I had a feeling he wanted to talk about something else, not ministry.

He cupped one of my cheeks. "You know you are a part of me. This is our ministry."

I froze. "Pastor Love," I stammered.

"John is not going to propose to you. You know that don't you?"

I shrank and his hand knew to withdraw from my face, but he placed it on mine where I kept both on the table. I stole a glance at him and quickly looked away. His eyes glowed like someone on a strange fire. His hand on mine was suddenly cold, and I started feeling tension cover all of me.

"You are mine," he said, and he wasn't whispering either.

The three people seated on the other end of the table, with only one chair separating us could likely hear, not to speak of the young men and women in the room. Love didn't seem to care.

"I'm not even going to ask his permission. He's a figment of reality. Something that should be but is not and can never be." Love sighed. "Now that you're done with school, we can plan our future."

"I want to go for Youth Service, get a job in Oṣogbo when I return." I blurted the plans John had sanctioned before we met Pastor Love.

"That's before. We need to discuss this when there's less distraction in this house." He looked around. "This house is too small."

John lived in a one-bedroom apartment I was so eager to share with him. This was a three-bed. How could he say it was small? I was tempted to follow his gaze around the room, but my neck was stiff with fear and shame at the closeness we shared so publicly.

"We need a bigger house." He sighed. "Will you stay till Monday or Tuesday? We can go house hunting."

What? House hunting? No. I don't want to house-hunt with you, sir. "No, I'm sorry but my parents will expect me back today."

I needed to put my foot down here. I wasn't marrying Pastor Love or sharing a life with him. He had to understand that. Even if John wasn't the one, it wasn't Love either. Fine,

I was a little flattered such an anointed man liked me, but I totally disagreed with his audacious style.

"When you come next week, then. Prepare to stay a week."

No. But my lips were sealed, and I only stared at him.

"Come and get some rest." He pulled me up. "Come."

We walked to the guest room, hand in hand. People acted as though it was the most natural thing to see us in that way. There were at least six ladies fast asleep in the guest room. The other room had men. His room had two brothers.

"I'll ask them to use the second room."

Before I could stop him, he woke them, his two closest ministers, and asked them to use the second room. I prepared to stop him as soon as we were alone. It was inappropriate to touch each other so intimately, though he never touched me except for touching my cheek and hands just today. He never touched me previously.

"Sleep. Bro. John will soon come for you." He walked to the door and turned. "From today, our future starts. Call me daddy. I call you mummy."

Chapter 6

Mummy.

Even on my campus fellowship as the "mama" of the fellowship, I wasn't called "Mummy." The name stuck on me faster than lice on a child's head and longer than super glue. Even John started to call me Mummy. If Pastor Love had machinations for a whirlwind romance, he had me caught and entangled in it. There was no profession of love or proposal, and I was planning a wedding. Mine. He was feverish when he talked about it. He had a date, a design and I just seemed to tag along. The following week, we went house shopping, and we got a five-bedroom duplex on Thursday. Someone in the ministry offered to pay for the first year.

I expected Love to be excited, but he was not. I thought it was a fantastic thing to have a member of the ministry offer to pay for your accommodation, but it was a lesson I was learning about my "fiancé's" attitude to material wealth. He had no emotions attached. We returned to his house that evening and he asked to be left alone to prepare for the night vigil the following night. There were at least five of us in the house. I went into the guest room, where another sister was staying. She was a random member I couldn't remember her name. There were many people like this always in Love's house. In the early hours of the morning, someone knocked on our door. The other sister woke up and woke me.

"Pastor Love wants to see you," she said.

I was disoriented but not enough to fear why. My consolation was that there were people around. I hoped this was not for a massage.

I found him in the parlour, alone.

"Have you been kissed before?"

It was about four o'clock in the morning. He woke me up to find out about kissing?

"No." I folded my arms across my chest defensively.

"I don't want to kiss you now, but I will enjoy being your teacher." He blew me a kiss and nodded. "Go back to sleep."

Like someone under a spell, I did, my heart thudding, questioning what sort of relationship this was. After night vigil on Saturday morning, I returned to Oṣogbo on the ride with John, Sunbọ and Jide. But not before a very disturbing occurrence. After the night vigil, as usual, people returned to Love's house. I did as well, and with my friends. The men went into the second room, while Sunbọ went into the guest room. There were no other members of the ministry around, which was strange. Love excused me, and I went to his bedroom with him.

"I wanted to do this yesterday, but I couldn't." He panted. "I want you, Bettina. I want you badly."

I willed my feet to run but they disobeyed. "No. Please."

He frowned as though he didn't understand me, and then scoffed. "I'm not going to rape you. Never. I just want you to touch yourself."

I had never heard anything like that. "Touch myself."

"Yes." He went to sit on his bed. "Sit on the chair and touch yourself."

There was only a single couch in the room, and it looked like something that was brought in from the parlour, because it had the same upholstery.

"I don't know what you mean." I refused to acknowledge what I thought he meant. In the wake of a powerful night vigil? To masturbate?

He chuckled. "I thank you, my God, for a beautiful virgin! Mummy touch your body for me, please. Don't make me ask again."

I sat in the chair. I should have left. It was wrong, but I obliged him. I touched my breasts slowly, tentatively. I had never masturbated before, and definitely not before another human, but I knew all about it.

He moaned. "Slowly. Yes."

Within a month, I was giving instructions on how I wanted my sitting room decorated and arranging my bedroom. I think I did two sensible things. The first was to invite Sunbọ and Jide to stay whenever they were in Lagos. John invited himself. The second was to bring my younger sister, Alexandra, who was just twelve and in secondary school. Daddy immediately secured a spot for her in a very expensive and popular private school, against the following school session. Since we were not yet married, and school was still in session for Alexandra, we came only on weekends. She was my chaperon, a decency Daddy flouted sometimes, by holding my hand in my sister's presence. I was just glad he never asked for a massage.

"I don't believe in long courtship, Mummy. We need to get married within three months."

And I told my parents. I expected Maami to question such a swift decision, but she was probably just tired of John's silence too.

Whatever the case, with John still picking me up to Lagos, and Daddy bringing me back, Maami might have just kept her silence out of respect. She approved of Love, though. Who wouldn't? My fiancé had a way with words. It's as if he was permanently anointed with a word in season. I could never understand.

By the way, Sunbọ got married and got pregnant with her first child.

My family was a humble one. My father's father had moved from Akwa Ibom state at a very young age to be a houseboy in Ibadan, and later Oṣogbo. He returned home after many years of servitude, and no education, to marry my grandmother, who he brought back to Oṣogbo. My father and his five siblings followed the same path after primary school, and worked as a houseboy, watchman, gardener and later as a messenger in government offices.

Like his father, Baami married my illiterate mother, an Akwa Ibomite like him, who was at some point a housegirl, but Maami's business was food, and she sold "Mamaput" as a wife and mother. It was from this lifestyle they had me and sent me to school. I was the first university graduate in my family, and my parents were happy to see me succeed.

Love's family, on the other hand, was middle class. He had two married sisters and two single brothers. He was a middle child. His brothers lived with his parents in a nice neighbourhood in the suburbs of Lagos. His father was a retired surveyor and civil servant, while his mother was a retired teacher. I saw him sweep them off their feet about me too. He spoke with audacity, gave them a wedding date, and told them the role he wanted them to play. Simple and straight forward.

Where? How? How would I start to tell my mother Love was...sudden! He swept her off her feet the same way he did to everyone. The same tone Love used to command demons out of a person he used for me, my parents, and his family. I was consoled.

Masturbation continued every week. He never touched me, but we both touched ourselves. I convinced myself it was not fornication, and it was better than sinning like kissing or necking. But each time we did it, it became more intense. Daddy wanted me to make some sound too, he said it made a difference.

"Sound as if we're kissing," he said. "Like this." And he made the sound, and then moaned.

"Touch there. Down there."

I did.

"Take it off. Yes. Yes, please. Your bra too, please!"

I did.

We never kissed, we never touched, but if there was any other way to have sex without intercourse, this was it. If sin could be coded, this was it. I felt awful.

On the night before our wedding during our "testimony night", someone asked how we were able to keep ourselves, if we did.

Daddy laughed. "We kept ourselves. I never touched you, or did I?"

I smiled. "No, you never touched me."

"It's grace, brethren. It is a level of grace," Daddy said.

Chapter 7

CHLOE SAT IN IRENE'S hospital room and read through a user's manual for her new washing machine out of boredom because she never did any laundry. Her daughter slept peacefully. A nurse walked in with a small tray bearing Irene's medication.

"Good morning, Mrs. Pedro," the nurse said in a sing-song voice. "How are you today?"

"Good morning, Wunmi." Chloe shrugged. "I feel the same. Should I feel different?"

Nurse Wunmi smiled and checked Irene's vitals. "There's some good news. We go home today!"

"Home, hmm." Chloe snickered. "Advise me. What do I do with my evil twin? I just want to drive her to a far place and leave her by the roadside."

"Don't do that, ma. She's just a child."

Irene stirred awake and started to cry. "Mummy."

"She cries every morning when she wakes up. How do I deal with that?" Chloe sighed. "Maybe I should just abandon her here for you guys."

Nurse Wunmi arched an eyebrow. "If I didn't know you better, ma, I'll call social welfare officers." She tickled Irene's cheek. "Good morning, sweetheart. Doctor says you're going home today. Are we happy?"

Irene cried. "Mummy!"

"Don't scare my baby, jọ! Go home, wo?"

"Ma, you're just paranoid. They'll be fine. They're still babies." Nurse Wunmi smoothed her hand over Irene's bald head absently. "And the psychologist scheduled to see Serena is the best in Lagos."

Chloe tipped her head backwards. "When are we going home?"

"Doctor will be here before noon. As soon as he arrives, he will discharge you," Nurse Wunmi said. "Sweetie," she cooed to Irene's face and quietly administered the injection into the line already set on Irene's arm.

Irene screamed.

"It's not painful, darling," Wunmi said softly.

"I hope I don't have to do this at home." Chloe snapped. "I don't have the patience."

"Chief already hired a nurse to return home with you today. You didn't know, ma?"

"How will I know when he doesn't talk to me." Chloe clicked her tongue. "You know what happened to him, don't you? Everybody in Lagos knows."

"Mrs. Pedro!" Nurse Wunmi shook her head. "We thank God it wasn't worse."

Chloe scoffed. "Small girl, o. Fifteen or so."

Nurse Wunmi smiled and hurried out of the room. Chloe alternately flexed and curled her fingers into fists. *As if this one will not fall for Yọde if she had a chance*, she thought. Irene sobbed softly on the bed and Chloe glared at her. She wished she had a little sympathy for the girl, but she just couldn't summon it. She still hadn't been able to set her eyes on her quiet, but evil twin, Serena. She really needed to talk to Elijah about this. The man was a well of knowledge and she liked being in his company. Maybe a little too much.

Elijah clasped his hands under his chin because when he relaxed them on the table, Mrs. Chloe Pedro's hand tended to wander and caress them. She knew exactly how uncomfortable her flirting made him, and it gave her weird joy.

"I can't even look at her, Elijah." She sighed. "I've thought of several things. They said it's not good to allow twins to grow up together. It…"

"Who said that?"

Chloe shrugged. "I can't remember where I heard it from. I mean, I'm living the nightmare of it. Maybe I should send her to a boarding school."

"Have you thought of getting a psychologist for her?"

"That's why I'm talking to you. The hospital scheduled a psychologist but I'm not taking her if I have a say in that," Chloe said.

Elijah snickered. "I'm not a psychologist, Chloe."

"You are everything."

"Exactly. I know a little of a lot of things, but Serena needs expert help. If the hospital scheduled…"

Chloe laughed suddenly. "Do you know after breaking the bottle and jabbing her head severally, she was going to stab Irene in the stomach before they grabbed her off. At seven? Where did she learn that?"

"A good question for a great child psychologist. I can recommend a friend if you don't want the one at the hospital." He took his phone. "Take this number."

"Text it to me."

He punched on his phone. "Okay."

"Is he as sexy as you?"

Elijah arched an eyebrow. "And let you replace me? She's a woman."

Chloe laughed and tweaked his moustache. "You're so sweet."

"Give her a call. I'll send her a message as well." He wagged his finger. "Treat as urgent."

"I don't even know...you know...is this in her genes or what? I'm thinking this is what my mother could do!"

"Your mother?" Elijah gasped. "Why would you say that? I mean, we all probably..."

"No, my mother didn't have the species of wickedness anyone had. She was special."

Elijah leaned back. "In what way?"

"Talking about her depresses me."

"Maybe you need a counsellor too. Talk about your mother. It may help you understand Serena if you really think she has your mother's genes."

She pulled his locked hands away from under his chin. "You."

"I have a good listening ear, but I won't help you much."

"But you're helping Pedro. He thinks his thing will start working again." She giggled. "The big fool was asking me to come into his bedroom yesterday."

"Chloe."

"Hahaha! I told him to go online and find a minor." She widened her eyes until they gave her a wild look. "Disgusting old man."

"You always find a way to talk about this. I'm not interested in your sex life."

"Why? You should be. Don't you find me attractive?" Chloe winked.

Elijah shook his head.

Chloe stood abruptly. "I thought of dumping the evil twin at my mother's doorstep." She rubbed her hands together. "But I don't know where she lives."

Chapter 8

"I'd rather be married to a pastor than any other type of man. You ladies are lucky."

The woman, Ugo, sat with me, Sunbọ and a few of the women from the church we started shortly after I got married, just relaxing and chatting after church on Sunday, the way I have come to spend Sunday afternoon as Mrs. Bettina Jaja, Mummy, for short.

Sunbọ smiled. "A pastor is a man, like every other man."

"Why won't you say that when your husband is a man of God. Does he lose his temper?" The one called Antonia, who is also our chief usher, said.

"Of course, the fact that a man is used of God does not make him less human," I said. "Didn't you even read in the Bible about Moses and his temper?"

"Ah, Mummy, don't even go there. You of all people have no problem," Ugo shouted. "Your life is perfect."

Perfect. What a word to use for my life.

Sunbọ nodded. "I agree."

"You agree?" I exclaimed. "Ah, my sister has forsaken me."

Everyone laughed.

"I think Pastor Jide is the sweetest man on earth, and as Daddy's wife, my life is not perfect." I shrugged. "Of course, I agree it's been good."

"Of course, it must be good!" Abike, a quiet woman in the church laughed. "Some of us are praying to God to give us husband like Daddy or Pastor Jide."

Sunbọ rolled her eyes. "How did we even get into this conversation. Let's talk about children, please." We all laughed again.

"That reminds me, Sister Abike, what can I use for ring worm?" Ugo clasped her hand. "All my children are sharing it like Tom Tom."

I shook my head. "Tom Tom of all things."

"Shey, every sweet is Tom Tom for these children," Abike laughed. "First, make sure they don't share towels and bathing sponge."

From talking about children, we talked about food. Then fashion. Then Bible. Back to husbands.

"I wish my husband was even a teacher or a pastor," Ugo said. "This bank work that he comes home twelve midnight and leaves five in the morning. I am tired."

"Pastors do night vigil, and cast out demons from covens," Sunbọ said. "Are you ready for that? Plus fasting seven days, eleven days, and seventeen days dry!"

"Ewoo! A teacher then," Ugo said.

"Teachers strike and are not paid for months," Abike laughed.

Then the women left one after the other, and only Sunbọ and I remained, waiting for our husbands to be done with all the meeting after meeting, fellowship after fellowship... counselling after counselling.

"Jide wants to leave," Sunbọ said.

"Leave?" I raised an eyebrow. "Leave what?"

"Leave church. He thinks God is calling him to itinerary ministry."

"Aha, since when? Has he told Daddy?"

"I'm not happy with the decision." Sunbọ sighed. "What is the meaning of itinerary ministry? Is God not using you here?"

"Did you tell him?"

Sunbọ looked down at her hands for a second. "No, and I don't plan to."

"Why? You should."

"Hmm." Sunbọ scoffed. "Does Daddy allow you to discuss his decisions?" She stood. "Ever since my husband started submitting to your husband, he hasn't listened to anything I have to say. Total submission. Isn't that what Daddy teaches us?" She sighed. "Before we came here, Jide carried me along." She walked away.

I stared after her, unsure of what to say or do. She was right. Daddy never discussed anything with me. Not even the names we gave our first son, Adam. I don't like Bible names, especially the very direct ones. I ~~rub~~ rubbed my stomach. I'm expecting another child and thinking, ~~will~~ would he allow me to at least do a scan this time?

His short, sharp answers make me frustrated. What is it like, being married to a man who allows you to contribute to the matters of his life, and ministry and the church? A perfect life, right? Is the perfect life defined by a man of God who knows everything because he is the man of God and head of the house? Would John have been such a husband? I shook myself to keep in tune with my life. In all sincerity, I hardly think about John now. I love my husband. He provides for me. We never ~~fight~~ fought. Never. He makes love to me as though my body is a temple. Pure worship. And he loves his son like the world belongs to him. Our church is strong and growing, fast becoming one of the biggest in Lagos.

I now preach. Daddy made sure he shared his pulpit with me. A perfect life.

Really, if Pastor Jide feels God is calling him to something else, he owes no one an explanation. It is fair to carry his wife along, but her main responsibility is to support him in every way. That is what Daddy teaches us and practices in his own home. I have never felt entitled to any information. My husband is the head of the family, and he is the one God holds accountable.

I rub my head because all of this is tiring. Did I also notice Sunbọ accusing me or Daddy of her predicament? Or ~~*is was*~~ *is it my imagination? She's had been my best friend since we started coming for the night vigils. We told ourselves everything, even the silly details in our marriage. I was her chief bridesmaid at her wedding, and she was mine even though she was married and pregnant. Am I missing something?* ~~*Can*~~ *Could she suddenly turn on me and think my husband is the reason she's not having the sort of marriage she wants?*

"Sunbọ!" I raised my voice. "Sunbọ?"

She waved and shouted. "Don't worry. We'll talk later."

Two things filled my mind at the moment. We need to talk, and later may be late.

I hurried after her and caught her at her car. Our drivers normally ~~*took*~~ *take the children and house helps home with other cars after church so we can have our time with brethren – fellowship after fellowship.*

"Sunbọ. Aha. Talk to me, jọ. What is it? You know you can't hide anything from me." I put myself between her and her car. "Are you blaming me and Daddy for Pastor Jide's behaviour?"

Sunbọ sighed. "Mummy. I don't know."

I still can't get used to her of all people calling me Mummy but that is how my husband wants it and everyone complies. But I never let that stop our friendship. It is something I consciously work on because my mother once told me I should never discard my old friends when I begin to climb high in life. I'm glad Sunbọ has been climbing with me, though as a housewife, she has everything she needs. Pastor Jide takes good care of her, and Daddy takes good care of Pastor Jide.

"I'm pregnant. Again."

"Ehn!" I jerk back as though I have been hit. "Again?"

Sunbọ sighed. "Yes. So, I don't know anything anymore."

It's the fourth baby in four years. Number one is three years, number two is almost two, and the third is seven months old.

"You forget that we can't do family planning. I think God is kind to you. You have supernatural child spacing."

I ignored her jab. "Isn't there something you can do?"

Sunbọ looked pointedly at me. "Help people like us beg Daddy to allow some of us to do family planning." She pressed into me, so I am forced to step aside.

Sunbọ opened her car door and drove away.

I think that was just a bad day. Sunbọ and I are sweet together. Two days later, we were in our house, chatting as usual. Over the years, we had moved from the duplex to a bigger house. Daddy wanted us to have a place where many people could come and have accommodation if stranded, so, although my family was just three, and my sister Alexa, and two housemaids, we sometimes had up to ten people in addition. With so many people always in the house, Daddy did not allow me to cook or do any chores. My main duty was to do whatever he needed me to do, and doing chores, or keeping house was not included.

Daddy would keep the guest parlour private to us alone, though. And this is where I hosted Sunbọ. We both sat on the couch and drank juice. She wanted to apologize for her brash behaviour on Sunday and let me know that she had a discussion with Pastor Jide.

"He wants to join another church." Sunbọ shrugged. "But Daddy has offered him a branch church."

I exclaimed. "Really? That is very good. If all he wants is to be pastor-in-charge, then it is wonderful."

Sunbọ smiled. "That's it o! You know my husband will not talk straight. He will come from all angles."

I laughed. "And Daddy knows him well."

"Very well." She sighed. "So, at least, we're not going far. Daddy told him he will start a branch at Lekki."

"Wonderful! I am so happy for you." We laughed and hugged.

Sunbọ rubbed her stomach, though it wasn't showing yet. "The only problem now is this childbearing and rearing. My husband thinks sex is food. Breakfast, lunch, and dinner."

We both laughed aloud as Daddy walked in with one of his proteges, Pastor Oye, who had a small ministry in Ibadan.

Daddy arched an eyebrow. "You women of God are here?"

We both stood, as had become a custom in our church whenever Daddy walked into a room.

Sunbọ curtseyed. "Welcome, Daddy."

"Daddy, welcome." I greeted though he had been in the house all day to my knowledge. Just another tradition everyone had grown used to. Greet Daddy anytime you come across him at home or in church. On the street.

"Good evening, Pastor Sunbọ. Mummy." Daddy walked over to the other end of the large sitting room, where he could see us, but likely not hear us.

"Let me start going home. It's getting dark," Sunbọ said.

I walked Sunbọ to her car.

She snickered just before she got in. "Did you notice that Pastor Oye did not even greet us."

"Hmm, he's so full of himself. I don't bother myself anymore with people like them. Already see how he looks. God just called him to ministry o, when? Last year?"

"It's still shacking him. When the demons start flying all over, he will calm down," Sunbọ said.

We laughed and Sunbọ got into the car. "Please beg Daddy to allow us to use condom o, at least."

I covered my mouth. "Sunbọ! I don't know about that ooo!"

I was still smiling when I entered the sitting room to find Pastor Oye on his knees in front of Daddy, his head bowed. What a humbling picture of the same man we just described now, and I felt a little remorse.

Daddy snapped. "Mummy, excuse us!"

"I'm sorry, Daddy," I whispered.

I turned, feeling the humiliation to my toes. This ~~has~~ had happened before, but I just feel Daddy is under some pressure or there's a problem, or he wants to be alone. But it is very demeaning especially when he uses that harsh tone for me in the presence of visitors.

I have learned to understand and love my husband. He is a great man. He loves me and is very tender with me in our private times, but I also know he is a man under God's consistent influence...but when he snaps at two-year-old Adam, I feel shame. And fear. He expects too much from the little boy.

"You cannot be fingering little girls and expect me to be quiet," Daddy said. Then raised his voice. "Oye!"

"Daddy." I could hardly hear Pastor Oye's broken voice.

The statement halted me in my tracks as I walked through the corridor by the sitting room to our bedroom. Daddy said something and I could not hear it, so I pressed myself to the wall.

"She's sixteen. An elder's daughter. She only came to my house a few times and…"

"I don't want to hear your dirty details," Daddy said softly. "Stand up and clean your face. I don't want to hear about this kind of thing again."

"Thank you, Daddy."

"Return to Ibadan. Fix a meeting. I will come and preach and that should dampen all the clamouring."

"Ah, Daddy! Daddy, thank you."

"Go back to your ministry and behave yourself."

I hurried into our bedroom, shaking from head to toe. Adam was asleep in the adjoining room, and I went to check on him. My son hated sleeping alone in a big room but that is how Daddy believes it should be. I try to push the conversation I just heard from my mind. It didn't sit well with me that Daddy would just tell him to go and sin no more. But then, what would Jesus do?

It's at times like this I remember John. John would always ask, what will Jesus do?

NOTE: I am sorry about the errors in this chapter. Writing is not my best talent and I feel too depressed to edit at times.

Chapter 9

"I told Idong what happened."

Chloe jumped from her seat. "Why would you do that? You know he will tell Daddy and..."

"He did." Calli squirmed. "I'm sorry. He kept asking questions about where I went. He was persistent. I didn't know when it came out." She scratched her head.

"Oh my God, Calli, why are you such a dunce?"

"But it paid off. Daddy said you need some time off the twins, and wants you to bring them..."

"Never!"

"While you go on a cruise for a week or so."

Chloe gasped. "Daddy said that?"

Calli laughed. "Yes! I was surprised too. I thought he will be very angry."

"On a cruise to where? Which ship?" Calli started to speak but Chloe interrupted. "I'm not going on his ship."

Calli sighed. "That was what he suggested."

Chloe paced the cosy space between her seat and Calli's, the two white fancy chairs in her anteroom where she met Calli after she was told her sister was visiting. It wasn't lost on her Calli never tried to enter all the house in her brief and far-between visits.

Chloe snapped. "I'm so not going on a cruise on your father's ship."

"I suggested the Allure. He agreed," Calli said softly.

Chloe twitched. "The Allure is boring alone. And I'm not taking my penisless husband."

Calli winced. "I'm sorry, Chloe." She shrugged. "It was just a suggestion, you know."

OPJ chose that moment to come into the house from being out biking with his clubmates, dressed in a black leather jacket and trousers and carrying a black helmet.

"Hey, ladies!" He gave Chloe a peck on her cheek. "Callista Jaja! How are you?"

"That is Mrs. Calli Idong Asukwo to you. I'm fine, Ọlayọde," Calli said.

OPJ laughed. "The only woman on earth who calls me that. Hey, are you ladies on your way out?" He gave Calli a once-over. "If it's a party, give me a second to change."

Chloe sneered, followed by a bark of a laughter. "Calli was on her way home."

"As usual." OPJ snickered. "See you later, babes." He sauntered off into other parts of the house.

"You could take him on the cruise," Calli muttered.

"I don't fu...sleep with him, Calli, contrary to what you all think." Chloe squared her shoulders. "I'm going on a cruise for a week, I'm going with a man I can...huh, bed." She laughed.

"I can't stand his guts. I don't know how you live with such a slimy fellow." Calli shuddered. "So disrespectful. Giving you a peck. You're his father's wife!"

Chloe gasped, and then burst into laughter. "The most opinion I've ever heard you have about another human, Calli. You amaze me." She flung her hand in the direction OPJ just disappeared to. "Look at him. He's an imbecile. Forty? Forty-three and still living in his father's house. What do I look like to you?"

Calli stood. "I need to leave. Daddy said you should see him to discuss the treat he wants to give you."

Chloe scoffed. "I expected you to leave as soon as you came."

"I'll see you, Sis dearest." Calli pressed herself to Chloe in a one-sided hug. "Bye."

Chloe rolled her eyes all the way through the house to her bedroom, and then back to the dining room to have dinner alone.

Chloe walked into the lobby of the offices of Drs Elijah and Joyce Aina, Physiotherapist and Child Psychologist. The cool welcoming colours drew her in but seeing those two names on the signboard at the reception on the ground floor of the fifteen-floor building made her stomach turn. Her first instinct was to turn back, but she wanted to know what Elijah's wife looked like. Although, she had stalked the cool guy on social media, she still wanted to see for herself. So, she walked to the lift, pressed number six and rode up, uncomfortable about what this first visit could end up being.

At first sight, seeing Joyce clad in a simple floral dress, with a wide smile that diminished her chubby cheeks, and such bright eyes, Chloe hated the woman. And Elijah for deceiving her into thinking she was just a friend.

"It's so good to see you, Mrs. Pedro." Joyce stretched her hand for a handshake. "Where's Serena?"

Chloe ignored the hand and looked around the office. It had quite a space, a lounger, two single couches, a fluffy beanbag, all in calm, friendly colours, light shades of yellow, green, purple, blue, and pink. Against a white wall was a long table, the only part of the office that resembled a hospital. Joyce's desk was placed in a corner with only a chair, and a computer. Pushed against the desk on the other side were two kiddies' chairs. The rest of the office could be someone's playroom and parlour.

Joyce came to stand beside her. "Would you like to take a seat?"

"Yes, please. Not those baby chairs."

"Sure." Joyce walked to one of the single couches. "Please, make yourself comfortable. Tea, juice?"

"What I need now is a shot of whiskey, but I'd sue you if you could give me that." Chloe scoffed and sat on the edge of one of the couches. "I didn't bring the child you speak of. I haven't been able to set my eyes on her since the day she tried to kill my daughter." She heaved a heavy sigh. "I wanted to know if…well, first to meet you, and see if I would be hiring you. And, to know if someone else can bring this child."

Joyce sat on the second couch. "If you are unable to come with her, yes, her father could bring her."

"Her father is Elijah's patient." Chloe grimaced. "Don't tell me you don't know what happened to him. All of Lagos…"

"Oh, okay."

Chloe snapped. "Don't interrupt when I'm talking, please."

Both ladies were quiet for a moment.

"Her father can't bring her," Chloe said.

Joyce shrugged. "Huh, maybe your mother?"

"Why are you pretending you don't know about me, and my family, you b*tch?" Chloe scoffed again. "Or that Elijah hasn't filled you in with the little bits of my dirty details?"

"Huh, I'm sorry. I don't…"

Chloe stood. "F*ck you!" She strode to the door and turned. "You billed me for this session already, didn't you?"

Joyce stood. "I believe my secretary may have sent..."

"Elijah's secretary, you mean? You two work together, don't you?" Chloe raised her voice. "Did he tell you I was hitting on him, and hitting hard? Even in the presence of my husband?"

Joyce followed her to the door. "Calm down, Chloe. The whole world knows who you are, why do you make it harder for yourself by being mean?"

Chloe jerked the door open. "F*ck you!"

"You are the reason Serena tried to kill Irene! You swear at her, at them!" Joyce raised her voice to match Chloe's. "You spew so much hatred at your children and yourself, you reek of it."

A door Chloe hadn't noticed to the right side, opened, and Elijah stood by it. "Are you okay?"

Chloe licked her lips. "Your *friend*, was just giving me a lecture about how f*cked up my life is!"

Elijah waved at her. "Come over here, and sit down, Chloe. Let Joyce help Serena."

Chloe laughed. "I can't believe this. I can't believe you keep mentioning her name when I've told you not to. And you sent me to your wife, instead of a friend. Elijah! I can't believe you."

"Come here, Chloe. Come and sit." He turned to Joyce. "She won't leave. Have your one hour with her, okay?"

Joyce nodded. "Sure, but she's not my patient."

"Sure." Chloe threw her hands up and walked back to her seat. "Sure!"

Elijah winked at Joyce.

Joyce took a deep breath. "Tell me about Serena. Call her name."

Chloe yawned. "The evil twin. Aw, here we go."

Elijah stepped back into his part of the office and closed the door quietly.

Chapter 10

CHLOE WAS BORN IN the early hours of a Sunday morning. Daddy would normally not be anywhere away from church on Sunday, and definitely not in a hospital, but Chloe's birth was exceptional. He said God prompted him to be with me all through the process. He wasn't allowed in the delivery room, but he was by my side the second Chloe was handed over to me in our private ward. Elder Elizabeth, the sister who once used to lead praise worship during the night vigils back in the day, handled service that day. She still wasn't married though she was older than me but had been growing in the church as one of Daddy's main ministers.

My baby was the most beautiful thing on earth. Her skin was smooth, and she had a head full of dark curly hair. I couldn't stop staring at her. Neither did her father. I had thought Adam, who daily looked more like Daddy, was a beautiful baby, but nothing compared to this fresh, dark, soft bundle.

"Her name shall be called Chloe Ẹwaoluwa Jaja," Daddy said, staring at her.

I had never seen him so enthralled by anything. Not even when God did stupendous miracles, or someone gave us a brand-new Mercedes Benz E-class. Each morning when he woke up, and evening before he slept, Daddy would come to Chloe's cot and prophesy on her and pray on her. Things he never did for Adam. It infuriated me and set me off against my new baby.

Chapter 11

CHLOE CHEWED GUM AS she walked to the lobby before Daddy's private parlour. Two protocol officers stood by the door, one of them in a police uniform.

"Hi." She reached out to open the door.

"He's in a meeting, Ms. Chloe." The one not wearing a uniform, Deacon Goke, said.

Chloe shrugged. "So?" She opened the door and walked in, closing the door behind her.

Daddy sat in his favourite chair. Bishop Oye, Idong and two other ministers sat in conversation with him. Like the king Ahasuerus, he hated being interrupted and if he had not summoned you, you dared not come into his presence. Chloe walked straight to him, ignoring the other men, and went to kneel at his feet.

"Chloe." Daddy smiled. "I'm busy."

She caught Daddy's eyes and made a fake "pouty" face. "Me too."

The men laughed.

Daddy looked at Idong. "Excuse me. We'll resume after my daughter leaves." The men all bowed and left. "Now, tell me, what has Bettina been doing? Calli said she wrote a book? And gave her a copy?"

Chloe gasped. "Calli? That traitor. She told me she hasn't heard from her mother since."

"Have you?"

Chloe looked at her hands. "She sent me the book, but I threw it in the dustbin without reading it."

"My poor daughter! You didn't know what else to do with it." Daddy sighed. "I'll get a copy. Don't worry."

"Did Calli not give you her copy?"

"She said she threw it away too. But I know she's lying." Daddy moaned. "She just has too much of your mother in her."

Chloe pouted. "Her mother."

Daddy laughed. "I will get a copy. I want to know what Bettina thinks she can ever write."

Chloe sniffed. "Even if she writes, she can't sell it. It will just be as though she's trying to defend herself."

"She will sell it alright. My name will sell any day. But people know the truth." Daddy pulled her to sit beside him. "Now, tell me all about Irene and Serena. And then we can discuss the cruise you're going on."

Chloe hugged Daddy's neck. "Thank you, Daddy. I love you."

Chloe sat in Joyce's office, her lips pressed together, her eyes half-closed, though she heard every single thing being said, and knew every gesture, while Joyce explained the practices she'd been going through with the twins in the last one month of visits.

"I want to show you their drawings." Joyce took two drawing books from the top of her desk and opened the first one. "Irene. She's been drawing a lot of undefined images. When asked what they are, she talks about the hospital, and the nurses and injection."

Chloe hissed. "Because that's what she's had to pass through."

"Serena has been drawing a lot of flowers."

Chloe winced. "What does that even mean?"

"Usually children love to draw, and paint. The colours they use let you know what's on their minds. Irene's images were painted white and red and blue and black. Serena used only yellow and green and pink and purple..."

Chloe snapped. "Because those are the colours she's seeing in your office. She's visual, has no creativity like Irene."

"Those colours coupled with the flowers show she's in a happy place."

"A happy place?" Chloe's eyes bulged. "A happy place! She almost killed her sister three months ago. I haven't set my eyes on her since then."

Joyce's tone remained calm. "Where did you keep her?"

Chloe leaned back in her single couch. "In my BQ with her nanny."

"She's happy there."

"And so, she won't remain there!"

Joyce shook her head. "What's more important should be reuniting the sisters. They are so alike, yet so different. Irene hardly talks and Serena is very vocal."

Chloe arched an eyebrow. "The opposite, you mean?"

"No. Irene doesn't talk. Serena does. Irene curses."

"I know Irene sometimes says nasty things but she's the vocal twin. She says what's on her mind." Chloe sniggered. "A little too much in fact."

"That's not what I found. Serena told me she likes Dara…"

"That's the nanny she's been staying with."

"Makes sense." Joyce nodded. "Uncle OPJ likes me, and Mummy likes him. So, Mummy hates me and like Irene because Uncle OPJ does not like Mummy."

Chloe sat up. "What are you talking about?"

"I record all our sessions. I can play it for you. Hear Serena say so."

Chloe gasped. "What?"

"Irene refused to tell me about anyone in the house. She would just pick up her book and draw circles, and squares and paint them red."

"Irene is a chatterbox."

Joyce sighed. "I will like to continue seeing both separately for another month or so. Then I will hope to see them together."

"Look, Joyce." Chloe sat straight. "I don't have a problem paying you, but you don't seem to have a grasp on these girls. I mean. I don't know what your qualification is or how many years' experience you have, but you have my twins mixed and messed up." She stood. "Is Elijah available? I want to talk with him."

Joyce clasped her hands. "I don't have his schedule."

"Good day." Chloe stomped to the connecting door Elijah used the first day she was in Joyce's office. She turned the knob, but it didn't work.

"You'd have to use his front office," Joyce mumbled.

Chloe knocked on the door as though she didn't hear Joyce. She knocked again. "Elijah! Are you there? Open up, it's me. Chloe."

No answer came, and Chloe turned around and marched out of Joyce's office. She refused to acknowledge the brisk way Joyce scratched the hair at her temple, or the soft smile about her lips.

"That door opens to a corridor," Joyce said a moment before Chloe exited and slammed the door behind her.

Chapter 12

CALLISTA'S BIRTH FOLLOWED BY Benjamin's were sort of hurried. Daddy wanted us to be done with babies so I could get into ministry fully. The marriage ministry he had in mind was as a direct instruction from God. As usual, my husband ~~does~~ did everything according to divine leading. We started the marriage series on TV and in form of monthly devotional. I had a clear insight and was excited about it. Each month, we had a title we delved into in detail. Some months we had the same title but dissecting it from different angles. The marriage ministry was an utter success, just like everything else Daddy laid his mind to do. Sometimes I would stare at him in awe. People from all over the world watched the "Marriage series with Daddy and Mummy" and every month, hundreds of thousands of copies of the devotional with the same caption was sold. Other churches placed orders and used it for their congregations.

Before the marriage series, Daddy refused to have a TV programme, but after three months of being in it, a station handed over a whole channel to us. Like many things in my life as "Mummy", I did not know. Daddy walked into our bedroom one evening as I prepared to sleep.

"You need to start a prayer meeting with women. One that will go on the channel," he said.

I sat up. "On the channel?"

"Yes. We have a twenty-four-hour cable channel, and I have ordered everyone according to the wisdom from God, to create content. It is going to be the best Christian channel the world has seen. Though the prayer team are going to be there, I want women to pray." Daddy jabbed the air between us. "Right there."

"Wonderful, Daddy! A whole channel? Of course, we will pray. I will let the women know." I giggled. "Sister Sunbọ is very prayerful. I'm sure she will…"

"Sunbọ will not be involved. Talk to other women, and pastors' wives." With that, no question or discussion or explanation, Daddy walked out of the room.

I know my husband didn't explain a lot. If I wanted to know why Sunbọ would not be involved, I'd have to ask Sunbọ herself. It was late, and I didn't think it would be fair to bombard her with a message. Besides, it would be best to see her. So, I simply sent a message to ask when she would be home. Sunbọ had never worked as a married woman, so I knew her time was flexible, just like mine.

The following day, I went to Sunbọ's house. Her two older daughters, Bolu and Folu, had gone to school and only the baby, who was almost five, was at home with her. Pastor Jide was not home either.

"Why didn't Lolu go to school?" I asked when I saw the child asleep on the couch.

We hugged. "She had a little temperature. I just decided she should stay at home," Sunbọ said.

"She shouldn't be sick o." I walked over to the child. "I know Pastor Jide has prayed but let me pray too."

Sunbọ smirked. "Prayer cannot be too much."

"Yes, my sister."

After the prayer, Sunbọ offered me a drink, which I declined. I delved into the details of my visit. "That's why I say I need to ask you directly. Why would Daddy say you won't be involved?"

"Hmm." Sunbọ sighed. "Jide is no longer going to be a pastor. He wants to do itinerary. He told Daddy."

"But how does that affect you being on the women's prayer meeting?"

"Ah, Mummy. You and this your naïve way. We are not members of your church again. What will we be doing on the TV with you?" She laughed. "In fact, I can go back to calling you Sister Bettina. That Mummy thing gives me headache."

I laughed. "Kai! Sister Sunbọ. I don't even know whether to cry or what. You know you pray more than me. I want you on the prayer programme o."

"Unfortunately, that decision is not yours. Our husbands have decided."

"Let me try and talk to Daddy to…"

"Mbanu! No. Jide wants to disgrace himself. And I have finally decided to watch him go and crash."

"Ah, Sunbọ! How can you say that? Your husband is…"

"He's nothing but a man. And I don't even know if he hears from God anymore. I'm…" She drew in a sharp breath. "I'm just tired. Right now, I am looking for a job."

"A job? You are a pastor's wife. What will you be doing with a job when you have women's ministry and other duties?"

"Hmm. I am over all that, my sister. When my husband had regular income, I could do ministry. Now, we depend on honorarium to survive. I need to get a job." Sunbọ squared her shoulders. "In fact, I got an offer with a community bank in Oṣogbo. I'm just..."

"Ah, ah, ah! Wait a minute. When did all this start? You didn't even tell me anything going on. I know I've been a bit busy having Callista and then Ben coming soon after, but how can so much be going on and I don't know?"

"I'm sorry I didn't tell you. It hasn't been easy."

"Going to take up a job will not be an option. What about the children? And Pastor Jide?"

"He'll be fine. At least, you remember that time I went to Oṣogbo for about three months. He was visiting me then, and he will visit now."

"It's not the same. Then you went for a surgery. Now, you want to..."

"There's even something I've been wanting to tell you. Don't tell your husband o, please, before God," Sunbọ said.

"I won't tell, what is it?" I won't tell, as though I had much of a choice if the matter came up and Daddy asked me.

"I've been feeling guilty, and hmm, though I have asked God to forgive me." Sunbọ paused.

I pursed my lips. "What is it, Sister?"

"That time I went to Oṣogbo and stayed for three months, hmm? It wasn't appendicitis operation I went for. It was abortion, and to tie my tubes."

My mouth dropped open. "Ehn? Sister Sunbọ? You lied such a big lie like that?"

She shrugged. "What else will I do? Three babies in three years, and the fourth on the way. Jide must have sex every day, whether I'm in period or not. He doesn't use condom..."

I exclaimed. "But I told you to do the natural thing I do! Count your days..."

"Count what days? When my husband is like a dog in heat every day." She stood. "Wo, Bettina, you can never understand. At least now, five years, everybody has rested. Is it easy to be getting pregnant every year?"

I didn't know what to say. She had an abortion? A married woman, pastor's wife? How could she deceive her husband like that? What if he wanted more children? What was this world turning to? Was Pastor Jide deceived too, or he was an accomplice?

Sunbọ sighed. "I don't expect you to understand. Your husband is a perfect man. He also makes all the rules because they don't affect him or his wife."

Her words annoyed me. "Those rules are ordained by God. In His word. We are not to tamper with the temple of God."

"Oh, stop it, Bettina." She turned her back to me. "Anyway, I'm getting a job. I'm moving back to Oṣogbo. Let me try and get my sanity back."

"You're backsliding, Sister Sunbọ!" I gasped. "Ah, we have to pray for the devil not to get your soul."

It did not slip my notice that she had switched to calling me by my name directly. Something we both never did.

Chapter 13

"Mummy is going away for a few days with Uncle OPJ. Okay, darling?" Chloe kissed Irene's nose. She straightened and glared at Serena, who stood by the wall, beside Dara. "Be good."

OPJ sauntered to the waiting Jeep, a smirk on his face. "Let's get this party going, baby!"

Chloe wagged her finger. "Don't get into any fights. No name calling."

Serena folded her arms across her chest. "Take her with you!"

Chloe snickered. "Dara, if anything happens, I'll kill you."

Irene burst into tears. "I want to come with you, Mummy! Please don't leave me." She clutched Chloe's thigh.

"They will be fine, ma." Dara smiled. "Irene, come with me."

"No!" She pressed her face into Chloe's jean-leg. "No, Mummy. I want to go with you."

Chloe sighed. "Pack some of her clothes, Dara."

"Ma, she will be fine, I…"

Chloe sneered. "Are you mad?"

"Yes, ma." Dara held Serena's hand and walked back into the house.

"Come. And behave yourself." Chloe opened the door to sit beside OPJ at the back and pushed Irene inside.

OPJ gasped. "The heck?"

"She's coming with us." Chloe sighed again. "And don't say anything. You all are giving me a headache. Dara is packing her bag."

"On a cruise?" OPJ threw his head back. "She should just stay away from me."

Chloe scoffed. "She usually does, pedo."

OPJ squinted from the force of a grin. "She's my sister, duh!"

"Oh my, I usually forget. Then your father is the paedophile." She snickered. "He really is. How old are you? Forty? Fifty?"

"I should be Irene's father. If you hadn't gotten really greedy."

"You're stupid, OPJ. That's why you're not my daughter's father. Idiot."

"Is this how you'll be rude while we share a room on the ship?" OPJ arched an eyebrow. "Huh?"

Dara came out with a small suitcase. "I didn't know how many days, ma."

Chloe snapped. "Put it in the boot."

Dara did and the driver pulled off. Just before the Jeep got to the massive gate of the mansion, half a kilometre from the house, the driver stopped, and OPJ came out with Irene. The Jeep zoomed off.

Chapter 14

A MEMBER OF THE church gave Daddy a one-hectare piece of land with a five-bedroom duplex on it, and this is where we moved to, basically living in the middle of nowhere in a developing suburb of Lagos. Daddy acquired an additional fifty hectares of land next to the property where we lived, built a low fence to secure the enlarged property, and a higher one still only about four feet high to demarcate our house, and raised a temporary structure for our church. Daddy was sure we were about to build a city.

"Mummy!"

"Mummy!"

"Ma."

Left, right and centre, someone needed my attention.

Guests were coming to the church for a retreat from another ministry and I wanted to oversee everything along with the other pastors' and ministers' wives. This was going to be the beginning of our world-renowned camp meeting, but I didn't know this at the time. All Daddy told me was that we were going to host ministers from another church. The general overseer of the church had been someone who claimed he followed Daddy from the early days.

Well, we now had a big campground and Daddy prophetically named our house the Jaja Mansion even though it was just a five-bedroom duplex. The four feet fence though encircled such a huge portion of land and Daddy spoke constantly of seeing the building expanded so much we'd have different "wings" of the house. I knew he meant it because he never spoke empty words. The church building, which had been built on the grounds, too had lots of space for expansion and it was easier to have people come and fellowship, and worship, and serve.

Over the years, many people followed our church, and Daddy, though didn't believe God called him to branching, had two other satellite churches in Lagos. The one Pastor Jide used to oversee was now under a young man called Pastor Ọ̀emi, who was still a single man, and making great moves for God.

I had been trying to find a wife for Pastor Fẹmi for a while, and thought my Alexa would be a great fit, but Pastor Fẹmi didn't seem too interested in my sister. The other satellite church was where we had started at the beginning before we moved to the camp, and one Pastor Joseph was in charge.

The first day of the camp meeting started in the evening with a worship and deliverance service. Daddy ministered to all the ministers. Again, I marvelled at the work of God as people's pastors fell like packs of cards, demons shouting out of them.

"We are going to start fasting from now on. Until the end of the retreat," Daddy said as he wrapped up the service.

I could only think of all the food we had cooked for dinner that evening. Who would eat it all? Why didn't Daddy tell me the guests would need to fast? Of course, it may have been a sudden instruction from God but how was I to cope with this?

I hurried to the central kitchen where all the food were in coolers. The minister-in-charge of hospitality, Pastor Edwina, and some of the other female pastors followed me out.

My head pounded. "We need to share the food tonight. Who knows where we can take them to?"

What sort of a dilemma was this? Food prepared for two hundred people would now have to be distributed at such a short notice. I still needed to figure out how to share the other ingredients and vegetables specially bought for this occasion.

"We can go to motherless babies' home or hospital," Pastor Remi, Pastor Joseph's wife, said.

"Prison," Pastor Edwina said. "We can just leave it there."

"Ah, okay," I said. "Let's share all the food into three. And share ourselves into three too." I looked at Pastor Edwina. "Please get three drivers."

It was just about eight o'clock in the evening. Too late ideally to start going out, but that was what we did. We went with all the food, and some of the foodstuffs, and shared everything.

I did not get back until close to eleven o'clock. When I entered the house, it was all quiet. It was only then I realized I hadn't taken permission from Daddy before I left. I had only acted on the spur of the moment.

Daddy sat in the private parlour to our bedroom, clad in his pyjamas.

"Where are you coming from?"

"Hmm, Daddy, I am so sorry I left in a hurry." I curtseyed, as we all did to him. "It was the food..."

"Did I not know there was food before I called for a fast? Mummy?" He stared at me, his voice soft and gentle. "Mummy?"

I went on my knees. "I am sorry, Daddy, honestly..."

"Do you know you just incurred curses on your head? That food was meant for something else."

"Ah, Daddy, please. It's not like that. I was not..."

"Whatever befalls you is totally your fault." He walked into our bedroom, and gently closed the door.

Cold covered my body.

"Lord, please, mercy. Forgive me. Please, Lord. I am sorry." I wailed and rolled on the floor.

After several minutes, I stood. Fear still gripped my heart, but it was late, and I was tired, and whether I liked it or not, the judgement of God was on me and there was nothing I could do about it.

Chapter 15

THE CAMP MEETING LASTED *seven days and I tried to stay out of Daddy's way because I knew he was still angry with me. I showed up at every meeting as expected and did nothing brash again. Still, my husband ignored me and frowned every time he had cause to look my way. This attitude, or the fast, did not affect our sex life, though. At least, I had that. The joy that my husband loved my body and even if he disrespected and intimidated me otherwise, it gave me pleasure that I remained the woman in his heart. He never looked at any other woman, never insinuated interest or flirted or did anything inappropriate to the best of my knowledge.*

On the last day of the camp meeting, Daddy had me pack some of the remaining dry foodstuff for the pastors who came. When I was done, I walked to our house to do other things, and stumbled on a meeting. It was obvious I wasn't invited on purpose.

Daddy sat on his highchair in our guest parlour. The general overseer of the visiting church sat on a couch to one side, while several of his pastors knelt beside him. Before anyone saw me, I stepped back out on to the corridor. I hated to eavesdrop but over the years, it was the only way I got to know a lot of things about our church, about my husband. Even about my children, at times.

"You. Next," the G.O. said.

There was some silence, and then I heard a man's voice. He said, "We have eighteen parishes in our area."

"Eighteen plus twenty-five, Daddy."

Silence.

"You next."

Silence.

"I am a district pastor with sixty-two parishes. Four are oversees."

It went on for a little while and then the G.O said, "By divine instruction, Daddy, we have come to submit all."

I gasped. All those churches will be under us? It humbled me. I pressed myself to the wall, and thanked God for committing such a great work into our hands. It was expansion like nothing I knew. How would I cope. With only three churches, I had a hard time leading the women, and children's groups, which was what Daddy wanted me to do, besides our women's prayer programme and marriage series. I would rather be in the music ministry singing in the choir, but my husband knew where he wanted me to be.

I straightened. Daddy would not appreciate if I walked in now. I heard loud amens from the men inside and knew I needed to move away from there before I was discovered. My heart thudded. Who could I speak to, who would understand my position, my fears, my excitement? Only two people in the world understood me: Sunbọ and John, and both now lived so far away in Oṣogbo. Though they were just a call away, it wasn't the same. I missed my mother too. She always had something positive to say.

Maybe it was time to visit home. I have not seen my mother since Ben was born and she came to help. That was almost five years. It excited me. I would also visit Sunbọ who moved to Oṣogbo about two years earlier. John lived there too, but I had no plans to see him. Daddy should let me stay a week at least. I could take Ben with me if it would be too much of a problem leaving him, although we had more than enough people living in our house who always help to care for him.

Early the following morning, I told Daddy I wanted to visit my mother, since the camp meeting was over and there wasn't much to do. He gave me permission, to the glory of God. I packed a small suitcase, and Daddy gave me one of the drivers in church to take me to Oṣogbo with a plan to stay the week with me. I was elated. Before leaving Lagos, I entered Apọgbọn and Balogun markets, and stocked the boot of the car. God had blessed me with abundance, and I could only share with my family and friend.

Chapter 16

I DID NOT LIKE the way I found Sunbọ. She worked at a small private nursery and primary school as the principal, but her income barely paid their house rent. Pastor Jide was hardly at home. He travelled all over the country to preach but hardly ever gave anything to support Sunbọ and the children.

"He keeps saying things will get better, and I wonder when." Sunbọ sighed. "When will he come home to me and the children?"

"Look, one G.O. just handed over all their churches to us. Let Pastor Jide come and talk to Daddy. You don't have to live like this," I said. "Daddy can give Pastor Jide a church to…"

Sunbọ snickered. "That is a tale for another life. Jide does not want to serve any man. He wants to serve only God." She sighed. "And where is the God we are serving? I went back to our former church. Sometimes I get welfare to feed these children."

My heart broke. "Okay, you know what, at least, let me help. Every week, my store is stocked with orisirisi. You know how full the house is all the time, too many mouths to feed. Though, I am not in charge of my kitchen, I can always send something every month."

Sunbọ shook her head. "For how long?"

"Of course, forever. If need be, forever, please, my sister. My friend." My heart bled. I felt guilty. I totally forgot my friend all these months. "This is my responsibility. If the tables were turned, will you not help me?"

Sunbọ laughed. "If the tables were turned, will you accept my help, you this proud girl!" We both laughed.

"Ah, now I know I will accept your help. Table can turn anytime o!" I hugged her. "See, my spirit just made me bring things. I entered the market without even knowing why."

Sunbọ was truly surprised I brought milk, milo, juice, rice, beans, yam, sugar, toilet roll, bathing soap and some nice fabrics for her. I knew, with my level of comfort, I could take over maintaining her and her three children, but I only needed to start from somewhere. At least, they would not need to buy food.

"Thank you so much, my sister. God bless you," Sunbọ said with tears in her eyes. "I love you."

It was rare for anyone to say this to me. Well, with the way Sunbọ said it. People who called me Mummy, virtually everyone I knew, always told me they love me, but I had a sad feeling it was all for who I was. How dare you not love Mummy? Daddy would say. This felt different. It was genuine.

"So, tell me everything that has happened since I left," Sunbọ said.

"Hmm, every day something is happening. Where do I start from?" I sighed. "Daddy and church is all I do. Busy busy busy."

"So, how are the children, anyway? At least, you have time for them."

I covered my face. "I am guilty."

"Ah, you must have time for your children. I'm even surprised you left them for this trip," Sunbọ said.

"Daddy has the best hands in children's church take care of them. In fact, our minister in charge of children ministry comes to the house regularly..."

"Is she their mother?"

"He. A man."

Sunbọ raised her hands to her head. "Haba! Sis. Bettina! You should know better. Don't you have a certain time you take care of them every day?"

My heart beat faster. Some weeks, I didn't see my children more than once a week. Daddy ensured he did the devotion with them daily, and sometimes looked into their homework after school, but I was always so busy with one thing or the other. My husband kept me fully occupied with ministry, sometimes I didn't have time for myself. Since we got married, all I did was whatever he assigned.

"We do devotion..."

"O ti! Bettina, no! Devotion how?" Sunbọ howled. "Every day, you need to talk to your children. When they come back from school, talk to them. Before they sleep at night, when they wake up. That's how you will do nothing, those girls will not know how to cook, keep home!"

"Ehn, cook! Daddy does not want his children doing chores o!" I smirked. "In the morning, they wake up and leave for school by six-thirty. I am still sleeping. When they return, I'm in the studio recording or listening to the edited something, until around ten-eleven when they are already asleep." I could see what she meant but how was I to wiggle out of all the work my husband expected me to oversee. "Sometimes I don't close my eyes until 2am!"

"There is a problem o. You are first a mother before a studio something o," Sunbọ said. "Can't other people do studio?"

"Hmm, you are right. Thinking about it, Daddy dumps everything on me. He is freer than I am. How is my own like that?"

"Good question, my sister. Tomorrow, those children will not want to hear about studio. The question will be where were you when I needed you?" Sunbọ said.

Long after I left her and got to my mother's house, I couldn't shake off Sunbọ's voice from my head. She was very right. Adam was twelve, Chloe nine plus, Calli seven and Ben almost six. I didn't know what my children liked or did not like. Whenever they needed anything, other people were sent to get it. Daddy would say we had people; why were we not using them?

"They will be blessed," my husband would say. "You are robbing them of their blessing when you don't let them use their gifts."

And so, someone cooked for us, cleaned for us, shopped for us, drove us around, did our laundry, took my children out for recreation, did their homework, took them out to parties they were invited to. Someone ensured they went to bed on time. People. We had people for everything. People around me in my house, in my family in my brain! I was tired.

"You look worried," Maami said when I returned from Sunbọ's. "Is your friend okay?"

"Sunbọ is coping, though she's not in the best place but..." I shrugged. "My problem is not Sunbọ. It's Daddy."

Maami sat down on the lone sofa in the sitting room. "Your husband?"

"Yes." I dropped my bag and sat with her. "My husband."

"What is the problem?"

Maami's simple question just overwhelmed me. Everything was the problem, and I never even saw this. My parents lived in the same old rental they had always lived since I grew up, and I had so much at my disposal, yet, I couldn't see beyond my nose, as they say. Why were my parents still in this house? Daddy sent them a stipend every month, but what about get them better accommodation? I had no say in even this.

I burst into tears. "I am tired, Maami!"

It was all I could say. I had never felt so stifled. The reality of my being had never been so obvious to me. I wanted to run away from my life. How could I have been so carried away from my own existence. Who could even understand? Everyone saw me as the chosen one, the lucky one. Married to almighty Love Jaja! Thirteen years of marriage and I was lost to myself. I needed a break. Not for one week like this, but for a year. I needed time to recalibrate, to find who I was and be who I was supposed to be. No one would be able to understand me or what I was going through. Every woman around me thought I was blessed beyond any curse.

My mother's next words confirmed my frustrations. "He beat you?"

"No. Never," I stuttered. "No."

"Ah, thank God. Then you should be grateful my daughter. Ile ọkọ, ile ẹkọ." Maami sighed.

Ile ọkọ, ile ẹkọ. I didn't want to accept this as a good answer. The verbatim translated to "a husband's house, a house of lessons" but what lessons was I learning when my husband had totally taken control of my mind and my life. I was like a robot. How did I get here? Bettina Silas, who as a sisters' coordinator mentored young women to be strong and independent, like Deborah, taking the lead in their homes and families; like the virtuous woman of the book of Proverbs, hard-and-smart-working...where was that brave, spiritual woman?

I looked at Maami, and thought what could she ever offer me in the way of marital advice? She had only my father, who stopped working due to a disability before I got married. The family leaned on my mother's business until after Daddy married me and started sending them money. Enough money to sustain them and a little to spare. What could my mother ever think was my problem?

I sniffed. "I know, Maami. It is well." I smiled for her, but I knew what I had to do.

Take my life back.

Chapter 17

THE GIRL CHIEF PEDRO was with on the night of the accident died, and her parents came to the mansion ranting and raving and wailing. She was just fifteen years old. Chloe returned from her one-man-one-week cruise on her father's luxury boat, feeling refreshed, only to come and face this. The girl's parents sat outside the door and refused to go inside on Chief's invitation, eat or drink.

Chloe stomped into Chief's private parlour, where he sat alone on his wheelchair, while OPJ, clad in pyjamas in the middle of the afternoon, leaned against the wall and stared into space.

"You have to call the police, Yọde," Chloe said. "They are messing up my garden."

"Why don't you call them yourself," Chief said.

Chloe shouted. "Then give them money. Send them away."

OPJ gasped. "Their daughter just died, Chloe, don't you feel?"

"Feel. Feel what? Feel the pain I went through when I heard what my husband was doing with their daughter?" Chloe snapped. "Is this what you choose to sympathize with, OPJ?"

Chief Pedro shouted. "Get out of my sitting room, Chloe!"

Chloe stepped back as though she had been hit. "That aggression should be for them, not me."

"Get her out of my house, Junior," Chief said. "I've put up with enough."

Chloe glared at Chief. "Meaning?"

"Meaning my dad doesn't want you anymore." OPJ came to her and invaded her personal space. "Come on." He grabbed her upper arm.

"Let go of me, OPJ. Are you okay?" Chloe snapped. "I'm not going anywhere. This is my house too."

"Since when?" OPJ laughed. "Come on, let's go." He tightened his hold on her arm and dragged her along. "You should know Dad is tired of you. As I am!"

"Make sure she doesn't take any of the gold or diamonds," Chief said. "Only her clothes."

Chloe shrieked. "Let go of me, you imbecile!"

She struggled but OPJ's grip was firm. Chloe never imagined OPJ was so strong. He did build his muscles at the gym to meet up with how his fellow bikers looked, but never had he used this kind of strength on her. He dragged her through the house to her room.

"Pack what is yours, and get out," OPJ said. He flung her on to the bed and went to stand by the door.

"You are stupid to talk to me like that." Chloe stood and headed towards OPJ.

When she got to him, he dealt her a hard slap that sent her reeling across the room and on to the floor in a corner.

She screamed and clutched her face. "You bastard."

OPJ walked to her wardrobe and found a leather belt. Before Chloe could realize what he was about and run, he trapped her to the corner and whipped her until she stopped screaming.

"See Chloe to her old room," was all Daddy said when a nurse from the church helped her to the Jaja Mansion.

"My name is Debbie," the nurse said. "And I will be helping you."

"I don't need your f*cking help," Chloe said.

She couldn't walk on her own and based off of Daddy's ban on wheelchairs in the camp or his house, Nurse Debbie had to help Chloe to walk.

"You know Daddy must not hear curse word in this house, or he will send you back to where they beat you up like this," Nurse Debbie said softly though Chloe clearly heard the tinge of contempt in her voice.

"No one can send me back to anywhere!" Chloe shouted. "I'm in my father's house."

Debbie helped her up the stairs to her old room, which at one time was one of five rooms but now in the east wing of the mansion and one of thirty rooms.

"We thank God for fathers." Debbie lay Chloe on the bed. "You have medication to take."

Daddy walked in with Idong and two other ministers, just as Debbie straightened to get the medication. "Leave us, we are going to pray for her."

"Yes, Daddy." Nurse Debbie curtseyed and left.

"I don't need prayer, Daddy. I want you to deal with Chief Pedro and his useless son. And I want Irene to come and stay here." Chloe cried. "She doesn't belong in that horrible house."

Daddy nodded at one of the ministers. "Go ahead."

One after the other, the men prayed over her. The last Chloe remembered was Daddy praying. She woke up ten hours later without a single hurt or pain in her body.

Chapter 18

My routine did not change.

When I got back from Oṣogbo, Daddy had other responsibilities for me. We now had over four hundred churches to oversee. Daddy wanted me to coordinate all the women groups and children's groups up to twenty years old. To do this, he wanted me to fix meetings. I did as my husband ordered. It was as though he was an oracle. Anything he uttered from his mouth became law. He spoke, and I obeyed. Everything about identity was lost. Anything about waking up to talk to children disappeared.

In my quiet moments, I remembered my resolve but courage to face my husband failed me. He never used force. Just a word, a phrase, a sentence, and we were all doing what he wanted. And why not? Wind and waves obeyed Love Jaja. Sicknesses disappeared at the mention of the name of Jesus. Dead were raised without fanfare. It was taboo to enter the camp, not to talk of the sanctuary, in a wheelchair or with crutches. No one was permitted to commit sin in camp and at the mansion. Miracles were a norm where Daddy was. He never had to shout. He only commanded. Who was I to then claim I wanted my life? What life? And so, I continued according to the pace my husband set for my life.

We had people begin to buy property and build on the camp and as more people came, we acquired more land. With the new number of members, stewards, ministers and pastors under our watch, my role as Mother-in-Israel increased and I naturally became a part of a certain set of pastors' wives. Daddy encouraged me to be a part. He wanted me to understand what it meant to lead multiple thousands of people and to carry myself as a leader.

The first meeting I had with some of these other ladies was really a surprise to me. It was a pastors' wives meeting but when I got to the venue, which was a popular five-star hotel, and was led to a very beautiful conference room, I knew then it was not an ordinary meeting but a gathering of the high class. Suddenly I realized I was now a part of an elite group. A caucus of sorts. The women all had someone carrying their bags. Some had more than one. I was the only one who walked in alone.

I found a seat and one of the pastors' wives walked up to a stylish podium. She was the wife of one of the trendiest pastors in town and everyone knew her as a fashion leader.

"Good evening, ladies." She smiled. "All the assistants should please excuse us. Thank you."

The PAs, and assistants left, and the coordinator proceeded to introduce herself and ask us to do the same. We all did. I later understand this was a culture for the sake of new members but for some meetings we would not have a new member but would still all make introductions. I had never been in a meeting with such important religious leaders. I felt like a little girl, though by age, I was older than some of them.

The meeting proceeded with prayer, the word, and some deliberations and Q & A, then light refreshments was served. We were encouraged to walk up to people we didn't know, and two ladies walked to me.

"Hi," one said. "I am Pastor Sharon."

"I am Reverend Faith," the other said.

"I am..." I wasn't used to introducing myself. Mummy, I was going to say, because Daddy never ordained me anything. But that would be ludicrous. "Sister Bettina Jaja."

"Huh." Pastor Sharon laughed. "Pastor Bettina, you mean. I watch your program with your husband once in a while."

"Thank you," I smiled.

"You have time to watch TV, Pastor Sharon? How? No offense to you, my dear," Reverend Faith said to me. "But I don't have a single breathing moment to do anything. Our people out there think being a pastor's wife is yam."

"And beans. Hmm. I just take off and do what I like. My husband has come to just agree with me that Mama has a life and must live it," Pastor Sharon said.

I loved her immediately. She seemed easier to relate with.

"What about you, Pastor Bettina? I understand your church is now very big." Reverend Faith touched my hand. "Do you know how many members you have now?"

It was an uncomfortable question for me. I shrugged. "I haven't even gotten to know how many churches we have."

Pastor Sharon laughed. "If I say that kind of thing to my husband, he gets so upset. For goodness's sake, how will I know how many churches?"

"Ah, aren't you lucky? I am in charge of all the missions, so I have the numbers on my fingertips." Reverend Faith groaned. "But what a joy it is to serve and see people blessed every day."

"Indeed, God is faithful," Pastor Sharon said.

"He is," I mumbled.

The conversations about ministry continued until I started feeling choked. When the first two ladies moved on to other people, others came to me.

I met a big pastor's wife who said she was not involved in her husband's church and was only wife and mother. "I dress up and look pretty for him," she said.

I met another who seemed to be the head of the ministry even though people saw her husband in front. "He can't peach a full message if his life depends on it," she said.

One thing that resonated though, was that we did not have a single down-to-earth conversation. I first thought it was because I was new, but this meeting held every quarter, and soon I found there were caucuses and I got sucked into one with Pastor Sharon and Reverend Faith. Soon, I made the rounds too and made small talk. We discussed as though church, ministry, husbands, and children were only about good things. No one seemed to have any problems at all. Their husbands were perfect. They were perfect. No one had any struggles. Some came to show off new churches, new jewellery, new cars.

We shared the word and prayed but nothing seemed authentic or real to me. Not like the way I could speak to Sunbọ and she to me. Well, I concluded these meetings, contrary to what they were created for – fellowship and bonding – was just to know whose level was where, and to compete. Unfortunately.

Every month I sent money to Sunbọ for her upkeep and to help with rent, and she remained grateful to me. I asked if Pastor Jide was going to come back to our ministry, and she kept telling me he would, but he didn't.

One day, I got the best call of my life from Sunbọ. She sounded so excited. I was in the middle of a leaders' meeting, but I just had to excuse myself because of how my friend sounded.

"Sister Sunbọ! What is happening? This one you have called almost five times in ten minutes," I said. "I am in a meeting..."

She laughed. "Ah, let me not disturb you. I will call back."

"No o. I have picked up already, and the first thing you did was laugh so I must hear you out."

"Jide. It's Jide. He came home early this morning with a fat cheque," she said.

For a minute, I wanted to hiss, or say something disgusting. That was it? All this excitement was about money?

"A fat cheque?"

"You know, the honorarium he got. It was really good, and they even want him to preach in some churches oversees. All-expense paid."

Okay. I could relate with the joy a little. "Wow!" I said. "I am so happy for you. This is really good news."

"I wanted to thank you for helping us through all of these stressful months. It is as if your gift made room for us." She laughed. "How fantastic."

"My life has been tremendously blessed too, Sunbọ. This is great news. I am happy for you."

"Jide just wants to travel, and now it is beginning to happen, hallelujah!"

"Are you going to be traveling with him?"

"No o. Heh. I can't leave the children. Who will stay with them?"

I drew my words out. "It's true. You are all alone." The exact opposite of me.

"All alone." Sunbọ sighed. "Well, I just couldn't keep the news. I had to tell you."

"Thanks for sharing this great testimony. You have made my day," I said. I did feel really happy for her.

I had been sustaining her for seven months, and it didn't feel like anything special, but with this call, I realized how much the situation affected my friend. She must have been far from happy taking alms from me.

Chapter 19

SUNBỌ'S LIFE IMPROVED TREMENDOUSLY. The change was rapid and beautiful to see. I was happy to hear Daddy tell of one of our national programmes Pastor Jide was invited as a guest minister. I called Sunbọ immediately.

"I was just about to call you," she said.

"I hope you are coming with Pastor Jide," I said. The program was three months away, and I reckoned she could plan to attend.

"Ahhh, I wish. It's just that no one will be here with the children and..."

"Haba! These children are not that small again now! Is Bolu not turning sixteen next year?"

"Seventeen," Sunbọ said. "Wow! These children are big, ehn."

"True. So, you can't use them as excuse," I said.

"Maybe we can even take a trip." Sunbọ chuckled. "The whole family. It's been so long we came to Lagos."

"Yes, right? You must stay in the house with us o! The girls will be happy to see their friends again," I said.

Though thinking about it, Chloe was such a rude and snobbish girl to the children in church, and Calli was very reserved. But they should get along. Sunbọ's children were a little older. Still, I believed children would gravitate to one another, especially since they did at much younger ages.

"It's been long sha." Sunbọ sighed. "But I will be very happy to see you. So much to catch up on."

The week came and Sunbọ and her three girls arrived our camp. I had the east wing of our house prepared for them, which was one of two ensuite two-bedrooms and a parlour. There was also a kitchen if they wanted to cook for themselves, but I invited Sunbọ to come and have their meals with us.

It was Thursday evening, which meant the girls would miss school on Friday, but Sunbọ didn't want to come on Friday to jump into the program. Another big man of God was going to open the weekend special healing service, then Pastor Jide would preach on Saturday night and Daddy would round off on Sunday morning. There was going to be a small ministers' recouping service on Sunday evening, but Sunbọ and her family would not stay for it.

When they arrived, I was in the middle of a meeting, but I excused myself to welcome them. I had asked a sister to bring my children so we could all go and see Sunbọ and her family. Chloe refused to come, and Ben was asleep, so I went with Adam and Calli. I regret having my children that day. Adam snubbed the girls and Calli just refused to smile or play. It was really awkward, and I asked the sister who brought them to take them back.

Sunbọ grimaced. "Chai, children."

When my children left, she asked hers to go into their room as well, so we could freely talk. Pastor Jide had locked himself up in the other room to pray, and we had the sitting room to ourselves.

"I said I should tell you when we see," Sunbọ said. "To God alone be the glory. We started our housing project."

"Oh, praise the Lord! I must come and see it with my two eyes," I said. I moved closer to her and hugged her. "In Oṣogbo, right?"

"Yes. Hmm, Sister Bettina..." Tears pooled Sunbọ's eyes. "It wasn't easy. It hasn't been easy. Hmm, but God is faithful. Jide is doing well, finally. God is faithful."

"What a mighty God." I laughed. "What a glorious God. He always comes through for us."

"He does. And you know, Brother John, hmm, he was the one that really helped. He pushed Jide to do this. Found the land and bought it on our behalf." Sunbọ smiled. "The irony of life. You supporting me this way, and John supporting Jide."

I sighed. "We all come a long way, so why not."

"And umm, the support for that upkeep, I don't need it anymore..."

"Ah, no o..."

Sunbọ raised her hand. *"Someone else will need it. Believe me. Honestly. Since things got better now..."* She looked up. *"Five months at least, and you have continued to support. I don't need it anymore, please. I appreciate you, thank you."*

"We thank God. You are right. Everything will be fine with all of us. Ah, my sister, let me gist you about this quarterly meeting I attend with some pastor's wives."

I proceeded to talk about those high-class prayer meetings we had. How I was so out of my league there and could not even form a true friendship. We were all always so guarded. Sunbọ laughed and gave suggestions about breaking the ice.

"Ask about their sex life, one day," she said, and we laughed. *"Or if they have a teenage daughter, ask them if she's still a virgin!"*

"Ewoo! Sister Sunbọ! How will they respond? With a slap, I'm sure."

Oh, we laughed and laughed. We talked about food, about the awkward way our children behaved, government, ministry in general, and so on.

Sunbọ, my best friend, my confidant, my prayer partner...the times we had together were few and far between, but we talked every week on phone. She had all the time in the world, and I didn't, but she remained solidly behind me. I could tell her anything. At least, except about my marriage.

I wish I could tell her about my marriage, but I couldn't. I couldn't actually tell anyone about my husband. My relationship with him. Who would understand that not having a problem was a big problem? He never said, *"I love you."* Never. He was not romantic but rather quite sexy. He made time for sex. He liked my body and remained faithful to it. Was that enough, though? We never discussed, he just gave commands and orders.

I wish I had a relationship like Sunbọ's. She and Jide were first friends before they became lovers and then husband and wife. Sunbọ could discuss anything about her life with her man. Their marriage was not always easy, and they didn't always have money, but they roughed the weather together. My case was not so. I had a rich, talented, anointed, sexy husband, and that was it. We could never sit down and chat and laugh. I didn't have anyone to joke about church service with especially after Sunbọ left. Was it normal? I didn't even know if any other pastor's wife had my same challenge.

Was it normal for husband and wife not to quarrel over anything? Daddy and I never had a disagreement. He used the same tone with me, as he used for demons. He ordered all of us around. Only Chloe...Chloe chatted a lot with her father. I sometimes thought it was *absurd for them to have things to talk about, but I'd seen it many times. They enjoyed each other's company so much.*

There was a time I walked into Daddy's office, and he was playing Ludo with Chloe. I nearly doubled over. Daddy never played any games with anyone.

Was it normal?

Chapter 20

Chief Alejolowo, SAN, was on his knees in front of Daddy when Chloe walked into Daddy's private parlour. She curtseyed and went to sit on one of several white couches in the exquisitely furnished, medium-sized room.

"Ah, here she comes," Daddy said. "I was just telling Chief what happened to you, Chloe. Sir, please have a seat."

The senior advocate stood, bowed to Daddy, and took a seat on another couch. "Thank you, Daddy."

"Go ahead. Think of me as not being here," Daddy said.

Chloe ground her teeth. "Good morning, Chief."

"Hello Ms. Chloe." Chief Alejolowo smiled. "It's great to see you looking so good. Umm, Daddy said you had some problem at your husband's place."

"His stupid son beat me up." Chloe snapped. "I spent four days in the hospital. And now the crazy old man has refused to let me see my twins."

"That is terrible," Chief said. "We definitely must sue. I will send my lawyer to come and see you, and..."

"No, I'm speaking to you alone," Chloe said.

Chief arched an eyebrow. "I don't personally handle cases. It will be better if you speak to the lawyer who will prosecute on your behalf."

"No! Daddy?"

Daddy shrugged. "I am not a lawyer or a judge. I have brought the big man for you, learn to do what people say."

Chloe snapped. "F*ck."

"Language," Chief said.

"Okay, umm, call the lawyer to come now," Chloe said.

"Okay," Chief said. He dialled a number on his phone and made a call speaking softly. "He'll be here in two hours."

Chloe stood. "Send for me when he arrives." She stomped out of the room.

Two hours later, Chloe returned to the guest sitting room. Daddy was no longer there, but the senior advocate was, with a handsome lawyer who would be in his early forties.

"Ah, welcome back, Ms. Chloe." Chief stood. "This is Barrister Nathaniel. Barrister, you know Ms. Chloe. Daddy's first daughter."

Nathaniel stood. "Very well. Happy to meet you, Ms. Chloe."

Chloe half-smiled. "Can I call you Nat?"

"Of course," Nat stammered. "Of course, ma."

"Ma." Chloe scoffed. "I'm Chloe to you, please." She walked to the couch she sat on previously. "Please, sit."

The old man, and the handsome man, sat.

"Chief just briefed me about what happened to you. I will draw up the report, and we will commence with a suit immediately," Nat said.

Chloe sighed. "Good. You look like a very smart lawyer."

Nat opened an iPad. "I have a few questions. Can you just retell what exactly happened?"

"Sure." Chloe swallowed. "Daddy sponsored a cruise for me for a week. I enjoyed myself thoroughly. The day I returned, right in front of my porch, messing up my garden, was this family of the little b*tch my husband f*cked."

Chief moaned. "Language, please."

Chloe grunted. "They said she'd died. So? I stomp into the private parlour my husband was in and asked him to send them away! His stupid imbecile bastard son chose instead to beat me up."

Nat arched an eyebrow. "Had he or his father ever laid a hand on you before?"

"Never. OPJ is retarded." An unkind smile slowly spread over Chloe's face. "He's forty-something. He doesn't have a wife or a child or a pet. He wakes up in the morning and eats popcorn while watching a movie. He's just waiting for his useless billionaire father to die so he can take over."

"Does your husband have other children?"

"My twins," Chloe said.

"Any others?"

"What has this got to do with OPJ beating me up, and his father refusing to let me see my girls? Well, girl, because I am not ready to see the evil one right now." Chloe yawned.

Nat shrugged. "Background information."

Chloe snapped. "Get your background information on Google, please."

"Of course. One moment." Nat tapped on his iPad, and with a slight frown, his eyes darted over his screen. "Several wives and women. Two sons overseas. One son, OPJ, the oldest. A daughter runs his businesses here. Good." He looked at Chloe. "Have you ever had any encounter with the other children of your husband, besides your twins of course."

Chloe threw up her hands. "What has this got to do with anything?"

"I'm trying to establish precedence."

"None!" Chloe shouted. "I have never seen any of those strangers before. OPJ has never done anything more than tickle me, duh! You don't want to know details of what his father has done to me, but beating is not one of them. Gosh."

"Thank you." Nat bit his lower lip. "What happened after OPJ beat you up? With his hands or what?"

"My leather belt. I was screaming at him at first, but it got too much, and I kept quiet." Chloe breathed through her mouth so she would not cry. "He probably thought I had passed out. He whipped me a little more." She shuddered.

"And then?"

"And then took me to the hospital and dumped me there in the lobby. I was recognized and attended to. I spent four days there, and then discharged, I came here," Chloe said.

"Did you make a police report?"

"No."

"No? Why not? How can we press charges if...?"

Chloe cut in. "It didn't occur to me! I've never had to deal with criminals."

"Do we have pictures?"

Chloe narrowed her eyes. "Pictures?"

"Yes. It will be evidence of the beating. It's barely a week ago and," Nat shrugged. "You don't look beat up. If at all, your face," he scanned through her body, clad in a spaghetti top and short skirt. "Your arms, legs, all look pretty smooth and nice."

Chief pressed his lips together and glared at Nat.

"When I got home, my Daddy decided to pray for me." Chloe retorted. "I came home with a nurse. She was going to give me my pain medication and Daddy sent her off and prayed instead." She sat forward. "And you know what? I didn't sleep at the hospital. For four days. Daddy prayed. I slept like a log. Woke up. No pain. No scratches. Nothing!"

Chief clapped. "Hallelujah!"

"No, sir. Daddy took all the evidence away. My face was bandaged, my arms, my legs, my back, my butt!" Chloe gasped. "All the scars are gone. No pains!"

"That is the miracle of God!" Chief said.

"It doesn't help your case, Chloe, if you don't have any physical evidence, or pictures," Nat said.

"Are you f*cking kidding me?"

"Language, language!" Chief said.

Chapter 21

PASTOR JIDE WAS BUILDING a six-bedroom duplex in a suburban and new area in Oṣogbo. There were quite a few new and big houses in the area, and the first thing that occurred to me, was to get a piece of land in the area and build too. I ran my thoughts by Sunbọ as she walked me through her uncompleted building. She loved the idea.

"Should I tell Brother John to get one for you. He is friends with the state surveyor-general." Sunbọ winked. "Or you want to tell him yourself."

I chuckled. "Abeg, tell him for me. I will inform Daddy when..."

Sunbọ gasped. "Heh, no o! This is your house, your property! It will be in your name. What are you informing Daddy for?"

My eyes widened. I had never done anything without Daddy's knowledge and approval. "How can? I have never done anything without telling Daddy!"

Sunbọ scoffed. "What if he says no?"

I shrugged. "Then I won't do it."

"Ahhh!" Sunbọ shouted. "My sister, you have been married how long, and everything you own is your husband's."

"The church's actually," I said. We owned almost nothing to our names.

"So, God forbid, Daddy dies, where will you and your children live?"

"In Jaja Mansion, of course," I tapped my fingers against my leather handbag. "Where else?"

"What if the new leader of the church wants to live there?"

I laughed. "Which new leader? Who will lead the church if not me?"

Sunbọ stopped walking and bent over, laughing. "Who told you? How many times do you preach? That Pastor Oni, who is second in command will be watching you take over?"

"Pastor Oni is not second in command o."

"Be there, ignorant. You think all those people who started with Daddy will let you step in?" Sunbọ clapped. "Even that Elder Elizabeth, or what is her name? Pastor Fẹmi, hmm. Better get sense quick. Buy land, build house. You can even buy it in your father's name."

"First, I am not buying a land and building a house in my name without Daddy's consent." I raised two fingers. "Second, if I am buying in my father's name, it will be from my husband. And," I raised three fingers. "Third, I don't even have all the money for that if at all I want to do something so wrong."

Sunbọ folded her ten fingers around her head. "Ah, aye mi. How are you so naïve? All the people surrounding your life are just there for what they can gain and fear of Daddy. When he's gone, who will you have?"

"My life, Sunbọ!" I shouted. "I have my life, and it is beautiful, and I am content!"

For a second, we both kept quiet. All my insecurity was right there, out in my voice, and in my anger. In truth, I had only what Daddy gave me, which was much more than enough but really, if he died, who controlled things? Not me right now, anyway. I wasn't even in the board of the church. What if Daddy died? God forbid. What did I have?

"Daddy is not going anywhere, anyway," Sunbọ said softly. "Abeg, whenever you decide you want a house here, let me know. We may even be able to get land close to us here for you."

I exhaled. "Thank you, dear." I was glad she deflated the tension.

We continued a tour of the house. I oohed, and aahed at how big the project was. They had almost a full plot of land at the back, and Sunbọ planned to have a small farm there, and rear goats and chickens.

"When do you think it will be done?" I asked as we walked out to the car that brought us. The driver, one from the church, waited for us in the car.

Sunbọ shrugged. "We are going to do the roof next week. Once that is done, hopefully, we can complete everything and move in say two or three months. By Christmas."

I waved to the heavens. "Ah, from your mouth to God's ears in Jesus' name. Amen."

We dropped Sunbọ at her rented house, and I went to visit my parents briefly, before returning home.

Maami was home alone as usual. My father, who couldn't work anymore, now found his recreation in the neighbourhood, sitting with other old men, playing draught, or talking about the state of the country.

"Hmm, Mummy," Maami said as soon as I sat down. I still found it awkward she also called me Mummy. "Your sister, Alexa, will she not marry?"

I chuckled. Skola, the older of my younger sisters got married at the age of twenty-one to a Yoruba man who lived in Port Harcourt, and they had four children already. I had married at twenty-three, so it was no surprise that Maami worried Alexa at twenty-nine was still single.

"Maami, when Alexa gets husband, she will marry."

"She have old o! At her age, Skola have born all her children finish. You sef, you have born all naw. Except maybe Ben."

"Who will she marry when husband never come?" I gasped. "Maami, don't worry."

I couldn't let her know I was worried as well. Alexa only wanted one man, Pastor Fẹmi Ezekiel, pastor of our huge church in Lekki, and Fẹmi didn't want her. What could I do?

Maami shook her head. "I worry. Find husband for her. In your big church. Please, my dear."

When I got back home, I asked my husband I needed to discuss something important with him. In my heart, I just wanted to get his opinion, and advise. Alexa still lived with us and worked full time as a graphic designer for the church. She was a beautiful and talented woman who loved God with all her heart.

Alexa was bold and knew what she wanted for herself. She would be a much better pastor's wife than I. She made me so proud. It was my duty to fight for her, though, Fẹmi Ezekiel wasn't my cup of tea; I thought he was too handsome and too proud, and too successful for his own good. Many of the ladies in his church were just there to gaze at him. Alexa deserved better. But he was what she wanted. In a bid to discourage her once, I told her he looked like someone who would cheat on her, and she laughed it off. Fẹmi enjoyed the company of ladies but there was no indication he womanized.

After dinner, Daddy invited me into his private parlour.

"You had something important to say."

"Yes, Daddy." He sat on his special chair, and I sat on the couch closest to him. "It's about Alexa. I'm concerned about her getting married."

"Have you spoken to her about it?"

"Yes, Daddy. She only wants Pastor Fẹmi. She thinks he'll come around, but it's been so many years now." I shrugged. "I've tried to talk to him but he's not thinking about that at the moment."

"Fẹmi Ezekiel?"

"Yes, Daddy."

"Hmm." Daddy sighed. "Fẹmi is in his mid-thirties. He should be thinking about it." He nodded. "Bring Alexa. Tell her to look very nice. I will ask Fẹmi to come here too. He's in the mansion somewhere."

I curtseyed. "Yes, Daddy."

As I walked out, I was amazed by this development. I could never predict what my husband would do or say. I should have asked but we never communicated in that way. Goodness gracious. Excitement built up in me. Would Daddy ask Fẹmi to date my sister or what?

Alexa was already in bed reading a novel when I knocked her door and she bid me to enter.

"Ah, Sister." She knelt to greet me and sat back on the bed. In public, she called me Mummy, but not when we were alone, which was a great relief to me. "Hope everything is okay?"

"Get dressed. Look beautiful. Daddy wants to see you," I said.

"Ha, yeepa! What did I do?" Alexa leaped off her bed and started dressing up.

I laughed. "You are not in any trouble, I hope."

"Sister, please tell me. What happened?"

For the life of me, I felt ashamed about taking her matter to Daddy without first telling her.

"Look beautiful, maybe you are meeting your husband today," I said.

"Yeepa!"

We both laughed. She truly was beautiful with a dark cream chocolate complexion she kept shiny and highlighted with light make-up. She had lovely almond-shaped, sleepy eyes, high cheek bones, and soft sensual lips. When she smiled, two dimples showed up on her cheeks. Her teeth were small, white, and even, and I reckoned she was the most beautiful of my parents' children. She had the longest list of suitors too. And an inspiring sense of humour.

When we walked into Daddy's parlour, Pastor Fẹmi was on his knees before Daddy.

"Dide, Fẹmi," Daddy said, and Fẹmi stood.

Daddy pointed at a couch and Fẹmi went to take his seat. I led Alexa to the couch closest to Daddy's seat, and we sat.

"Good evening, Mummy." Fẹmi greeted. "Good evening, Sister Alexa."

"Good evening, Pastor Fẹmi," Alexa and I chorused.

"We all have church tomorrow, so I will make this brief," Daddy said. "Fẹmi, have you considered anyone for wife?"

Fẹmi involuntarily glanced at Alexa before he shook his head. "No, Daddy."

I thought he looked really nice too in a striped dress shirt, and blue jeans, and a pair of loafers. He was almost as dark as Alexa, slim, tall, with an angular face and dark, impressive eyes. He had a full beard and moustache that only added to his appeal. Alexa looked right with him, but a man had to want a woman. My thoughts.

"Well, go and think about it. Your church needs a first lady. You need a woman," Daddy said.

Fẹmi bowed. "Yes, Daddy."

Daddy glared at Alexa for the first time since we entered the room. "Alexa needs a husband."

Alexa, poor girl, dropped her gaze to her hands. I felt some humiliation on her behalf. I wish she wasn't here to witness this. But how would I have known when Daddy didn't discuss, and I didn't ask?

Fẹmi turned his gaze on Alexa, and I was grateful my poor sister was just staring at her hands and didn't see the confused expression on the young man's face.

"Let us pray," Daddy said.

We all went on our knees, including Daddy. After a brief prayer for direction, we all dispersed quietly. I couldn't, out of shame, even talk about it with Alexa.

After church the following day, Pastor Fẹmi Ezekiel came to Jaja Mansion, and proposed to Alexa. She said yes.

Chapter 22

Sunbọ said they were moving into their house anyway. The roofing was all done, as well as the plastering. What was basically left would be the finishing, which she said they could do with time. She couldn't give me a clear explanation for the rush. It was just two weeks to Christmas, and everything had gone a little slower than she envisaged because Pastor Jide's trips were more frequent. Pastor Jide was now so busy and known all over the country and abroad. I even heard that people paid him honorarium ahead of the program they invited him to.

I couldn't visit when they were moving because the church annual end-of-year-camp meeting was just a few days away, but I spoke with her on the phone, and she sounded bright and excited. I promised to visit first week of January.

A mere wish.

In the early hours of December 13, at about 3a.m., Bolu called me on her mother's phone. She sounded hysterical. I had never heard a voice so terrified in my life. I couldn't make out anything she was saying. Much as I tried to calm her down, I could not. My whole body shuddered in fear and trepidation. Something terrible had happened. But what? Why was Bolu calling with Sunbọ's phone? Where was Sunbọ?

Where was Sunbọ? My sister. My friend.

I cut Bolu's call and dialled Pastor Jide's number. It rang out. Confused, I stood from my bed. Daddy was in his prayer room. I went there and knocked, knowing he would never answer until he was done praying. He did not. Who could I turn to? I hurried down the hall to Alexa's room and knocked. She opened the door groggily.

"Sister?" Alexa yawned. "What? What time?"

I stepped in and burst into tears. It must have driven all the sleep from Alexa's eyes.

"Yee! Sister, what is it?" She cried.

"I don't know. Bolu called now and was crying so loud; I didn't hear what she was saying. She used her mother's phone."

"Bolu? Aunty Sunbọ?"

"Yes." I sat on Alexa's bed and sobbed.

"Hah!" Alexa paced. "What can we do? Daddy?" She moaned. "Maybe he's praying and Pastor Jide, nkọ? Ummm, yee!" She picked her phone. "Let me call Pastor Fẹmi."

She paced and called Pastor Fẹmi and put it on speaker.

He moaned. "Sweetheart?"

"Honey, it's Pastor Jide Ọlaolu's wife. The daughter called and was crying. With her mother's phone. We don't know what happened."

"Huh? What happened?"

"We don't know. We can't get information."

"Let me come to the mansion," Fẹmi said. "Give me an hour."

"Okay, honey." Alexa hung up. "Sister, Fẹmi is coming."

"Ah, my God. Sunbọ! What happened to my friend?"

I knew it was really bad. I didn't have Lolu's number, or I'd have called. I tried Pastor Jide again and got no response. I tried Sunbọ's number, and it was switched off. I didn't have Bolu's number either. Frustrated, I stood.

"I have to go to Oṣogbo. I can't stay here." I headed for the door.

Alexa yanked me back. "Huh, Sister! It's middle of the night. Who will take you there? The drivers are all asleep. We have to wait till morning."

I sat down and scrolled through my phone and saw John's number. I couldn't remember ever having it. I was just thinking I could call Maami, though she would not have any way of getting to Sunbọ's house at this time. John!

I had not spoken to John for the sixteen years since I got married. The beginning of my life with Daddy marked the end of John's love and admiration of my husband. John simply stopped showing up around us.

"Hello, Brother John, this is Bettina."

"I know, Mummy. How are you?" he said.

He wasn't aware of anything? I screamed. "Yee! I am done for. I don't know what is wrong with my friend. John, help me."

He seemed to come awake. "What? Who? Sunbọ?"

"Yes. She huh, huh, huh…"

Alexa took the phone from me and explained what happened. John agreed to go to her house immediately and call back to let us know what the problem was.

It was the longest half hour of waiting, but alas, John called back, and it was the worst news I had ever heard.

My friend was dead. Sunbọ was dead. She was only forty-two!

Chapter 23

"Do you like me?" Chloe winked. "Hmm?"

Nat half-smiled. "I'd like you to get justice."

Chloe scoffed. "Are you married?"

Nat looked up for a minute from his iPad, and murmured, "Was. We're separated." He sniffed.

"Huh." Chloe pouted. "Shame."

"My investigator got a nurse at the clinic, one of the first ones who received you. She's very articulate too," Nat said.

Chloe stood from her chair opposite him in his modest office at Chief Alejolowo's chambers, and circled round to where he sat in his black swivel chair.

"I really like you." Chloe moaned. "I couldn't stop thinking about you." She stood behind him and wrapped her hands around his cheeks. "You're free to date, and so am I."

Nat grunted. "The last time I checked, you are still married."

"Separated." She giggled. "Like you."

"I'm not free to date, Chloe. And maybe it's a bad idea to have this meeting in my office. Daddy was fine having it at the mansion."

"Oh, please! You think Daddy will appreciate my touching you like this in his parlour?" She kissed the top of his head. "Or anywhere there for that matter."

Nat swung around. "Chloe, no."

She placed her kiss on his lips. "Yes." And moaned. "Hmm, oh my god!"

Nat took over the kiss for a moment and drew back. "No, please." He stood. "I think we can continue with this meeting in the conference room."

Chloe lowered her eyes and they widened. "Oh, by the gods. You are bulging."

Nat's gaze dropped too. He stepped out of his seat and walked to the door. "Look, Chloe..."

"I wondered why I was cursing so much that first day I met you. I do that. I curse when I see what I like. Daddy thinks it's a bad habit." She shrugged. "Come on, Nat. Come here."

Nat breathed heavily. "Chloe…"

"Come here." Chloe signalled with one index finger.

Like a dog after its own vomit, Nat ambled over to her. They kissed for some time.

"We both can't resist this, as you can see," she said.

"You are so beautiful, Chloe," Nat murmured. "Too beautiful."

"Thank you, darling." She pushed him into his chair and sat on his laps. "No kidding, it's been long I felt like this."

"Me too." Nat took small bites off her neck and chest.

Chloe further pushed down her off-shoulder dress, until parts of her bosom were exposed, and Nat dug down, both moaning. Then, she started to push him away.

"Not here," Chloe said.

Nat looked up with dilated eyes. "Why? Please."

Chloe laughed. "No!" She stood and staggered to her previous seat. "Let's talk about this case. Then we can have lunch somewhere. Then we can go back to the mansion. And do the needful." She blew him a kiss.

Nat breathed through his mouth. "You really planned to kill me, right?"

Chloe giggled. "Yes. Sudden death. In my arms."

Nat gasped. "No. I'm not going to the mansion to sleep with you."

"Why not?"

"Your father lives there. "I'm not going to sin in God's temple."

Chloe's mouth dropped open, and then she burst into laughter. She bent over and laughed until tears came off her eyes, and she sniffed.

Nat's eyes twinkled. "Call me backward, naïve, anything. I'm not going to be in your arms while Daddy lurks behind your door."

"Do you." Chloe coughed and sniffed. "Do you know how large that house is? There are at least twenty rooms. Thirty. Or thirty-five! Daddy lives in the west wing, and I live opposite in the east wing."

"Are you sure about this?" Nat glared at her. "Honestly, I'll do better if you come to my house."

"No offense to you, babes, but what can possibly be cool in your house? Your wife left you."

Nat arched his eyebrow. "Throwing jabs when you see how weak I am for you?"

"Hmm, I love it when you arch those beautifully shaped eyebrows of yours." Chloe groaned. "Do you think we should go to your house now? See if I like where you live?"

Nat jumped to his feet. "I'm a twenty-minute drive away. Come on."

"We take your car. No way is my driver knowing I left here for a bit." Chloe sneered. "All of them are Daddy's spies."

Nat laughed and closed on her. They kissed again for a bit. "Come on. Let's go. I need to get back to work as soon as possible."

Laughing like two kids at a carnival, they left Nat's office.

Chapter 24

ONCE PASTOR FẸMI ARRIVED, *he agreed to take Alexa and I to Oṣogbo, that early morning of Tuesday, December 13, 2005. I wept all through the journey. John was calm when he broke the news over the phone, but I knew tears were not far from that voice. Kind Fẹmi, I saw the way he consoled Alexa. In the few weeks after their courtship started, I had never seen him or my sister so happy. Alexa truly knew what she wanted, and I respected her more. For a man to leave everything at 4 a.m. and drive from the outskirts of Lagos to Oṣogbo, was a lot to tell about him.*

We got to Oṣogbo roughly three hours later. John had arranged for a hearse to take Sunbọ to the mortuary. Bolu was at home, and Maami was there too with her. Bolu had cried so much, her eyes were red, her nose was blocked, and her voice was gone. I couldn't bring myself to ask her what happened. Not yet.

"Where are your sisters?" Was the only thing I could say.

"They are still in school. Boarding school. They are supposed to close on Friday," Bolu said.

"Sister, we need to tidy the house," Alexa said. "People will soon start coming. Maami, maybe you need to cook or something."

I watched my baby sister take charge like a queen. She and Fẹmi swept the house, which was a regal mess as though there had been a battle there. It kept me wondering what happened in my friend's last few hours. Did Bolu know? The most pressing questions were the "hows" and "whys?" Would they ever be answered?

Alexa checked out the pantry and fridge, and Fẹmi gave some cash for Maami to buy things to cook. Bread, yam, and fish stew. Then we all sat in the sitting room to wait for the inevitable throng of criers, and mourners. And they were not a few.

Sunbọ had been a friend, a sister, a life-support for many. When John returned, he had some people I didn't know with him, and we never got to sit down to talk about Sunbọ. Then Sunbọ's parents came, and I had never seen so much pain on any shoulders like I saw on her mother's. Wailing, screaming, rolling continued with no one able to stop it. Pastor Jide was still nowhere in sight and when I tried to call him, his number didn't go through. I wish I could be of any sort of support, but it dawned on me that though I might have thought Sunbọ was my closest ally, I wasn't hers. Definitely. It was all coming through, and soon, it was obvious there were people who knew more about her, and the people around her, for instance John.

Pastor Fẹmi, Alexa, Maami, and I were soon part of a throng. When Pastor Jide finally showed up later in the day, there were too many people to surround and support him. I didn't even have a chance to register my presence. Alexa signalled for us to leave, and we did. The drive back to Lagos, much as the journey to, was silent, punctuated by my uncontrollable tears.

Daddy had left a message that I see him immediately I return. Weary and tired, I sauntered to his private parlour. He was on his seat. I curtseyed and sat on the couch I normally took.

"Mummy, stand up and come here. Face me," Daddy said.

Did he know what happened? I guess he would. Pastor Fẹmi would tell him. Pastor Jide too, even in his grief. Why then was my husband sounding so indifferent, as though he was not aware?

I came to stand in front of him. It was custom to obey whatever he said.

"Where did you go all morning, and all afternoon, without telling me, and you are just coming back?"

Oh no! He didn't know?

My heart thudded. "I went to. Sunbọ. Sunbọ died and..."

"I know Sunbọ died. Where were you?"

My teary eyes shot to my husband's. He knew? And he was still asking questions in that bland tone? First, anger, and then disgust melted into my heart. What sort of human with no feeling was this?

"You know? Daddy! My best friend, my sister just died this morning." I burst into tears.

A husband would stand, come close, hug, comfort. Right? Mine just sat there while I cried myself dry. Until there were no tears anymore. My knees felt weak. My head, heavy. I just wanted to lie down and do nothing else. My stomach hurt because I had not put any food in it, and this was night already. I wanted to scream at my husband, but that would not go down well with him.

When I quietened, Daddy said, "You got me worried. Next time, leave a message at least. And don't travel without letting me know. No matter what!"

I sniffed. "Yes, Daddy."

"You can go. Get some rest."

I wanted to ask what he knew about Sunbọ's death. I knew he'd have more information than me. But I was too weak, and sad to probe. Not that I would normally anyway. It was too distressing. This was beyond me. I lacked the energy or spiritual will to process the fact that the only woman I could be myself with was dead. Suddenly. We still talked yesterday morning. She was hale and hearty. She was forty-two! Living her best life. She finally had her own house! How could she be dead?

I didn't want to sleep in my husband's bed tonight, yet it was what I had to do. I took a bath, and on my empty stomach, took two pain relieving tablets. Someone knocked on my door, and I asked the person to come in. It was Alexa.

"Sister, are you okay?"

I nodded. Then I shrugged. I just wanted to cry but all the crying had come out of me. I didn't know if I had any energy left to be sad. Alexa sat on the edge of the bed, and massaged my foot, which was closest to her. So soothing, so thoughtful of her.

"It is unbelievable what we are hearing, Sister. I don't know if this will ever pass." She reached out to hold my hand. "Chai, Aunty Sunbọ."

The way Alexa spoke, it was obvious there was something new. We came back together barely three hours, and she didn't sound like this previously.

I moaned. "Hmm. Sunbọ."

"Sister, did Daddy tell you anything?" Tears gathered in her eyes. "When you went to see him?"

I sat up. What more horrible news could I take? "No. What happened again?"

Alexa swallowed and huge drops of tears fell down her smooth cheeks. I just started crying too. I sobbed hard though I didn't know what it was. Was Sunbọ killed? By Jide? Or what worse news could there be?

"Sister, they are saying Aunty Sunbọ killed herself." Alexa sobbed. "That she drank..."

"Heh! Yee! No, it is not true." I jumped from the bed. "Who told you?"

Daddy chose that moment to walk in. Without a word, Alexa hurried out of our bedroom. I dropped back on the bed, and wept, unable to hold myself. When I thought there could not be any more tears.

Why? God why? I wailed.

Daddy came to me and held me in his arms. I surrendered, relieved my husband wanted to share my grief. But his hand went to the slim sleeve of my nightgown, and he buried his *head in my bosom. And I knew he didn't come in to console me but to perform his conjugal duty.*

Chapter 25

Sᴜɴʙọ's ᴅᴇᴀᴛʜ ᴄʜᴀɴɢᴇᴅ ᴇᴠᴇʀʏᴛʜɪɴɢ *in my life.*

Inward, I felt empty, useless. The mere fact that suicide was suspected made me more miserable than I imagined I could be. Why would my friend kill herself? In the wake of all the tragedy and controversy, Daddy ordered an autopsy, but he did not reveal the result to anyone. However, it was announced to all our pastors and leaders that Sunbọ's cause of death was food poisoning.

The following morning after the horrible day December 13, I rushed to Alexa to get details, but she had little more than that Daddy told Pastor Fẹmi there was a rumour and that he would get to the bottom of it.

I began to hold on dearly to Sunbọ's words. What I could remember of them. There was no hint of suicide. Stories trickled in but nothing to show the state of my friend's heart. One thing was sure, though. No one saw it coming. Which made the situation worse. Did Sunbọ have a mental condition no one knew of? What about Pastor Jide? Did he have a clue this could happen?

It was difficult to concentrate with all these questions. I started questioning everything I was. Would I wake up one morning and poison myself? How could God let this happen? What were the issues Sunbọ was dealing with that she had to eat things that would end her life? What about hope, and faith? Didn't she have love in her life? Was she mentally sick? And I could not answer or get answers.

One week after Sunbọ died, Daddy presided over her funeral. We all stood at a corner of her compound where she'd earmarked for her chicken pen and committed her to mother earth.

"Do not mourn like people without hope," Daddy said. "Sister Sunbọ served God with every inch of her spirit. She has done her part. Think about yours."

For some weird reason, my husband's gaze came to rest on me.

Daddy's eyes pierced my soul. I stared back, tears gushing from my eyes unbidden. I looked at Bolu, Folu, and Lolu, all in black. Young women who would never see their mother again. She was the one always there for the children. Pastor Jide travelled all the time. He wasn't even there at the end for Sunbọ. What a life.

My eyes rove to my friend's husband. What was he hiding from the world about his wife? I wish I could sit with him but there had been no chance for this. Camp meeting already started, and he was in attendance. He had driven down for his wife's burial, what kind of man was this? Were these? Him and my husband. How could they live life as though nothing awful just happened? Was Sunbọ so soon pushed aside for important things? Didn't she deserve even a day off the schedule? What was important? A day to mourn a wife and cancel events to honour her? Or end-of-the-year camp meeting that reoccurred every year amongst several other believers' meetings. Was this how important I was to my husband too? It indeed was quite disturbing to me.

After the burial, Daddy asked that we return to Lagos immediately to re-join the campers. When I think about the number of hours' break taken to dedicate to my friend's burial, I calculated about nine altogether.

"I want to see the girls," I said. "I will come before Friday."

I couldn't believe I was opposing him right there in the open, with his pastors standing all around us by the grave.

"Hmm." My husband walked away from me, and his men followed him.

Alexa walked up to me. "I will go back with Pastor Fẹmi."

"Okay dear, I'll see you tomorrow or next."

Daddy and his entourage left. There was light entertainment. People dispersed one after the other. I felt like a sore thumb. People milled around me, most of them members of Sunbọ's family. I sat with some guests who seemed not eager to leave like me.

Pastor Jide came to where I sat. "Mummy, I'm going back to Lagos for camp meeting, first thing in the morning."

I gasped. "What about the girls?"

"They will go and stay with Sunbọ's parents. Here in Oṣogbo," Pastor Jide said. "They will return here when I come back."

"So, who will be here?"

Pastor Jide sighed. "I'm locking up the house, when we leave."

I clasped my hands. This meant I had to leave too. Was this done because of Daddy? The thought seemed silly as soon as I had it. Surely Pastor Jide made his plans regardless of what

I or Daddy wanted. Or did he make his plans just because Daddy asked him to? Nothing made sense to me.

"I guess I will go to my parents, then," I said.

"That will be a very good idea, thank you," Pastor Jide said.

Before I could say more, he turned to someone else and continued talking and making plans. I may forget to talk about Pastor Jide again, but he never remarried. Perhaps that was his tribute to my friend. He cut me off too. We never had a chance to ever talk again.

I saw Brother John head towards the door, and I followed him. "Brother John, I need to speak with you," I said.

"This is not a good time, Mummy." He continued on his way.

I had not said a word to him in sixteen years since I got married until the night Sunbọ died. When would be a good time?

Chapter 26

CHLOE WORE A KNEE-LENGTH sundress for the first time since she turned eighteen and got her independence, like she enjoyed saying. All her dresses and skirts were mid-thigh. She'd had to buy this dress at a shop in Lagos, just for this outing with Nat. She still couldn't believe herself. Doing something for someone else. Because she lived so far from civilization as she referred to the camp, they'd agreed to meet at a mall on Mainland, a safe place for Daddy's driver to take her, and then Nat would pick her up.

It worked perfectly. She entered the mall through one entrance and exited with Nat through another. They went to an exclusive strip club famous for having rich patrons. Nat had booked a nice cosy table for two in a corner far from the entrance where they could have their privacy. The only snag was that they had a curfew. The mall closed at 10 pm so Chloe had to be out and back with Daddy's driver before then. It was seven o'clock and at least, they had two hours of uninterrupted time together.

"I love the dress," Nat said, as he seated her.

"About time you noticed," she murmured.

"You will soon find out I am quite slow to speak, my love." He chuckled and sat opposite her. He took her hands in his and rubbed his thumbs over them softly. "Thank you for doing this with me."

Chloe smirked. "I can't believe myself. Daddy Jaja's daughter in a strip club."

"It's the only sane place to hide and date. You know that." A waiter came to take their order, but Nat waved him away. "I want so badly to be with you every day. It's been long I felt like this," he said.

"I have never felt like this." She sighed. "With anyone."

He rubbed his forehead. "With anyone?"

Chloe laughed nervously. "I was a wild child as you may have noticed. My daddy was always trying to get his noose about my neck. I did everything he preached against."

"Why was that?"

A muscle tic jumped in Chloe's jaw. "Why else? I wanted to push the boundaries. I'm curious." She laughed. "And forget the sarcasm. I've been to more strip clubs than any pastor's child, I think."

"Being curious gets you in a lot of trouble, you know." He bent and kissed her palm. Chloe felt it all the way to her toes. She moaned. "Don't tease me here."

"There's just so little time. I'm dragging your investigation as much as I can, but," he shrugged. "It's bound to come to a head soon. We won't need to meet again. Then what?"

Chloe lowered her voice. "What?" She had never felt so vulnerable. So in need.

"I don't want to lose you," Nat said.

"You still have to divorce your wife." She giggled. "Or kill her."

"God hates divorce, and so does your father." He breathed through his mouth. "Even if I divorce Charity, how will I be able to marry you? Your father will never let me marry you."

"Forget about Daddy. I know how to handle him," Chloe said. "I have to get a divorce too. He won't stop two divorcees from remarrying."

"You make it sound so straightforward."

"It is." Chloe shook her head. "Tried and tested."

"What do you mean?"

"So, when I was thirteen, I had a huge crush on this guy in the choir. Daddy did not allow children to join the main choir, but I insisted, and he let me."

Nat laughed and shook his head. The waiter returned but stood at a distance. Nat waved him over and he took their order of drinks. She wanted a margarita, he asked for red wine.

"He was my first lay," Chloe said.

"Hmm," Nat moaned. "I wish I was in your church at the time."

"Where were you when I was thirteen?"

Nat put his index finger on his lip for a second. "Sleeping around, I think. Charity was a brave Christian woman when I met her." He snickered. "She defied her parents, her church, her pastor, to marry me. We joined Daddy's church as a truce after almost ten years and three kids, and begging, praying, fasting."

Chloe threw back her head and laughed. "She was begging you. For what?"

"To come to church with her."

"Ten years! What changed your mind?"

"We had our last baby, and Charity almost died. Lost so much blood. I panicked and ran to church. Chief Alejolowo took me to Daddy. Daddy said, your wife will not die. He prayed for me. Ces't fini."

"I believe you. How many years ago was this?"

"Almost five. Charity thought that would settle all our issues, but this dog went back to his vomit." Nat sighed. "I hate to cheat on her."

"But you do. And you will cheat on me too, right?"

"I'm falling in love with you, Chloe." He bit his lower lip. "That's all I can say. I've never said that to anyone. Not even my wife."

For a moment they just stared at each other.

"I'm falling in love with you, too," Chloe whispered.

Nat raised their hands to his lips, but Chloe's phone rang, jolting both out of their reverie. She freed her right hand and found her phone in her dress pocket.

"It's the driver! Goodness. It's not even nine!" She freed her other hand from Nat's. "Yes?" She snapped.

"Ma, the mall is closing," the driver said.

"That is not true. I am inside!" Chloe said.

"Ma, they are rolling the something. The gate or something."

Chloe groaned. I'll come out now." She hung up. "We have to go back. I know he's lying but...aahhh!" She grunted.

"We have to find a way to see each other," Nat said. "Waiter!"

The waiter ran over. "Ready to order, sir?"

"Bring the bill, we're leaving."

"Yes, sir." The waiter left with a small bow.

Chloe stood. "They are so respectful here." She looked towards the pole where a young woman danced, patrons eating and drinking, the music soft and sensuous.

Nat stood too. "How am I going to see you tomorrow?" He licked his lips. "We need to find a way."

"Come to the mansion. That's all I can say. It sucks that Daddy won't let me own a car or drive one, and the mansion is so far out that I can't call a cab or..."

The waiter returned, Nat paid and led Chloe out. In the car, he pulled her into his embrace and kissed her until her phone started ringing again.

Grudgingly, he drove her back to the mall.

Chapter 27

WITH SUNBỌ GONE, *I tried to put my life in perspective. True anyone could die anytime but death had never seemed so real to me. No one close to me had ever died and the reality of that shook me to my roots. I had been going through life oblivious of living it. I did only the things expected of me. I never took charge of anything. I prayed because it was time to pray, ate, slept, woke up, took decisions only because it was the normal or expected. I lived like a part of a closed community. On a schedule. Refusing to take liability or responsibility. I was invisible to my own existence. I was going through life, but life was not going through me. I was in a dream.*

Sunbọ's death woke me up!

Daddy probably saw what was happening. Days, weeks, months after Sunbọ died, I moved around myself like a ghost. Then, he called me into his private parlour. I walked in, curtseyed, and took my seat.

"Your fortieth birthday is coming up, and I want us to throw a party," Daddy said.

He wasn't one who believed in birthday parties. In all my sixteen years of marriage to him, we never celebrated a birthday. Not his, mine or the children's. The birth date was a day for prayer and reflection, though Daddy never stopped anyone from attending other people's parties.

My mouth fell wide open, and I would have protested but he raised his hand.

"Hear me out." He leaned forward. "We don't need to pretend that Sister Sunbọ of blessed memory was your only friend. You need a new friend. And how best to connect than through a party? Forty, for that matter. Hmm?"

He was asking for my opinion? It sounded weird even in my own ears. Daddy pronounced, not ask. He ordered, not request.

I shrugged. "Whatever you say, Daddy."

"Good. I will call, umm, this boy, Elijah. He'll come and draw up a list. He's good with such things."

Daddy pressed the bell beside his seat. It normally rang the intercom in his home office where he had a full staff separate from the ones in the church office.

"Daddy." The secretary, Sister Theresa answered through the speaker in the parlour.

"Ask Elijah to come."

"Yes, Daddy."

Elijah was a young man, probably in his late twenties, who Daddy had recently taken keen interest in. He was a computer scientist at the time he joined the church, working for a food manufacturing company. Several months after he became our member, he joined the pastoral armour bearers. We called them PAB. Daddy must have noticed him. He was kind, had a serious face but a warm smile, and he was very loyal.

I didn't concern myself much with Daddy's team because they were fine without me, and I had mine to cater to. Daddy took care of his team, and there had never been a time any one member wanted me to intervene in their case. It surprised me a little though that Daddy would want someone on his team to plan my party. Did he see me as someone who did not have such capacity?

"I also want you to get close to Oye's wife. She's a very gentle, submissive woman, but she has great ideas about a whole lot of things," Daddy said.

Again, this surprised me. Oye was Daddy's son in ministry from before I got married, then a pastor, now a bishop. He rarely said anything to me, so how could I "get close" to his wife. I didn't know anything about his family beyond his wife's first name, Oluchi. This attempt by Daddy to socialize me was new. He had never bothered himself about who I was or was not close to.

Elijah walked in momentarily and went to kneel before Daddy.

"Stand up, Elijah." Daddy signalled. "Mummy's birthday is coming up in two months. Work with Oluchi, Oye's wife, and let's blow Mummy's mind." Daddy smiled.

His smile always melted my heart. If there was one thing I loved about my husband, it was his smile. He rarely smiled, but when he did, it touched me.

"Yes, Daddy," Elijah said.

I beamed. "Thank you, Daddy."

"Yes o, my dear wife. Your face has been too gloomy."

My fortieth birthday party was the talk of town for many months to come. As expected, Daddy did not spend his money on it. The moment it was known Daddy was throwing a party for me, everyone came on board. Elijah was an excellent planner, and as Daddy said, Oluchi was something else. I never knew she was so bubbly and capable. She had taste to cap it up. I was more of the old school, always so conservative but Oluchi would have none of it.

We had a garden party at the mansion and every important person in Lagos both spiritual and temperate, were invited. A few people came from the national too. It was not lost on people that Daddy had never thrown a party before. He also made it clear, that this was not a norm, but a direct order from God.

Oluchi had me change outfits five times through the course of the night. From a long flowing white heavy lace to heavily beaded blouse, with two wrappers (my native outfit) to a long red evening gown, dressed in the Yoruba "buba and iro" and lastly a beautiful flowing "adire" tunic. It was a parade of affluence like I'd never seen before. Glam magazines had me on a red carpet and paraded me in front of guests several different times as the evening progressed, and I wore something new, taking hundreds of pictures alone and with friends and family.

And so, I turned forty with style. For the first time in a very long time, I felt joy in my soul. My husband smiled all through the party. Many said they had never seen him so relaxed. Food and drinks were unending. Our church band played, but then, they were also acclaimed internationally. We had this new, dashing minstrel, Ayanbode, who led the band. He was young, charismatic, the most talented singer I had ever heard, and he knew how to move a crowd.

Most unlike what Daddy would have ever agree to, Ayanbode started singing a popular praise song and putting me and Daddy's names instead of God's. We were lured to the dance floor and people threw money at us. Unbelievable. Honestly. I had never seen my husband so relaxed, his guard down. I thought Daddy would end the party there and then. But he laughed and danced along.

When we got back to our table from the dance floor, Pastor Sharon walked over with her husband, a bishop of one of the very big churches. They greeted me, and then her husband spoke briefly with Daddy. He walked away afterward with two of his men, but Pastor Sharon came to sit with me.

"I've been looking for a chance to come and visit," Pastor Sharon said. "I didn't know the late Pastor Sunbọ was your good friend. Eeya, so sorry."

I half-smiled. "How did you know Sunbọ?"

"Haba, the circumstances around her death just made everything come out in the open."

I couldn't believe this woman would say this to my face at my party. I wanted to scream at her. Shout, but instead I swallowed. I looked around and saw Oluchi walking towards my table. It was the perfect opportunity to send this evil woman away.

I stood. "Pastor Oluchi, please come quick." I turned to Pastor Sharon. "Please, I have to talk to other guests."

"I will come and see you during the week," Pastor Sharon said.

I couldn't tell her off, or that I didn't want to see her. I just moved away. Oluchi asked what I needed but I had no answer to give her. I just needed to get away from this crowd for a bit.

Chapter 28

PASTOR SHARON CAME TO *the mansion the following Monday after my birthday party on Saturday. I was still upset and didn't want to see her, but she first went to Daddy's office, and he directed her to where I was. It would be disrespectful to turn her away. Though our church was on the premises, and I had an office in the church building, I did most of my work and correspondence from our family sitting room in the mansion.*

After the party, Daddy instructed the head of the PABs to assign some members to me and draft all the stewards who previously worked personally with me to join the unit. It didn't go down well with me at first, but as always, what Daddy wanted, Daddy got.

One of the PAB members served my guest a drink and snacks before they came to call me.

"Hello," I said. "I didn't know you would come so soon after the party." I took a seat on a couch facing Pastor Sharon's single couch.

"Hmm, my sister, you know how our lives are. If I don't come now, busy-busy will not allow." She sighed. "I'm sorry I upset you on Saturday. I didn't expect you to be taken aback."

Her apology surprised me. She was one of the high-class ones in our meeting and though we sort of formed a caucus, it never stuck. Since Sunbọ died, I'd not attended the classy meetings anymore, and no one ever checked to know why, so this association left me wondering what could be in it for such a big woman of God.

"Sunbọ was very close to me and umm, any mention of her makes me very emotional," I said.

"I'm sorry for your loss. Hmm." She sighed. "How exactly did she die?"

She wanted to gossip? My heart skipped a beat. I really wanted to send her out of my house. How dare her?

Pastor Sharon leaned forward. "I mean no offence, Pastor Bettina. But I heard...what I heard is not good."

Despite myself, my disgust with this woman, I wanted to know what she heard. "What did you hear?"

"*That she killed herself,*" Pastor Sharon whispered.

I stood. "*Please, come and start going. Thanks for visiting.*"

"*I...*" She stood. "*I'm sorry. I did not mean to upset you.*" She smiled. "*Let me go.*"

I should walk her to her car, but I stood rooted on the same spot. And, I had no plans to say anything or encourage her gossiping but involuntarily, I took a step towards her.

"*Are you okay?*"

She stopped and turned, and there were tears in her eyes. "*Pastor Bettina, I don't know.*" Then she bent over and sobbed and ruined all the foundation of her make-up.

I hurried over to her and brought her back to sit with me. She tried to stop crying and talk, but it seemed impossible for her. I could only sit there and pat her back.

After several minutes, she pulled back and shook her head. "*I needed that.*" She sighed.

"*Do you want to talk about it?*"

Never in my life had I had to counsel someone I considered my colleague or even higher than me. I spoke to hundreds of women from our church every week. They all believed I had a perfect life, and a perfect marriage, so I told them what they wanted to hear. In truth, besides the emotional aspect missing in my marriage, I had everything. My husband provided for me, he never physically or verbally abused me, he had sex with me regularly, adored my body, which made me feel beautiful. What else could a woman want?

Except that I felt something seriously was missing in my life, and I couldn't even place my hand on it.

"*Hmm, I have two sisters. I'm a triplet. We're forty-three years old. We are all married to pastors. We are all abused.*" She sighed. "*Two weeks ago, I seriously thought about killing myself. Then I got to know you were close to Pastor Sunbọ.*" She shuddered.

I froze. What was this? Another pastor's wife considering suicide?

"*I wanted to talk to you. See if you knew Sunbọ killed herself, and why? And maybe you got help for her? Or maybe you didn't even know? Did her husband know?*" She shook her head. "*I am sorry. I'm rambling.*"

Tears came to my eyes. Had Sunbọ tried to speak to someone also, and just never got the help she needed? I realized this had to be my cross. Two suicidal women couldn't come my way around the same time, and women who really couldn't speak out. Pastors' wives! Endangered species, we were. And we couldn't even trust ourselves seeing the way we prayed at our meetings. We were like the upcoming social media. Everyone trying to put up only their best foot.

"You're not rambling, ma." I blurt out. "You should speak up. Sunbọ never spoke to me about anything. She always said I was perfect, and I had a perfect life." I bit my index finger. "Had I known. There was no sign she was not happy. I mean to that extent. I knew she was not happy but…"

"Was it about her marriage? I sometimes wonder if I married the wrong person. My husband and I were so close when we got married," Pastor Sharon said. "Then we started to grow. Grow apart."

I stiffened. "You said he abused you. That is, beating you."

"No. Emotional, psychological, financial, at a time, before I started my business in the church…"

I gasped. "You do business in the church?"

"I started day care, and it turned to nursery/primary. Now we have secondary. Pastor tried to take it from me when he saw it succeeding but I didn't let him. He then started his own school in another part of town and got many of the members to take their children out of my school to his own." She sighed. "But my school is still doing so well. At least, the financial abuse and control is over."

"Then why do you want to kill yourself?"

"I'm just tired. I have my own money now but…I thought if I had enough to cater for myself, I'll be fine. But money seems not to be enough, and…" She sighed. "I think I have taken enough of your time. I have to go."

I didn't want to push her. I could see she was uncomfortable. As though she had said too much already. Yet I couldn't let her go. What if she did commit suicide?

I would never forgive myself. "Please, ma. Pastor Sharon. Talk to me. I have a feeling this is a ministry for both of us. You have two sisters who are dying in silence, and I am helpless if you don't talk to me," I said.

"Does your husband still sleep with you?"

I froze momentarily. "Umm, yea, yes. Why?"

"My husband has not so much as hold my hand in sixteen months. I suspect he has a girlfriend, or he's addicted to porn."

I clasped my hand over my mouth. "Porn? Yeepa."

"Exactly. You see that you can't help me. I now even understand Sunbọ. She probably never found someone to understand her problem." Pastor Sharon stood. "Thank you for your time."

I stood too. "No, my sister. I may not understand. But I have my own problems too. It may not be as big as yours, but it is still my problem. Is it better to have a man who uses your body like food and shares nothing else?"

Pastor Sharon smiled. "I just needed to offload, and I am happy you were here for me. Thank you." She pulled me into a hug.

"Let us pray, ma," I said.

She pulled back. "Pray? Does it really work?" She shrugged. "Okay, pray."

I closed my eyes and tremulously prayed for her. I didn't know what to pray for or how to pray, but I prayed. She thanked me again and briskly walked out. I was too dumbfounded to walk her out. I lowered myself to my seat, and asked God what exactly was going on. Why would a pastor's wife kill herself or want to kill herself? Why would she ask if prayer worked? Wasn't this what we believed in all this while? The efficacy of prayer?

My phone started to ring. It was Alexa. "Hello dear."

"Hello, Sister. Are you in your office?"

"No, I'm at home, what happened?"

She sighed. "I'm in church office. There's news going round that Bishop Oye, that a woman came forward that she is pregnant for him."

"Hmm, all these rumours," I said. But my mind went straight to Oluchi.

"In fact, she has pictures and she's putting it on social media."

"Leave all this junk on social media alone." I couldn't even say she should not believe the rumours. I could clearly remember when Daddy reprimanded Oye years ago about inappropriate sexual conduct.

This definitely was a call of some sort on my life. Sunbọ could not be saved, but see Sharon, and now Oluchi would have to deal with all this rumours on her own.

"Maybe you should call Pastor Oluchi," Alexa said. "She will need someone to comfort her. It is really bad. People are believing the woman."

"Hmm, thank you, Alexa." I moaned. "I will try and call."

In my heart of hearts, I didn't want to call Oluchi. But how would she know I was a shoulder she could lean on in her times of difficulty.

"Okay, Sister. Bye."

I decided to call Oluchi immediately before I procrastinated it off.

"Hello, Mummy! Birthday Mama! How are you?" Oluchi screamed. "That your party is making serious waves o. Can you believe some of the guests are calling me, as if I am an event planner." She laughed. "Big people o. One senator's wife. In fact, two. How are you, now, Mummy?"

"I'm fine." Had she heard the rumour? "I'm still getting over all of it."

"Ah, wait until the pictures come out. Huh, me I'm not on social media o, but we will scatter it, believe me. Brother Elijah is so excited about that," Oluchi gushed.

I chuckled. "Is he?" I could not possibly bring up any rumours.

"The few pictures I saw are bombers! Chai! Mummy! You are beautiful ooo! No wonder Daddy fall scatter for you." She whistled. "I didn't even know. Brother Elijah said he's been managing Daddy's profiles and accounts. Shey you know me I'm not on social media. I cannot die over junk."

No wonder. "Me sef that I'm on it, what do I do? I don't even know how to navigate, and new ones come up every time. The one with the bird, I don't even know."

"Twitter? Hahaha." Oluchi laughed. "Mummy o, don't worry, Elijah said he will take over your account too so you can be seen by everyone in the world."

"But why are you not there, Sister?" I thickened my voice to show some mockery. "On social media, I mean."

Oluchi scoffed. "Mummy, leave matter for Martta."

Poor woman, she had no idea. We laughed over some of the events at the party and I hung up. When she would get to know, it became such a huge scandal that Daddy stepped in.

"You have to address this in your church," Daddy told Oye.

Oye cried on his knees before Daddy. "Ah, Daddy, how?"

"You are asking me?" Daddy snapped. "The Holy Spirit did not give me anything to say on the matter."

The following Sunday, Oye stood in front of his church and told his congregants the Holy Spirit had not given him anything to say to the matter of the scandal on social media. Oluchi sat on the podium behind him, with a straight face.

Chapter 29

Calli stepped into the general lobby of the east wing of the mansion and paused, unsure of whether to confront Chloe or not. Her sister had tried to be discreet, but it was impossible to not notice a man had been in and out of this side of the house and at odd hours too. Was it worth Chloe's angst to challenge this? For Calli, she hated that Victor had run into the stranger once, though the man disappeared before Calli got there. No, she knew he wasn't one of the men who worked in the PAB team, or he'd have not gone into thin air when she approached.

She paced. He parked his car in the multi-purpose shed close to the general kitchen door. Calli suspected he came in from there. Right now, the car was there and had been for most of the evening. She checked her watch. It was almost ten o'clock. Victor was asleep, and Idong could return anytime from his meeting with Daddy and other pastors. This was the best time to challenge Chloe if she had a man in her room. Keep this under wraps. If Idong got to know, Daddy would. Her dear husband kept nothing from her father, which was irritating to say the least but...she needed to decide now.

Calli marched to Chloe's door, which opened to the two-bedroom apartment her sister had used now for almost six months since she "returned" home. She pressed her face to the door but heard nothing. She knocked. She was going to knock again and then leave when the door opened, and Chloe glared at her.

"Yes, Calli?"

Calli pressed her lips together. "Are you free to talk?"

Chloe snorted. "About what?"

"The man in your room," Calli said.

"The man in..." Chloe laughed. "Oh, please. Good night." She started to close the door, but Calli put her hand out to stop the door from closing.

"Daddy must not know you have someone in your room."

Chloe shook her head. "Yeah, he can't dare have sin under his roof. Be there deceiving all yourselves. Will you step back and let me close my door?"

"Bringing him here is like rubbing sin in Daddy's face, and you know that." Calli gasped. "You push the limits, Chloe. Why?"

"Excuse me? I do what I like. I don't care what you think or what anyone thinks. Go back to your cute little family, and stay out of sin, little sister!"

Chloe slammed the door, and it would have caught Calli's hand if she didn't step back in time.

"Chloe!" Calli knocked.

She heard Chloe laugh out loud. For a moment her heart thudded. Maybe Chloe was right. She could do whatever she wanted. She was Daddy's favourite child. Had always been. Why care? Why bother? Grieved and angry, and not sure why, Calli turned, and bumped into Idong.

"Huh!" She shrieked. "Idong!"

"Callista," Idong said.

Behind him, Daddy stood, his arms folded across his chest.

Calli curtseyed. "Daddy!"

"Step aside, Callista," Idong said.

Tears sprang to Calli's eyes. Had she led Daddy to Chloe or how could they be here?

"No, Daddy." Calli cried. "Please."

"Step aside," Idong repeated. "Don't get Daddy upset."

Calli stepped back. Daddy hated sin, probably more than God.

Idong knocked on Chloe's door. Chloe opened the door and the smirk on her face froze. Idong marched past Chloe into the house.

"Excuse me! Where are you going?" Chloe followed Idong.

Calli thought Chloe probably didn't see Daddy, or just ignored him. Nonetheless, a moment later, Idong, Chloe and the strange man came back to the front. Chloe had a very angry look on her face, but the man looked sorry. He fell on his knees at the sight of Daddy.

"I'm sorry, Daddy," he said. "I will leave now."

Daddy did not raise his voice. "Nathaniel, you brought sin under my roof?"

"Ah, Daddy, no, sir. It is not like that. I planned to tell you, sir..."

"We were going to tell you tomorrow." Chloe snapped. "And we didn't bring sin under your roof."

"Fire burn you, Nathaniel," Daddy said.

Calli fell to her knees. "Ah, Daddy! Please, ẹ jọọ, Daddy! Ah!"

"How can you curse him, Daddy?" Chloe snapped. "What did he do?"

Daddy turned and walked away.

"Daddy! Ah, Daddy, please," Nat said. "Ah, Daddy, I'm sorry."

Idong marched after Daddy. Calli sniffed. Nat bent over and wept like a child. Chloe pouted.

"Follow him, sir," Calli said. "Tell him to reverse the curse. Ah, God."

"Nothing is going to happen!" Chloe turned and walked into her room and slammed the door after her.

Nat followed Chloe.

Calli leaned against the wall and cried. Daddy's words came to pass. Didn't Chloe know this? She felt drained. Maybe this would be different, and everything would be fine. At least, now Daddy knew what was going on between Chloe and the man. It wasn't too surprising to Calli that Daddy knew the man's name. Daddy knew many people and sometimes, a word of knowledge revealed such information to him. Maybe for once nothing will happen like Chloe said.

Calli returned to the three-bedroom apartment she lived with her husband and son. She checked on Victor who was still asleep, and then returned to her room.

Idong was already in bed. So fast as though nothing important just happened. He sat up when she walked into their bedroom.

"Now, your sister will learn her lesson," he said.

"What do you mean by that?" Calli turned her back to him.

"You don't know? Daddy has spoken and nothing else will happen than as he spoke."

"Excuse me! You support Daddy cursing someone? You think this will bring an end to Chloe's behaviour?" Calli cried. "What if she moves out and goes to live with the man?"

"Is that what she plans to do?"

"I don't know what she plans to do. But what if Daddy's words come to pass? How will Chloe take it? Whether we like it or not, Chloe is the way she is." Calli turned and picked a new nightdress from her wardrobe. She loved her sister, but love wasn't something expressed around in her family, and she wished she could do something about it.

"When will she learn? She defies Daddy all the time. Is she not supposed to be in her husband's house...?"

Calli gasped. "Husband who kept quiet while his son beat up his wife...?"

"Who decided to marry the man? Did your father not warn her?"

Calli screamed. "Daddy said nothing! Nothing."

Idong snapped. "Why are you shouting at me?"

"Because if it was me, is this how you will take it?"

"I should stand against the oracle of God? I should risk the wrath of God?"

Calli yelled. "I am your wife!"

"And so?"

Calli could not bear his words. She ran into the bathroom and slammed the door.

Idong shouted. "Calli!"

The following afternoon, Chloe's scream disturbed the peace of the Jaja mansion as she ran wild, tearing at her clothes and throwing anything she could lift. Two PABs finally constrained her and held her down until a doctor arrived and gave her an injection that relaxed her, and she slept. Then she was carried to her room.

Nat had been killed on his way home the night before after the altercation with Daddy. His car got into an accident and caught fire. It burned to ashes with Nat in it before help could come.

For days, Chloe, confined to her room by PABs Daddy commanded to be stationed at her door, screamed, and banged on the door, and wept. Her tears tore at Calli but no one else seemed bothered by it. The east wing was on the outer end of the mansion, and besides Chloe and her attendants, only Calli and her family lived there when Daddy had no visitors from out of state. As long as Chloe remained indoors, she bothered no one. Calli related with this on a defeated level she didn't believe she could get to.

Chapter 30

SUNBỌ'S DEATH CHANGED EVERYTHING!

I realized how fickle life was. I must admit to my shame, I could not bring myself to face the truth. Sunbọ did indeed take her own life, and as the truth came out more and more within our circles, I hated Pastor Jide, and detested myself and Daddy for focusing so much on ourselves, we didn't realize our friend was in trouble. Pastor Jide though continued his life as normal, and soon, his daughters were back in school, living in the same house that held such horrible memories. I think I just sunk into myself and did not make myself available as a resource for my friend's girls.

There are no words to describe what dark, blank hole my life was like before my fortieth birthday bash. I however started paying attention at least to my children. The fear of dying suddenly, not knowing what would become of them overwhelmed me.

I ordered my schedule, just as Sunbọ advised before, around my children's. Adam had written his WASC exam and was studying for JAMB. He now attended an extra-mural school on Lagos Island and one of the drivers took him there in the morning and brought him back before three o'clock. He would then stay in his room, or in the library at home to study, or visit with his friends.

Chloe was Daddy's puppet. Once she came home from school, she went to his office and returned home with him. Calli was Chloe's puppet, and Ben was mine. Calli mostly followed Chloe to Daddy's office after school but would be made to sit in the general office with other office staff while Chloe sat inside Daddy's office. Ben came to my room after school.

In all, I made sure I was at home more, especially to be there when the children came home. I tried to build my relationships with Oluchi and Sharon, and Alexa, with the hope of connecting on social and emotional levels with others. I particularly wanted to start something that would help troubled pastors' wives. I could see many of us struggled. Oluchi's and Sharon's stories broke my heart and I ventured to be closer to both women. I visited them at home, created events and recreation we could attend with our children. I started a prayer movement for these women I wanted to reach out to – Sharon, Oluchi, and some others.

I think my ministry really took off after Sunbọ's death, after I turned forty. I believe that was when the scale of marriage and Love Jaja fell off my eyes and I started seeing Jesus for myself. Hard to accept, but it was my truth – the year after Sunbọ Ọlaolu died, I saw the Lord.

Chapter 31

ADAM HAD A FEW friends from church, who were mainly children of pastors, and a few friends from his high school too. All were elite, in a caucus of sorts, well-behaved children of prominent men of God. I was glad to see where my son was. I couldn't give myself a lot of credit for the young man he was, but at least, even in my feeling of redundancy, I may have done some good for him, raising him. Hard to describe I wasn't there for him because there were just so many things I was fazed by. Still, I made the effort to get close to him.

Daddy wanted him to school outside the country, but I prevailed because I wanted him to school in Lagos. I wanted him close by. It surprised me a little that Daddy was willing to accept my way. Probably because it was Adam. Sadly, father and son didn't agree on a lot of things and because no one successfully defied Daddy, Chloe excluded, Adam just did whatever was asked of him.

Truth told, about what university he would attend, and what course he would do, the decision rested on us, Adam's parents. At some point, I asked what he wanted to be, and he mentioned some course like artist, which I immediately discouraged him for. He needed to pursue a professional course so he would please his father. We ended up agreeing he could study law, since he wasn't good with science subjects.

I knew my son was smart, incredibly, and so when his JAMB result came out, and he passed well, I was so happy. I told Daddy we needed to celebrate, and so we did. We allowed Adam to host a few of his friends at the mansion. Someone had recently built an Olympic-standard swimming pool, and though our children were just learning to swim, when Adam requested he wanted his friends over at the poolside, Daddy let him. I got a caterer to serve light snacks and drinks for the boys, a total of ten of them.

One of the boys who came, Lucky Nedion, was new in church.

Lucky's family had made such a strong impression. When they first started attending, they were very committed. The father, a bit elderly, quite versed in the word of God, though he had never been a pastor, was a successful and wealthy architect. The mother was a nurse.

She was a beautiful woman in her early forties. Lucky and his sister, Olive, were the only children. At the time, Lucky was eighteen, and in his first year at the private Christian university Adam wanted to attend. Olive was fifteen. Besides the fact that Lucky's family quickly blended in church, Lucky and Adam hit it off too.

As evening approached, the boys moved the party to Adam's room. They played music and games and made a lot of noise. Close to dusk, Lucky left with some of the other boys. Shortly afterwards, Olive arrived with the family's driver to pick Lucky. By this time, all the boys had left, and Adam was alone in his room.

One of the PABs who Olive met at the door, had no idea if Lucky was still with Adam and simply directed Olive to Adam's room. Or not? Here, the twist to the story was reduced to a "he-said, she-said."

Three weeks after Adam's party, Mrs. Nedion came to the mansion to see me. Olive was with her. Even though the boys were close, Mrs. Nedion and I were not, and I didn't know why she wanted to see me. She was a beautiful woman who carried herself well, and someone I'd not mind being friends with, but my lifestyle did not permit such relationships. Daddy had told me from the beginning of our marriage that I could not, as his wife, make friends with members of the church.

I got one of my PABs to serve refreshments, but Mrs. Nedion declined. The moment she sat down, and Olive as well, she made her mission known.

"Mummy, my Olive is pregnant. For your Adam," she said.

I swallowed. The first thing that came to my mind was that Daddy must not hear of this.

"That can't be true." I exclaimed. "How?"

"The day of his party," she said softly, but I could see how hard she struggled to maintain calmness, speaking slowly. "Olive came with the driver to pick Lucky. She was raped."

I jumped to my feet. "Ah, madam, please. Please. Choose your words wisely. If Daddy hears this..."

She stood too. "Maybe Daddy should hear."

I laughed. "You want your daughter to die?"

Olive started sobbing and I think I noticed her for the first time. She was more beautiful than her mother. Very light skinned, with long, soft, curly hair. For her age, she had developed nicely. She had her curves already defined. I could see why Adam would be attracted to her but rape! It was too strong an accusation.

"Please, Mummy," Mrs. Nedion said. "Can you call Adam, and let him speak for himself?"

I shook my head. "No, ma. Rather, I will like for you to leave. Find someone else to dump the bastard baby on."

What an accusation!

Mrs. Nedion took deep breaths. "Three weeks ago, Olive came with our driver to pick Lucky from the party. She was sent to find him in Adam's room. Adam raped her repeatedly for more than thirty minutes, then he let her go. My daughter has never known a man. Now she's pregnant."

I stared at her. I was disciplined in that way, to just listen when people spoke regardless of how much I wanted to shut them up. Her lips puckered with each pause in between a recount she may have wept over. When she stopped talking, I pointed at my door.

"Leave my house before I throw you out, ma!"

Mrs. Nedion tapped Olive's shoulder. "Let's go," she said.

Without another word, the mother and daughter left my office. The family never came to our church again. I never saw Olive, or Mrs. Nedion again. Probably they left Lagos, I could never know. I didn't try to know.

After they left my office, shaking from head to toe, I marched to Adam's room. Before I could break his door down, I breathed in and out. I had only heard one side. What if they were wrong? Adam would think I didn't trust him. He would detest me. The relationship I was trying to build would be destroyed.

So, instead of unleashing my temper, I said a quick prayer and pasted a smile on my face, and knocked,

"Who is it?"

"Mummy."

"Oh, come in."

When I walked in, my son was in his boxers alone. It was late afternoon, and I didn't expect to find him like this. His room was a mess, clothes everywhere. We had PABs who cleaned the rooms daily. Was it that he didn't let them into his room? I never came here. And it dawned on me...I didn't know my son at all. I didn't know he was untidy because he did everything properly when he was in the rest of the house. I never tried to find out about girls, we only talked about school, and church.

"This is super strange," Adam stifled a smile. "Mummy in my room."

I cleared a small part at the foot of his bed and sat. "Mrs. Nedion was here."

He scrunched his face. "Who?"

"Lucky's mum."

"Oh, okay." He stood over me with his arms akimbo. "Um, is Lucky okay? I mean, I just spoke to him like an hour ago."

"Lucky is fine, but Olive is not."

I tried to gauge his reaction to her name. There was none. He just looked so unaware. Confused even. Was he pretending or he really didn't know how this concerned him?

"Sit down, Adam." I patted the space beside me. "I need you to tell me the truth and I will believe you."

"The truth. About what?"

"Sit down."

He did. "What's this about?"

"The day you had your party. Three weeks ago. Olive came to pick Lucky up..."

Adam cut in. "And Lucky had left."

Why was he getting edgy?

"But Olive still came to look for him," I said.

"No! Lucky had left. I didn't even see Olive. One of the guys later told me she came but he told her they had all left."

"Do you remember who the guy was?"

He shook his head. "No." Then he stood. "Why are you asking me all this?"

"Because Mrs. Nedion said you raped Olive..."

"What?"

"And she is pregnant!"

"That is total nonsense, Mummy. I didn't even see her that day!" He stomped around his room. "Oh my God, what a stupid liar she is. I never ever touched her."

I stood. "It's okay. I believe you. Just be careful because people are jealous, and they will say anything."

"Mummy, I swear, nothing happened." Tears sprang to Adam's eyes. "I can't believe this. Why would they? I still spoke with Lucky today. Why would his mum lie about me?"

"It's okay. Come here." I gestured and he moved closer to me, wiping tears off his eyes. "It's okay," I said. I pulled him into a hug.

Adam sobbed. "Thank you, Mummy."

I walked out of my son's room that day, afraid I had just finished feeding a monster because it suddenly came back to me, what happened on the day of the party. I was in my room down the corridor from Adam's and my door was open as I liked to leave it when I was inside so I could easily see the doors to my children's rooms. I saw Adam open his door and Olive walked in. I tried to stick around to know when she left, wondering if she was having an affair with Adam. But I had a meeting I had to attend. At least ten minutes after Olive was let into Adam's room, I left mine. I became engrossed and lost in what I went to do. I never remembered to ask Adam what Olive came to do or when she left.

And as I left Adam's room, I believed he had lied to me. He raped a young girl, and he was going to get away with it because I would never be the one to talk about this again.

What sort of mother was I?

Chapter 32

ELDER ELIZABETH'S OFFICE AS the director of missions looked like a home for antiques from every country of the world, with pictures, and keepsakes from different nations strewn in a decorative manner all over the place. Calli thought the woman was weird, but she had been a part of her father's church from the day it started and now she acted as though she was a shareholder. Calli knew she had a son her age, but no one had ever known Elder Elizabeth's husband or the father of her son.

The elder couldn't be more than five years older than Daddy, but she acted so much older. She hardly ever smiled, and everything she did was so business-like. Calli couldn't help but remember how she represented Mummy at her wedding with stoic professionalism, greeting people beside Daddy, giving orders like a soldier. It was the weirdest thing for Calli to be here now given her dislike of Elder Elizabeth, but she couldn't think of anyone else to go to.

"Welcome, Sister Callista," Elder said. She waved to one of several single couches in her office. "How may I help you?"

With the elder seated at the head of a conference table in her office, Calli suddenly realized how large the space was. Filled with so much furniture and antiques and shelves and files, how could this be an office. It was a well-arranged junk room.

Calli walked to the twelve-seater conference table and sat on the chair beside Elder. "Let me sit here, ma."

"I am surprised you are here. When I saw you booked an appointment..." the older woman narrowed her eyes. "Does this have to do with your marriage?"

Appointment. The earliest Calli got on the Elder's schedule was one full week. She'd had to call Daddy's office and get a faster day, still three days. How busier could a person be running such a mission as theirs. Well, Calli was learning.

"Elder, Mummy wrote a book." Calli cleared her throat. "A book of the story of her life. And she mentioned something I feel I should not treat lightly."

For the first time in all of Calli's twenty-nine years, all of which Elder Elizabeth was a part of, she saw the elder cringe and readjust her long flowing gown at the shoulders.

"I'm listening."

"Adam likely has a child, and I want to find the child," Calli said.

Elder jumped on her feet. "Ehn! How? Where did you find that? Does Daddy know?"

"Daddy, can't know, please ma. I told Daddy I didn't have the book." Calli stood, shaking. "I told Daddy I didn't read the book. Please ma, I have to go. Daddy can't know!" Calli pushed her chair back and turned towards the door.

In her hurry, the chair fell and made a thudding sound on the thick, carpeted floor.

"Wait, Callista. Wait!" Elder hurried after her. "Come and sit down. Daddy will not know you're here or talking to me. Come. Come."

Calli returned to her seat, eager to get the information she needed. "Elder ma, do you remember Architect and Mrs. Nedion? They were members seventeen or so years ago."

"I remember them very well. Ah!" Elder lowered herself to her seat. "She tried to report Mummy to me, but I would not hear of it. I knew it had to do with Olive's pregnancy, but you know, those days, it was speak no evil, hear no evil."

"Adam raped Olive. Do you know if she kept the pregnancy?"

"Oh, my goodness, God!" Elder sighed. "I don't know. I was upset with Mrs. Nedion. I didn't want to hear any details of what she had to say." She shook her head. "You see, they were relatively new in the church and the way everyone just loved and accepted them, and less than two years in, she was trying to spread a rumour. You understand, don't you?"

"I do. But do you have any idea how to find them?"

"Are you sure you want to? We should just let sleeping dogs lie."

Calli shook her head. "If my brother has a child, I want to know, and I want to find the child."

Elder stared at her fingers. "You are right." She pressed her palms to her eyes. "Architect Nedion is still very successful and has an office on the Island. I know one of his very close associates. She'll know how to find Mrs. Nedion."

Calli curtseyed. "Thank you, ma."

The Nedions lived in an exclusive estate in Ikoyi. If you were not looking for it, you couldn't find it because there was a school right in front, and the estate behind. Just a gate with a code on Turnbull Road opened to a narrow road that wound around the school to the estate. The main estate however had six grand houses, a massive sports field, a playground, and a swimming pool. The Nedions lived in number six.

A maid opened the door and led Calli to a small sitting room.

"Thank you," Calli murmured as the young woman left.

Calli looked around the room, cosy, private, it gave a sense of belonging in the house. It looked like a room you'd meet friends in. The pastel colours of the cane furniture, the curtains and Persian rug, left a warm feeling. Only one picture hung on the wall. It was of a young man Calli would easily call Adam. Her mouth dropped open, and she stared at the boy. It looked like a recent picture. Everything on that face was Adam Jaja's. Dark, smooth skin, a winning smile, inquisitive eyes with a touch of mischief.

"It was taken two weeks ago on his seventeenth birthday," Olive said behind Calli.

Calli jumped and swung around to face Olive. "Huh."

Olive smirked. "I hung it up here when I knew you were coming."

It had been close to eighteen years, but Olive didn't look a day older, perhaps more beautiful, and more mature. Clad in a small blue dress that shaped her figure, she was barefooted, and held two glasses of iced drinks. One looked like apple the other like orange.

"The last time I saw you, Calli, you were skin and bones. You fleshed out," Olive said. "Apple or orange?"

Calli blinked. "Apple, thank you. And thank you for seeing me." She received the glass of apple juice.

"I have prayed every day since my son was conceived that a day like this will happen." Olive sat on a single cane chair. "I don't want to guess but what brings you here?"

It didn't miss Calli's attention that Olive did not offer her a seat. She took one anyway.

"I, huh, I want to thank you for being so nice. I didn't know what to expect." Calli cleared her throat. "I was only eleven at the time. I never knew anything happened."

"I suppose."

"My mum wrote about it in a book…"

Olive grunted. "A book?"

"It's not yet out. I think she just wanted us all to read it first. A first draft, really." Calli sighed. "Umm, I'm not sure she'd want to publish it, you know. It has real names and places."

"The only way you could have found us." Olive glanced at her son's picture. "Thank God he's not in it, though." She scoffed. "Since your mother, the almighty Mummy threw us out and made sure everyone cut us off. My son was born without anyone in your circles acknowledging him."

"What's his name?"

"Hermon." Olive smiled. "It means truth."

Calli smiled. "Hermon Jaja."

"No!" Olive laughed. "He is Hermon Nedion. My father adopted him. A child must have a father, not so?"

"I am so sorry for what happened to you. And I thank you for seeing me, and for being so receptive," Calli said.

"What else can I do? Your brother raped me for almost an hour, and no one in that house of yours noticed. And when he was done, he told me, and I can never forget," she snorted. "He said, get out."

Calli clasped her hand over her mouth. "I'm so sorry."

"I just thank God for my parents. All their support and love. My brother. Everyone protected me." Olive drew in a shuddering breath. "I'd like to have that book your mum wrote. It will be my evidence that I was right. Then," Olive smiled. "Then, I can prosecute all of you."

Calli gasped. "Prosecute!"

"Yes, probably since then Adam has raped more girls. They'd feel safe to come out and speak. Huh?" Olive arched her eyebrow. "What do you think? You, being here, is additional evidence. I have cameras recording us now, audio-visual."

Calli swallowed. "Adam left home shortly afterwards. He went to university, but he didn't...he didn't finish."

"Tell me something I don't know. I have been following your family like a lunatic. I have done nothing else, believe me." She swiped at the tears in her eyes. "I knew when he was thrown out, expelled from Lucky's college, then he went abroad and disappeared into thin air. I know he didn't die, or it would have leaked." She sniffed. "I know when you all went to university, graduated, Chloe got married to the old man, you got a pastor, had a baby, Ben went into missions in some remote area in Asia, right?"

Tears sprang to Calli's eyes. "Yes."

"My life is the study of the Jajas! I do nothing else," Olive said.

"I'm sorry."

Olive stood. "Believe me, your father will soon hear from mine. We plan to prosecute and your presence here is all we need."

Calli remained seated. "You can't prosecute Daddy. He didn't rape you."

Olive snickered. "Yes, I know, but he will fish out his son."

"You can't prosecute Adam either." Calli breathed through her mouth. "Daddy will protect Adam with his life."

Chapter 33

WE BECAME A CREW of four. I, Oluchi, Sharon, and a pastor's wife close to Oluchi called Chinwe. Of the four, I'd say I was the one without serious marital problems. At least, my husband was not sleeping with anything or anyone like Oluchi's husband, nor was he sexually abusive and neglecting like Sharon's. Chinwe was a physically battered woman. Emotionally, I could say I wasn't balanced, because when Daddy made love to me, he reassured me and made up for all the romance he lacked the time and quotient for.

Our crew of four started a prayer and counselling meeting we tried to camouflage under Daddy's ministry because he was the "cleanest" of these men of God. The other husbands would feel offended because they were guilty of it all, so I was the president of the group. Soon, we had more pastors' wives join us. Alexa joined us too and became very involved and committed. We called it, "Praying for Leading Ladies." In the meetings though, we spoke about abuse, and how to overcome. We contributed money for women who did not have a means of sustenance, and for us pastors' wives, organized outreaches to prisons, orphanages, hospitals, and schools. We got so busy.

It worked a little for a while. Chinwe became one of our best success stories.

She was out of her house so much; her husband hardly saw her enough to beat her up. For weeks sometimes, she was not even in Lagos. I feel felt so happy for Chinwe because her case was worse than any I'd ever seen. Once her husband beat her up at night and pushed her out of the house. She was in her nightgown when her neighbour let her into their house to sleep. On another occasion, when her husband agreed to meet a marriage counsellor, it got so heated that he slapped and punched her in the face and walked out on the counselling session. Chinwe finally got a contract job with the UNESCO and moved to live in Uganda with her three children.

Her husband continued to pastor their church. Stories of the abuse went underground, and only her exploits became news.

Only God knew how Oluchi continued to do it. Bishop Oye was in and out of scandal. With the emergence of social media, it only got worse. One would hear of a girl rant on social media, and she would be pulled down quickly by members of Oye's church. Oluchi once signed up so she could connect with her friends and family and members of the church, but the gossips started showing up with tags to her name. People were calling her out to speak and warn her husband, so she deleted all her accounts.

Did God not answer our prayers at our pastors' wives' meetings? Yet Bishop Oye's churches expanded at alarming rates so much so that he could host international meetings. Daddy continued to be the rock-supporter and father-in-the-Lord, which further endorsed their ministry and church.

It couldn't get worse when the news went viral that fifty women had signed a petition against Bishop Oye on allegations of sexual harassment and statutory rape. Social media exploded. Bishop Oye came to Daddy, with Oluchi right beside him. Both panicked that if something was not done, Oye would be off to prison.

One of Daddy's members, a reputable lawyer, Barrister Alejolowo, had been in the limelight in recent times, making headlines in some big advocacy cases. Daddy called him to an emergency meeting.

"Lawyer. Do something," Daddy said. "Oye, mo ti ma n warn ẹ! You need to tame this demon!"

"Daddy, God will help me," Oye said.

Oluchi remained stoic, on her knees beside her husband. Could I ever be this supportive even in the toughest times? Because I was close to her, I knew she was genuine. She really loved her husband and prayed for him, but what a vice he had!

"Barrister, you have to do something," Daddy said again.

If Daddy said something once, it was law. Twice, it was an unbreakable law.

The lawyer nodded. "Consider it done, sir."

Bishop Oye fell flat on his face. Oluchi just stared ahead; no emotion displayed. Nothing. It left me cold. How did she feel? Oluchi had never been one to show any of her feelings in public. But when she was alone with Oye, did she cry, fight, refuse to talk to him, refuse to sleep with him? I would never know. Oluchi never discussed her marriage with me. I didn't think it was healthy because I was one of her closest allies. But did she talk to someone else? Maybe her mother? She had to find someone to confide in. There had to be a way to expunge all these negativities.

I don't know much about this but Oye's case never got to court. The civil suit by the women accusers didn't even succeed. It wasn't admitted on a technicality. The way the presiding judge struck it out, none of those fifty women could sue Oye for those crimes again. They scrambled around trying to do something, anything, but all just went down the drain, and the case died a natural death.

Oluchi was so elated, she celebrated during our meeting with a testimony. She compared it to how the red sea swallowed the Egyptians. It all left me wondering. Alejolowo was not a judge in Lagos where the case was filed, or Ibadan where Oye's massive ministry was. He was not even a judge at all, but he pulled it off. Whatever he did worked the needed magic. I believed Oye was guilty, but he never admitted to any of the accusations, or show any remorse in public, at least. Would so many women be lying? I didn't get it.

Sharon's story, I guess would be the worst in all our lot. Well, besides my story. Or maybe not. People would be the judge of this. Sharon had confided in me that she didn't have sex with her husband anymore. At least over a year. She didn't feel attracted to him and divulged in masturbation and porn. We were praying on this, believing God that she would be delivered from this horrible habit.

Nothing really changed at first. As accountability partners, I would ask her every week if she masturbated, and we'd pray about the results. Several months down the line, with so many activities, she was able to reduce the number of times, and eventually, stop for months.

As part of the programs she started in her church, she helped children off the streets. We sponsored children who were hawkers to return to school. It was really very impactful. So impactful, the state governor's wife took interest and sponsored some of our outreaches. Taking kids off the streets also entailed helping to set up their families and we did as much as we could. This turned out to be Sharon's sole commitment, and she became very engrossed.

On the fifth anniversary of her outreach, she brought ten families to church for thanksgiving, and invited me to her church to preach. Preaching wasn't always my forte. I was a minstrel, but I stopped singing in church after I became Mummy. It wasn't proper for the "Mummy" to be in the choir, Daddy had said, and that ended my music ministry. So, I started to pray, and to preach.

My message in Sharon's church, in an auditorium packed full, with over five thousand members, was on love. I spoke extensively on how love needed to be shown not only to those people we know, but also people we did not know.

Sharon came up after I spoke. "Thank you, Mummy. Our very dear Mummy, Pastor Bettina Jaja. I love you, ma. You have been a great encourager." She half-smiled. "Can we please stretch our hands to Mummy and pray for her."

The church did. I went on my knees and prayed for myself as well.

"Amen! Halleluiah!" Sharon shouted at the end of the prayer and the church applauded. "Now, to the main matter of the day. I would have called our dear pastor, my husband to come and share the blessing over us, and the church dismiss, but today is the day for Ichabod. The departing of glory from this assembly."

I gasped and looked at Sharon's husband. He scowled at her, which made me realize he was surprised at what she was saying.

A murmur went through the church.

"Yes, brethren. The glory has departed from this church. The pastor of this church has a concubine in the choir. Sister Mirabelle. She's pregnant. And it is not her first. She has decided to have this baby for my husband. Previously, she aborted!" She turned to her husband. "The church should know, sir."

A loud wailing rent the air, and several people joined in. Sharon's husband stood and to my shock, walked up to the pulpit, snatched the microphone from Sharon and stomped out of the church. Sharon raised her two hands in protest. People stood and started leaving the church hall.

Had she gone mad?

I hurried to her. "Pastor Sharon. Yeepa! What was that? Kilode? Why would you?"

Tears streamed down her face. "I'm free. It's over. I did it. It's over." She sobbed hard, and I pulled her into my arms.

I had never seen anything like this.

Sharon got home that day and packed all her belongings and moved to her mother's house. She continued with her outreach for a little while, but the scandal of what she did was too much. Her husband never returned to the church, and gradually, the other pastors left, the ministers left, the stewards left, the members left, and the church closed. It was the biggest ministry tragedy I had ever seen in all my life.

Alexa's issue was the one that came up as a big surprise for me. She was planning her wedding to Pastor Fẹmi months after my fortieth, and it was going to be big! Daddy was proud of the young couple, and so was I. One day, Alexa asked me to go to Balogun market with her to do some shopping. Pastor Fẹmi drove us there. It was a sunny day, and after hours, everyone was tired.

Finally, we were done. Alexa got some really good lace materials, and all was paid for by her fiancé. We decided to go and eat lunch somewhere, and that was when trouble started. Alexa wanted a particular restaurant, but Pastor Femi complained it was too far and there was tendency to get into a hold-up.

My sister got so angry, right there in the car, she slapped her fiancé twice.

I couldn't believe my eyes. "Alexa! Stop it!" I shouted. "Don't you have respect?"

"That's what she always does," Pastor Femi said. "Okay, we'll go where you want."

"I don't want to eat again," Alexa said. "Just take me home!"

My sister was abusive? I never would have believed.

Chapter 34

PART OF WHAT WE did in our PLL meetings was praying for our children and teaching one another basics about mothering even despite marital difficulties. I knew I hadn't been there for my children. Deep down, I prayed for God to forgive my absenteeism, and help me have good children. It's hard to explain because of my perspective and upbringing. My mother was never busy the way I was. She always made time for my sisters and I, and when we came back from school, though she couldn't read, she sat with us while we did our homework.

My children never had that closeness with me. Ben was always close by, but I never gave him much attention. I had my regrets and I wanted to fix things. I started getting into my children's businesses. I cleared my schedule in the morning and saw them off to school, and I made sure I was in the house when they returned, at least for one hour. On weekends, I planned my meetings around theirs. It began to show a little after a while. Calli warmed up to me more, and once in a while, they would come to ask my permission to do different things, which they never did prior. They always asked their Daddy or a PAB.

Shortly after Chloe turned thirteen, the church hired a music minister to take over the choir in the main church and help with other churches who needed assistance with grooming their choirs. His name was Dami Odami. People called him Minister Odami. He was a young, fervent, and gifted man who carried the congregation on his very first service. At the time, he was engaged to be married, and he joined the church with his fiancé, Sister Lili. Lili joined the hospitality department. She was a petite, light-skinned, and shapely woman. I thought she looked older than Odami, and I found out I was right. Lili was thirty-two and Odami was twenty-seven. But the two seemed great together.

Odami changed the whole mood and atmosphere of the worship in the church.

Three months as music minister, we were planning a city-wide music concert that would feature international minstrels. The whole church was provoked and explosive. It would be the biggest music concert of the year 2006.

Chloe walked into my room one Sunday morning as I was preparing for church. She had never done this before. Rather, she went to speak to her father.

"I want to join the choir," Chloe said.

My hand on the way to my face to rub powder, froze. "Choir? Why?"

"I want to be in the concert, huh."

I snickered. "Chloe, first you are in junior church. You can't join the main choir, or do you mean junior church choir?"

On one hand, I was glad she wanted to be involved in service but on the other hand, she had to do it with her age mates. The youngest person in the main choir was at least twenty because we had a vibrant teens church, and they had their own choir.

Chloe pouted. "Adult choir."

"Huh, it's not possible." I continued with my dressing. "Did you tell Daddy?"

"No! I knew you will say no." She turned and stomped to the door. "I hate you!"

"Chloe!"

My daughter marched through the door and slammed it hard. For a second, I wanted to follow her, but I assumed she would go and tell Daddy, and he would refuse. I finished dressing up, and we all went to church. Normally, Daddy went earlier than everyone else, and I went before the children.

To my greatest shock that day, when the choir stood to minister, Chloe, the youngest and shortest was right there in front, with them. My gaze shot to Daddy, but his head was bent, and his eyes were closed as he normally did when the choir ministered because immediately afterwards, he would stand to preach.

I couldn't wait for church to be over, and I summoned Odami to my office.

"Who allowed my daughter to join the choir?"

Odami frowned. "She came with a letter signed by you and Daddy. She's been attending rehearsals for twelve weeks as stipulated for newcomers."

My mouth dropped open. "What?"

"She bought all the uniforms." Odami gasped. "Ma, you are not aware?"

Heat and cold enveloped me. A letter signed by me and Daddy! The minister had such a sincere confusion on his face, I just had to cover up for my motherly disgrace.

"Ahh! This girl o!!! You know she came with the letter and was just ranting; I didn't know it was to join choir. Choi, this child. Isn't she too young?"

"She is but since she had you and Daddy's approval, I couldn't object." Odami smiled. "She was the first person I auditioned."

"Oh wow. I hope she's doing well?"

"She sings well. Not too matured, but she'll do very well," he said. "I heard Mummy that you were a powerful minstrel yourself."

"Huh." I smiled. "In the good old days o."

After he was gone, I sat for several minutes, unable to coordinate. Chloe definitely forged my signature, but did she do the same for her father? What was going on here? I know my children had access to money all the time. People gave them money they didn't tell me about. Daddy gave them money too, but the choir had so many uniforms. Would Chloe have afforded all of this? It took me to the question. Were my children born again? Not too long ago, Mrs. Nedion came to accuse Adam, and now this?

Daddy had preached to each child when they turned seven and "led them to Christ" but in hindsight, would any of these children have said they didn't want to accept Christ? What about a personal relationship? Did they have this?

The ideal thing was to call Daddy's attention; call Chloe and stop her from the choir.

I did neither. I stood back as though nothing was wrong. Daddy did not question Chloe being in the choir, and so I assumed he had signed his part of the letter and Chloe forged only my signature. If he gave her permission, then she should be there. The choir was one of our strongest church teams. They prayed every day and had night vigils every week. A member of the choir could not be lukewarm. It was a good department to grow as a Christian. With these in mind, I rested my fears about Chloe. I refused to consider Chloe's rude remarks and attitude that Sunday morning, or the fact that my daughter had been involved in the choir for three months without my knowledge...the height of my negligence.

The music concert came, and it was a glorious night. The crowd in church filled everywhere, inside, and outside, and Daddy announced it was time to build a stadium so we could have more of this. That very night, money to build a fifty-thousand-seater amphitheatre was raised. One of the guest ministers from Europe then invited the choir to a concert he was planning in Dubai. What a magnificent way to end the evening.

When we got back to the mansion, Daddy called a meeting with Odami to discuss the Dubai trip. The guest minister said it would be in a month's time and gave Daddy all the details. I would have thought this could be discussed the following day and not at almost twelve midnight when everyone was tired, but that wasn't Daddy's style.

Daddy took his seat, and out of curiosity, I sat on my usual couch too. Odami knelt before Daddy.

"Joko," Daddy said, and Odami took a seat on one of the couches. "The minister is not paying anyone's way to Dubai. I will sponsor ten people, or do you need more?"

"Ten people is good, Daddy. Two from each part, me and one additional soloist," Odami said. "Thank you, Daddy."

Chloe walked in. "I want to go too."

I stuttered. "Aha, Chloe, are you not supposed to be in bed?"

She walked to Daddy and fell to her knees at his feet, ignoring me as though I had not spoken. "Daddy, please. I promise I will do anything you want, please."

"Okay, Chloe. Go to bed."

Chloe stood and flung her arms around Daddy's neck. "Thank you, Daddy." She strolled out, making sure her gaze caught mine, and then Odami's.

The look on my daughter's face made me shudder. She didn't smile at me. In fact, there was a look that said, "it's me and you in this battle." I watched her walk away and noticed for the first time her round hips and the furious way she swung them. When did Chloe grow so big? How did my daughter turn against me at such an age? When I was her age, I was my mother's wrapper, and I remembered Sunbọ's girls all adored her and wanted to be around her and do whatever she wanted. How did I miss it so badly? How could I ever make amends?

Chapter 35

DUBAI WAS SOMETHING ELSE.

Since Chloe was going, I insisted I wanted to go too, and in the end, took Calli and Ben. Adam was soon leaving for school, and in order not to miss his resumption date, Daddy did not allow him to go to Dubai. The choir members lodged in the same hotel as us, and we were booked to spend one week even though the concert was just two days. Odami made it a retreat versus vacation for the members he chose. They prayed and fasted several of the days, and Chloe joined in.

I was comfortable leaving my daughter with the choir members. Altogether, there were five men and five women. Two of the women were single, and the others married. All the men were single. The women took care of Chloe, at least in my presence, they pampered her, and she succumbed. In my absence though, the story seemed different. Not seemed. In my absence, the story was totally different. Chloe proved her independence and didn't submit to anyone, as I would later come to know.

While Chloe was with the choir, praying, rehearsing, and sightseeing, I took Calli and Ben out, sightseeing and shopping. At first, I felt a little guilt, but once I offered Chloe to join us and she declined, with support from the sisters in the choir that they were having fun as well, I let her be.

On the last night of the vacation, Chloe told me there would be a choir meeting in Odami's room. I thought nothing of it. They had had meetings in different people's rooms. Mostly Odami's. At about ten o'clock, Odami sent me a message that the meeting was prolonging, and could Chloe stay until the end? He said he would walk her to our suite, which was just down the corridor when they were done. Fine, I replied.

Just before one in the morning, Odami returned my daughter. He knocked once and as soon as I opened the door, he left, and I didn't quite see him.

Chloe was bubbly, unlike how she normally was whenever she returned to the room. She went straight into the bathroom and took a shower. The woman's instinct in me rose like an angry mama-bear.

I knew at least a little about my daughter. She was lazy and dirty. If she had underwear on when she went for that meeting, it was likely on the floor of the bathroom. So, I waited until she was asleep and went into the bathroom. Her underpants was in the dustbin. I picked it up and smelled it. Tears sprang to my eyes. My daughter had the residue of a man's seed. The first awful thought that came to my mind was that they did not use protection.

"Oh my God!" I cried before I could stop myself. "Which of the men was it?"

Odami? The highly talented, highly spiritual music minister? I stomped back into the room with the pant in my hand. I didn't care about how disgusting this was. I picked my phone and called Odami's number.

"Hello, Mummy." He yawned.

"Odami! Did you rape my daughter? You bastard...did you touch her?" I screamed. "What did you do to Chloe?"

Calli woke up behind me. "Mummy?"

I ran into the bathroom and slammed the door. "Odami. Daddy is going to hear about this. Whatever you did..." And I realized he had hung up.

I looked for the number of one of the sisters in the choir, Maria, and called her.

"Mummy." Maria moaned. "Is everything okay?"

"Sister Maria, please do you know what has been happening to my daughter in the choir? One of the brothers is sleeping with her."

"Ye! Mummy?" Maria screeched. "How do you know?"

"What time did the meeting finish this evening?"

"Just before ten. Mummy, what happened?"

"Chloe did not return until one!" I cried. "Ah, Sister Maria, Odami has finished my daughter."

"Let me come, Mummy."

Moments later there was a knock on my door. I opened the door to Maria and another sister, Diana who shared her room. They curtseyed to greet and walked fully into the sitting area.

"Mummy, how is she now? Shouldn't we go to the hospital so they can flush her?" Maria said.

It was then I realized I still had the stinky pant in my hand. I excused myself and went to trash it in the bathroom. No, Chloe was not raped. All the choir members were there, and she could have left when they did. The joy in her face when she returned too showed no sign of force. My daughter fully consented. How would I now handle these ladies? I should not have called them. Calli remained awake and looking worried, but I ignored her. She just kept staring at me, hoping for me to say something to her, I guess but I had no words, not even to tell her to go to sleep.

"My problem now is the brother. Odami. Daddy will curse him," I said.

"As he should," Diana said. "I even can't still believe my ears. But how is Chloe?"

"The man used condom. She brought it back with her, that's how I knew," I lied. God forgive me. I was now such a good liar when it came to hiding my shameful parenting.

"Well, he will have himself to blame whatever happens to him when we return." Maria sighed. "What a demon!"

"Thank you so much sisters, I'm so sorry to wake you up from your sleep." I fake-yawned. "We're flying tomorrow. When we get home, we will solve this matter."

The sisters curtseyed again and returned to their rooms. Definitely, Odami was a goner. He had heaped curses on his own head. It didn't matter if she consented or not. He was more than double her age. No, Daddy had to hear and rain judgement. If Chloe was not raped, then I had a bigger problem on my hand because it meant there would always be an Odami to fight off.

When we all woke up the following morning, I pretended nothing happened. We went for breakfast and Odami was not there. I later learned when we went to check out that he had earlier checked out and left. Could he have changed his ticket? It was possible. The church paid him a good salary. But whatever the case, I planned to challenge him back at home unless he didn't show up there either.

We arrived home in the evening and Daddy was not available. He was locked up in his office and didn't want to see anyone. The following day was Saturday, his day of rest. Daddy didn't believe a pastor should pray and fast on Saturday for service on Sunday. When I woke up on Saturday, he was in my arms. We made love and made up for the one week I was away.

Relaxed and happy, and very unlike me after intercourse, still in Daddy's arms, I said, "Daddy, something terrible happened in Dubai. Minister Odami raped Chloe."

It was meant to be a bombshell. Instead, Daddy kept quiet for a long time.

"Daddy, did you hear what I said? Minister Odami raped Chloe..."

"Did she tell you so?"

"No! But I got the evidence. I found the..."

"If Chloe did not tell you, why are you making up stories about her? What exactly is your problem with your daughter?" Daddy shifted himself until I was out of his embrace and turned to the other side.

I couldn't believe this. "Daddy!" I tapped him.

"If you touch me one more time, Mummy!"

My jaw sagged. What was this? Did Chloe talk to her father already? She had behaved as though everything was normal. Sisters Maria and Diana had come to me in the morning to find out if Chloe spoke about it or not. I could remember how they exchanged a silent look when I said Chloe said nothing, and even the normal way Chloe behaved made me look like a moron.

The following day in church, Daddy praised the choir members who went to Dubai and welcomed them specially. Minister Odami led worship powerfully. I couldn't take it. I was not insane or rash. I knew what I smelled. I trusted my instincts.

Again, when church closed, I summoned Minister Odami to my office, along with Sister Maria, and Chloe. I wasn't a fool, and this man could not get away with defiling my daughter. I planned to get a confession from both ~~of them~~, and in the presence of Sister Maria.

"Minister Odami, what time did rehearsal end on our last night in Dubai?"

"Around ten, ma," he said.

I tried to keep my voice calm. "And what time did you return Chloe?"

Odami shook his head. "I didn't return Chloe, she left with the others."

I snapped. "If you lie to me, I will curse you!"

Odami dropped to his knees. "Mummy, I am not lying. Ask anybody. Sister Maria, talk now. You were there. Everyone left. Only me and Brother Akpan were in the room."

I remembered he did share a room with the Akpan. Why didn't I remember that? Or did the two evil men rape my daughter?

I turned to the sister. "Sister Maria?"

"When I was leaving, Chloe had already left and Diana and I left," Maria said. "Minister Odami and Brother Akpan were talking about something else."

Did Chloe leave and then later return?

"So, what was the message you sent about, that could Chloe stay longer?"

Sister Maria answered. "Yes, we were thinking we would rehearse a new song for today but now decided to do the song we did at the concert. So, we went through it, and didn't take time."

All this could be true, but I didn't trust my daughter. I couldn't trust Odami either. Chloe may have walked right past our suite and gone to wait until everyone left. She had a phone. Odami could have messaged her when the coast was clear. Akpan may have been in on the plan. I didn't know but I was sure of the smell on Chloe's underwear. I glanced at her, and she was just staring at the floor the whole time. Odami on the other hand, had his eyes on me, and there were tears in them.

"It's true, Mummy, please believe me," Odami said.

"So, why did you check out before everyone? Were you on the plane with us?"

Odami shook his head. "No, Mummy, I was told my mother fell into the well, I just changed my flight to an earlier one."

There was nothing more to say. I felt drained and cheated but I was fighting a battle I couldn't win. Chloe was not innocent, and neither were these choir members. Whatever the case, there was a conspiracy, and I was caught in its web.

I pressed my lips together. "Okay, I hear you. Just mind yourself, Minister Odami. My eyes are on you!"

Odami stood and left. Maria curtseyed and left.

Chloe stood in front of me and flared her nose, and hissed, and rolled her eyes. "Just leave us alone, Mummy!" She stomped out of my office and slammed the door.

I sank into my chair and wept. I had failed. God, please what can I do to redeem my daughter?

Chapter 36

MANY PEOPLE THOUGHT ADAM Jaja was in Britain, but he had been sent back home for years. On Daddy's request, his lawyer had argued for him to be deported rather than incarcerated on taxpayers' money at a government psychiatric prison. His condition was that bad. Only Daddy, Idong, and Elijah knew where he was. To the public, Adam's only failure was that he didn't want to be a pastor. He was touted as a very private businessman who had his chain fashion stores in Britain and Ireland. Some even rumoured he was gay because he didn't get married or court anyone.

Indeed, Adam's fashion stores existed. There were pictures of Adam posing in the stores. Photoshopped pictures. In truth, Adam was riddled in drug addiction and a few criminal indictments, and the worst part, mental breakdown. At thirty-four, he already had greying hairs on his head and beards, and though the private asylum he called home was in Lagos, he hadn't seen a street in at least eight years.

Calli initially didn't know any of this and had no clue how to get information about Adam. Daddy had clearly made talking about Adam or Ben a taboo. Going back to Elder Elizabeth was not quite appealing or even an option. The Elder would sooner or later think she was sinning by aiding Callista without Daddy's permission.

On her return from seeing Hermon, Calli cuddled in her room, and wept. Why was her family so messed up? She had friends who lived decent, normal lives and didn't even serve God half the way she and her parents did. Bosa's parent didn't have a quarter of Daddy's wealth, but they were happy, and their children did well. Except for Bosa's accident, which at one time Calli overheard his mother blame her for, everything went well.

She didn't know what to do. She couldn't tell Daddy about her discovery, and she didn't have such a great relationship with Idong, who probably knew everything she wanted to know. She had been "forced" to marry him. He was polite to her and a great father to Victor, but Calli never trusted him because his loyalty was to Daddy and not her. She thought of finding Mummy's number to contact her but that was somewhat awkward. Mummy probably knew nothing about Hermon, at least not in her book, and may not be willing to step into the situation. But, why did she add the rape incidence into her book? She could have easily omitted it. Maybe she wanted the Nedions to be found. Maybe Mummy wanted the story to come out!

Calli decided to try and contact Mummy. Yes!

She wiped her face and jumped to her feet, and startled at the sight of Idong, standing in the doorway. She hadn't heard him come in. He was supposed to be in his office at the church, and Victor's school had not yet closed for the day.

"Why are you crying?" Idong said.

Calli sniffed. "Nothing." She walked towards the bathroom to wash her face and Idong followed her.

He glared at her. "Why are you crying?"

"I said…"

"I know what you said, Callista." He closed up behind her. "You've been very withdrawn. What's going on with you?"

She stiffened. "Nothing."

He turned her around and searched out her face. "Look at me. I know what happened with Chloe must have upset you and…"

She screamed and burst into tears. "You don't know anything!"

He pulled her into his arms and let her cry her heart out. "It's okay, my darling. Ssh," He cooed. "Ssh. It's okay."

Calli had never been so vulnerable with him, and he had never been sensitive to her. All these years, she had never felt his comfort or love until now. She knew she would regret it. He was loyal to her father. But she desperately needed to talk about her discovery or go mad.

She drew in a ragged breath and stepped away. Idong pulled her back.

"Please, my baby. Tell me what's wrong." He cupped her cheeks. "I won't say a word to Daddy."

Despite herself, Calli chuckled. "He'll kill me if he knows."

"Then I swear on my dead father's grave Daddy will never hear." Idong made the sign of a cross.

Calli thought it was the cutest thing she had ever heard or seen from Idong and smiled. She sighed. "I… You know Mummy wrote a book, which she sent to Chloe and me last year."

Idong nodded. "Daddy said you threw it away."

"I didn't. Well, I started reading it some weeks ago. And," she swallowed. "Mummy wrote a lot of secrets in it. And," she sighed again, "I started following up on one of the stories. It's about Adam. He has a son."

Maybe Idong knew something because he did not exclaim or show surprise.

"You know?"

Idong shook his head. "No. But, I am just wondering if Daddy does not already know."

"Please. You promised he will never hear that I read Mummy's book."

"I promise." Idong pulled her into his arms again. "I am Team Calli. I know I probably never made that clear to you, but I am your husband, and I love you very much. I thank God every day for giving you to me."

Calli's lips trembled, and tears gathered in her eyes. "You never said that before."

"I know, and I am sorry, but I was scared that you hated me so much. I know about the guy you wanted to marry and what happened to him. What Daddy did to him," Idong said.

Calli looked away. Staring at him made her feel even more vulnerable than she already was. But this was the moment. She wanted to find Adam. Idong could know how.

"I want to let Adam know he has a son," she said. "Can you help me?"

His mouth dropped open. He stepped back and paced. "Calli, that is almost impossible. Daddy will…"

"I've gone too far. I'm sorry." Calli felt as though Idong had punched her stomach.

From the look on his face, she could tell he had information about Adam. She marched into the bathroom and slammed the door shut.

She leaned against the bathroom wall and fought tears. He could never be Team Calli. He was too loyal to Daddy.

Idong parked his Toyota jeep in the hidden lot reserved for Adam's visitor and turned in his seat to Calli. "You know your father will kill me if he knows I brought you here."

"Please, baby," Calli whispered.

Idong switched off the ignition and came out of the car. Calli followed suit. A part of a storey building had a door which opened to the lot, and Idong opened it with a key he brought with him. Calli entered after him, and he locked the door, and led the way through a short corridor to another door.

"He doesn't recognize anyone," Idong said. "You can talk to him, but he rarely answers. Daddy thinks it's good to visit him once in a while, pray with him, and prophesy to him. Read the Bible to him." He sighed. "We take turns doing so."

Calli licked her lips and nodded.

"They do those random photoshoots for his stores too. He always liked that," Idong said softly.

With another key, he unlocked and opened the door to a small bedroom, with all-white furniture. A double bed neatly made with white bedsheets and beddings, stationed in the middle of the room, was surrounded by four single couches each with a stool. The ceiling was quite high with large windows controlled by a switch. It felt like a prison.

Adam sat on one of the couches, staring into space, clad in kaftan and trousers. He was barefooted.

"Ah, Mummy, ẹ kabọ, ma." Adam prostrated. "Thanks for coming. Ẹ joko."

Calli burst into tears and Idong patted her back.

"Compose yourself. He's alright. He has those outbursts, but he'll sit and listen calmly. Greet him," Idong said softly.

"Okay," Calli nodded. She looked at Adam and smiled sadly, "Hello, Brother Adam."

"Ẹ kabọ, ma," Adam said. "Ẹ joko."

Idong pulled two couches together to face Adam. "Hello, Adam. Your sister, Calli is here to say hello." He motioned to Calli, and they both sat.

"Ah, Calli. Ẹ kabọ. Ẹ kabọ. Ẹ joko," Adam said.

"I didn't even know you were here in Lagos; I'd have forced Idong to bring me. I didn't know he knew where you were. But Mummy's book is revealing so many things I never imagined," Calli said. "You have a son, Adam. He looks exactly like you." She sniffed. "And if it is the last thing I do with my life, I'm going to give him the Jaja name."

Idong took out a vial from his pocket. "Spit into this, Adam. Go on." He placed the vial close to Adam's mouth. "That's good. Spit. Fill it up."

Adam nodded and did as he was told. Calli rocked back and forth on her seat. Before Olive prosecuted anyone, she was going to get evidence Hermon was a Jaja. She closed her eyes and prayed it come to pass.

Back in the jeep with tears she couldn't control, Calli tapped Idong's arm. "Is he getting better?"

Idong shook his head slowly. "I'm afraid not."

Calli slumped and sobbed into her hands.

Chapter 37

I WILL FOREVER BE happy with myself that the first time I ever spoke up for exactly what I wanted with Daddy, it was to fight for my daughter, Chloe. After we returned from Dubai, I watched Chloe and Odami as closely as I could. The minister continued planning his wedding and ministering, leading worship, and the choir. People loved him more and more and I hated just seeing him. I knew he continued to sleep with my under-aged daughter, the evil paedophile, but I could not prove it. Chloe had that swag anytime she was close to me. She swayed her growing hips when she walked and because of her closeness to her father, evaded my scrutiny. Daddy always gave her the cover she needed.

At first, I thought I could tackle this on my own, but I couldn't take it anymore. A whole year passed, and I noticed Chloe's dressing changed. She wore tighter clothes and stayed in "Daddy's office" longer than was good for a child her age. She didn't look like a child anymore. At thirteen, she was budding and used the small size of bras, but at fourteen, she was full grown and wearing a "D" cup. She also stopped allowing other people to buy her clothes. I knew I was late, but I couldn't keep quiet anymore.

Sharon at the time was still married and running her welfare programs. She was my only support, as Chinwe was too busy, and Oluchi...Oluchi was Oye's wife, and I felt she was not my contemporary.

"Pastor Bettina!" Sharon exclaimed after I told her everything. "Are you sitting and watching your daughter go down like that?"

I cried. "What will I do? Daddy does not want to hear anything negative about Chloe. I don't know how that girl managed to wrap him around her little fingers."

"How is not the issue now. The how we should be thinking is yours. How you will save your daughter and reveal the evil of that horrible minister," Sharon said.

I moaned. "She has grown so much, filled out everywhere!"

"Focus, Pastor Bettina. That musician is not fit to lead the church," Sharon said. "Is Chloe close to Calli?"

I shrugged. "Calli follows her everywhere."

"Is Calli close to you?"

"Not really." Tears sprang to my eyes.

Since Adam went to the university, I had lost total touch with him. Chloe was Daddy's and Calli was Chloe's. Only my little Ben listened to me. It was a shame.

"You need to pull Calli closer for two reasons. So, Chloe will not spoil her, and she may know about Odami and Chloe."

"You are right, Pastor Sharon," I whispered. "But should I not take this up with Daddy?"

"I don't know how to answer that question of yours." Sharon grunted. "It is where you should start, biko!"

When I got home, I took a bath and dressed nicely. Daddy wasn't swayed by sex or anything and I didn't plan to use anything besides my motherly concern for our daughter. It was a Wednesday and after midweek service, he would normally stay in his private sitting room for hours, seeing people and just making himself available. Aside from having him alone in bed, this was the second-best place to discuss important issues.

Daddy had Elijah and two other PABs in the parlour when I walked in. Intuitively before I said anything, he told them to go. They bade us goodnight, as it was already almost eleven, though they lived in the mansion as well, and Daddy could summon them anytime. I took my usual seat.

"Daddy, I know you love Chloe. She is a special child. But I am worried, and I have been worried about her for a long time." I scooted forward. "She is having sex."

"With who?"

My gaze shot to my husband's. At least he didn't dispute my allegation. This was a good sign.

I sighed. "I suspect Minister Odami. Since they came from that Dubai, I know it's been a year or more, but there is something going on."

"Do you know the meaning of what you are saying? This accusation? Chloe is fourteen, Odami is twenty-eight. It is a criminal offense." Daddy leaned forward. "Should I call both of them to come now and answer to this accusation?"

"Haba, Daddy. At this time of the night? Odami lives in Lagos..."

"He will come if I call him."

I sighed. "I know. But it's too late, and Chloe will have to go to school in the morning."

"So, why are you here? If you don't want the matter settled?"

"I want us to discuss it, Daddy," I said. "We are her parents, and this is a concern."

"If you want us to discuss like husband and wife, we should do it in the bedroom, not here," Daddy said.

I exclaimed. "But I tried to talk about this when we first came back, and you refused to listen!"

Daddy snapped. "You were accusing our daughter of having sex at thirteen, without any evidence."

"I had evidence. Her pant was stained and smelly." I paused. "Daddy, I am not here to argue. We have a problem. Chloe..."

"We? If you have a problem with your daughter, deal with it! I have been observing the way you treat all of them, only Ben is precious, and you are sowing discord among your own children. You never have time for them..."

I leapt to my feet. "Ehn, Daddy! After you were the one controlling..."

"Sit down!"

I remained on my feet. Almost twenty years of marriage and this was what I had to cope with? I couldn't talk to my husband. Was it too much to ask him to discuss our daughter? He didn't care about the allegation, my concerns, the man involved! This was not about me and how I related with my children, this was a serious matter about the path Chloe was taking in life.

"I said sit down, Mummy, if you want this discussion to continue," Daddy said.

"Chloe is doing something wrong, and that is what I want us to talk about," I said. "I have failed in many ways, but I cannot continue to do the same things and expect change."

I glared at my husband, and he glared back.

"If we have a problem, we solve it together. Chloe listens to you. You are close to her, please, can you at least talk to her? If she is in a relationship with Odami, it must stop, and both have to leave the choir." I breathed in. "I have tried to speak to them. Odami denied it, as expected and Chloe said nothing, also expected. They can't try that with you." I paced. "This is not even good. What if she gets pregnant? He can't marry her. He's going to marry Lili. This should not even be heard in our family. And what of Calli? She will think it is the right thing to do."

For almost thirty minutes, I continued to talk alone. Daddy just sat there, staring at me. Not a word came out of his mouth after I refused to obey him. It left me upset.

"If you want to sit there and refuse to talk about your own child, then, fine." I had never done this before, and my heart thudded in my chest. I faced him. Really stared into his eyes

and he glared back. "If that child does not turn out well, it is your fault. You will be the reason our child does not make heaven!" I stomped out of the room.

Several hours later, Daddy came into our bedroom, and as though nothing had transpired earlier, started touching me. For the first time in my life, I slapped his hand, and left.

That night, I slept alone in Alexa's old room.

Chapter 38

DARA HAD THE TWINS dressed the same way, which Chloe hated, and never did, but she wasn't here now, and anyone could do as they wished. This made Calli sad. She had only visited Chloe's twins once since their mother left her home, not because she didn't want to, but because OPJ didn't give her permission.

"Good afternoon, ma." Dara curtseyed. "Sir said you could see them for only thirty minutes, and I have to be here."

Calli smiled sadly. "That's alright. Thank you, Dara." Calli reached out her hand to the girls but neither moved in to embrace her.

"Sir said they should not hug anyone, ma," Dara said.

Calli sighed. "That's unfortunate."

She took several calming breaths. When she'd called OPJ that she wanted to see Irene and Serena, she had been given a long list of rules. She wasn't to bring anything for them, she would wait in the anteroom, which had now been changed from Chloe's design, to accommodate several chairs making it look like a waiting area, and she must come alone, among several other things specifying what she could or could not wear.

Dara made Irene and Serena sit down on a couch, and she stood by it. Taking the cue, Calli sat too, and smiled.

"Your mum sends her love. She wishes to be here, but you know, things haven't been the same and..."

Dara cleared her throat. "Sir said you can't talk about madam, ma."

Calli's face shot up to Dara's "Dara, help me take them out of here," she whispered fiercely.

OPJ waltzed into the lobby. "Ah, the beautiful, faithful, and ever seductive and alluring Calli!"

Calli jumped to her feet. "I have only thirty minutes, and I'll like to be alone with the girls."

"Huh," OPJ checked his Rolex. "That would be twenty...huh, twenty-four minutes and sixteen seconds left." He laughed. "How are you these days? It's been a while. How long ago was that last visit before Chloe ran off. Umm, eight months? Dara?"

"It's been one and a half years, sir," Dara murmured.

OPJ laughed. "Wawu! That long? Gosh. Geez. Mehn!" He scratched his balding head. "How time flies."

Calli held back from speaking, spitting her anger. At the beginning, she had thought it was not necessary to involve herself in Chloe's issues, but not with all she now knew. Daddy had shown he had no interest in anything besides his church and ministry and someone had to cater to the family. That someone had to be her. Callista. No one else was disposed. The weight of the responsibility crushed her but what could she do?

She straightened, resolved, and smiled at the twins. "I wanted to bring Victor to see you, Irene, and Serena, but he's in school and afterwards we'd have to go to church, and it would be too late."

"You couldn't bring anyone to see them without my permission," OPJ said. "So, how have you been? How's my delectable stepmother?"

Calli braced herself. "OPJ, please excuse us. I want time with the girls."

"Then answer my questions. You have huh..." OPJ checked his watch again. "Huh! Twenty...huh, twenty minutes and..."

Calli snapped. "Chloe is fine."

"I was going to say twenty minutes and huh, nine seconds now." He looked up. "Did you call me OPJ just now? Not Ọlayọde. You are finally getting the drift of it. I am boss in this house! You and your f*cking sister and your f*cking father need to know that." He yelled.

"OPJ, please," Calli mumbled.

"And every bozo out there who thinks I have no rights as my father's first born, just because I live in his house! Go read your Bible, f*ckers. The so-called prodigal son came back home and who did he meet? The f*cking first son!" OPJ hit his chest. "I am here! I aint going nowhere. F*cking s*itholes." He smiled at Dara. "What are we having for lunch? I'm famished."

"Rice and dodo with ẹfọriro," Dara said. "With stew, I mean."

"Uhh, again? I eat that delicacy every day. Anyway, Callista, come and start going. Thanks for coming and greet stepmom for me." OPJ pointed to the door.

Calli gasped. "You just said I have like twenty..."

"And now I say you don't. Get out." He turned to Calli. "Get the f*ck out!"

Calli picked her bag and marched out of the lobby without a spare glance at the girls. This was wrong. She fought tears as she walked the one kilometre under the morning February sun to her ride, which was parked outside the gate.

Idong sat in the driver's seat, reading his Bible, the engine humming since the car air-conditioning was on. He looked up when Calli opened the passenger's side of the car. He closed his Bible. "You're early."

"I can't do this anymore." Calli burst into tears.

Idong pulled her into his arms and patted her back. "What happened?"

"We have to take those girls away from there. We have to." Calli sobbed. "OPJ. He was cursing me out. In front of the girls." She hiccupped. "He didn't let me have time with them."

"It's okay. It's okay. Let's go home," Idong said.

Calli sniffed. "No, we still have the other place."

Idong sought out her face. "Are you up to it?"

She nodded. "Yes. I have to be."

Chapter 39

Bolu Mustapha lived in Ẹpẹ a suburban town close to Lagos, with her husband, Peter, and two sons. Calli had been peripherally in touch with her over the years, though in the last five years, the families had been somewhat disengaged. Her father, Pastor Jide Ọlaolu continued to submit to Daddy's leadership, and ride on his platforms as an itinerant minister. In at least three years, he'd been a constant guest speaker and facilitator at Daddy's annual convention, which attracted more than two million believers from all over the world. Bolu and her sisters, Lolu and Folu, however, stayed clearly away for reasons obvious to all concerned. It wasn't difficult to find Bolu, though. She had always lived in her deceased parents-in-law's family house since she got married.

Bolu smiled. "Calli. Pastor Idong." She stepped back and allowed them into a simple but modern parlour. "You're welcome."

Calli and Idong greeted at the same time. "Good afternoon, Sis. Bolu." And they laughed. The humour of the moment broke some ice.

In the past, Bolu had harshly criticized Calli for other people's choices. For some reason, she couldn't understand why Calli or her siblings remained on the side-lines as things deteriorated between their parents. Since then, the two had not spoken.

"I'm glad you came by," Bolu said.

"I am very happy you agreed for us to come," Calli said.

Bolu gestured the couple to the couch. "Why not? Whatever may have happened, we are still sisters."

Calli and Idong sat. Calli looked around. "You changed your furniture?"

Bolu smiled. "You are very observant. We actually just changed the colour." She sat on one of the single chairs.

"I remember, yeah. They were white or cream, right?"

"Cream. But the boys turned it to their colouring board." Bolu sighed. "It was too much."

Calli laughed. "I can imagine. This navy is beautiful, though. Matches the walls, curtains. Hmm."

"You always had an eye for interior designs," Bolu said.

"That's why she married me." Idong laughed. "I helped redecorate her apartment at the mansion."

Calli gasped. "That is not why! Sister Bolu, don't mind him o!"

"We all know the story, don't worry." Bolu laughed. "What can I offer you? Juice, soft, malt?"

Calli shook her head. "No, we can't take anything, thank you."

"Aha, why not." Bolu stood. "After all these years, you must…"

"No, Sister Bolu. Please." Idong raised his hand. "We are in a little hurry because we need to pick Victor."

"We came for something very important." Calli scooted forward. "About your mum."

Bolu snickered. "Huh. Well, you know we don't talk about that again." She shrugged. "And, when you called, I was in the school, I just didn't want you to meet me there. Huh, I need to get back too."

Idong stood. "Sister Bolu! We understand you're still hurting but we need to talk about this."

"Mummy wrote a book, and mentioned names," Calli said softly.

"So, how does this concern me? Even if I am in her book, I will be nothing." Bolu threw her hands up. "Mummy had no time for anyone or anything but herself. And when our Mummy died, she threw us away." Tears came to her eyes. "But we survived. God is faithful."

"How's the school doing?" Calli muttered.

"Great. We are now in primary three and turning down students." Bolu smirked. "God is good."

"Amen." Idong nodded. "And he will continue to help you."

"Why did Aunty Sunbọ kill herself?" Calli said softly.

"You think I don't want to know too?" Bolu burst out. "I was there that night! She couldn't even talk to me. I know I was just seventeen and perhaps she thought I was too young, but she killed herself thinking I was too young to confide in? But not too young to handle the pain and tragedy her death brought to us? The stigma even to this day? Did she even care?"

"You have done well, Sister Bolu," Calli said.

In one accord with Idong, Calli moved to Bolu and surrounded her in a group hug as she wept. When she was calm, they took her to the couch with them and flanked her. Idong handed out a clean handkerchief and Bolu blew her nose into it noisily.

"I will continue to thank God that we can at least start our school in her name. In her remembrance. She was passionate about giving us quality education. She will always be remembered in this way." Bolu sniffed. "For years, me Folu and Lolu couldn't understand. Our daddy told us nothing. People looked at us strangely. Family members avoided us, like we carried a plague."

Calli rubbed her back.

"Daddy took all her belongings and locked them up in two huge trunk boxes and threw the key away. The boxes remained in our Mummy's room for many years." Bolu swallowed. "No one could ask Daddy. Hmm. Then, after I got married, I went to the house with Peter, when we knew Daddy was out of town, and carried the two trunk boxes out.

"For weeks, we waited for Daddy to call and ask about it. He didn't. So we broke the lock, and looked through." Bolu stood. "Please give me a minute." She walked out.

Calli looked at Idong, who shrugged. They sat quietly for several minutes, and then Bolu returned with an old diary. She did not return to sit with the couple.

"My mother kept a journal. To the very last day," Bolu said.

"Oh, my goodness." Calli exclaimed. "Your daddy never mentioned it."

"He told your Daddy about it. I know because I got very angry with him for keeping it a secret." Bolu breathed through her mouth. "Your father advised him to burn it. Instead, he locked it up. Hoping no one will find it."

"Hoping someone would, you mean?" Calli sighed. "What do you plan to do with it?"

Bolu returned to her original seat slowly. "I don't know. Lolu and Folu thinks we should keep it safely and never make it public." She looked at the diary. "It is very telling, revealing. The many things pastors in our churches indulged in. Stealing money, sleeping with women, hating on one another. My mummy was tired of everything."

"It is not an excuse to take your own life," Idong said. "She should have gotten help. Spoken to someone. Anyone. What heaven did she think she would go?"

Bolu slouched. "I try not to think of those things. I try to think she overdosed by mistake. But how do you mistakenly overdose on a sleeping pill, when you should take one and you take a whole bottle? In her journal, she researched on it. On how to die." Bolu bent over the diary and cried.

Calli and Idong looked at each other, and in agreement, stood. Calli went over to Bolu and hugged her tight.

"I won't be far again, Sister Bolu. Thank you for sharing," Calli said.

Bolu did not stop crying or look up as the visitors left her house.

Chapter 40

MY FIRST REASON FOR starting a journal was to document my feelings about Daddy, Chloe, and Odami. But soon, I was writing everything about everyone around me. The more I wrote, the more the bubble my life was surrounded with cleared. I started to question everything. Why did we have so many churches, and our country was a mess? Why did people kneel to Daddy and only stood when he told them to? Why were we living on a camp so huge many other members now had big, beautiful houses on it too? Why was our house called a mansion? Why was our house so big? Why did Daddy acquire so much more land, almost double what was already there, and building a hundred-thousand-seater auditorium? Why were so many people living in our house? When was the last time I cooked? I loved to cook so why were PABs doing it for me? Why did we have so many cars? Why was Daddy planning to buy a private luxury boat of which one of his followers already donated half of the total cost?

Down to myself, why was I not able to feel deep connection and love to anything around me? This hit me the hardest. I was first lady of a Christian empire, yet deep inside, I was nothing. Again, I seemed to be breezing through the world. I was alive but life wasn't in me. I needed to get out of this. I needed to connect with my reality, and I always got that when I went home to my parents.

I decided to go to Oṣogbo to celebrate my forty-third birthday. Home was my reality. When I told Daddy, he refused to allow me. And in my journal, I posted one more question – why did Daddy tell me what to do as though I was a slave? It dawned on me that indeed I was a stooge. From the day he asked for a massage, and I gave him, I became a fool for him. He had a control over me like I could not even understand. And every night I lay in bed to write in my journal, I hated myself more. To think I was that firebrand sister, who prayed two hours daily, loved on God, sang for God...heard from God! Where was that spiritual sister?

The day before I turned forty-three, I got one of the drivers to take me to Apọgbọn market. I bought some drinks, and foodstuff like I normally did when I was visiting home. Then, I stopped at a cake shop and bought myself a nice cake and proceeded to Ọṣogbo.

Maami was very excited to see me. "Aha, you did not even call to say you're coming. Hope all is well."

"Yes, Maami." I knelt to greet her.

The driver helped to offload the things I brought and returned to Lagos.

"Will you spend your birthday here?" Maami said. "Huh! Two bags of rice. Who will eat all this?"

"Haba, don't you have neighbours again?" It felt so good to be home. This was where I belonged. "Ah, I want to give one to Pastor Jide. I should have just asked the driver to take me there before he returned."

Maami folded her arms across her chest. "How is Daddy?"

I shrugged. "He's fine. Umm, so tomorrow, I am going to cook jollof rice. I brought meat and chicken, I will fry, we will eat and be happy."

Maami somewhat slumped. "Sometimes when I see you on TV, I know you miss home."

I laughed to cover the pain her words brought. "Hmm, Maami, you know how Lagos is. Ọṣogbo is a breath of fresh air."

We sat and chatted for hours. Maami gave me updates about everyone.

"John has been very helpful with Bolu, Folu, and Lolu," Maami said. "I will call him and ask him to come and take their bag of rice to them."

John. The mere mention of his name still had my heart racing. He was getting close to fifty, yet he had not married anyone. He didn't have children. He lived alone. It broke my heart. He lived well though. This I knew because he was always in the news as the director-general at the state ministry he worked in.

"That's very kind of him. I will also find my way there tomorrow evening," I said.

The following day, Maami's friends came to the house. Bolu came as well. I cooked and we all ate and drank. Daddy did not call neither did Chloe, Calli or Ben. Adam sent a message in the evening. Though I was upset with my family, I still enjoyed great company.

Alexa and Pastor Fẹmi came from Lagos, and Maami chided them for driving all the way seeing Alexa was heavy with her pregnancy. She allowed them to stay for just a few hours and then sent them back. I saw from the way the two behaved that it had been Alexa's idea to travel. Sometimes I wondered if I didn't make a mistake. Pastor Fẹmi seemed too good for my sister.

Later in the evening, as we reminisced over the day, Baami, who had always been the quietest in the family, complained of chest pain.

"It has been on small small, since afternoon," Baami said.

"Maybe it is cold," Maami said. "This rain every day is very annoying."

"Baami, maybe you should go inside and lie down," I said.

Baami stood, and slumped. Confusion ensued.

Maami ran to his side. "Yeepa! Papa Bettina!"

I ran outside to get a taxi. The streets were nearly empty as it was later than nine o'clock and shops had closed. Several minutes later, I got a taxi, and with the driver ran back inside to help Baami.

"He's not talking, Bettina!" Maami screamed. "Ah, Abasi mbọk! God o!"

The taxi driver and I carried Baami to a good private hospital. He was unconscious and they immediately admitted him. What a way to end such a beautiful birthday but at the same time, I kept wondering if this was why I strongly wanted to come home. I wished my husband was beside me, but what difference would it have made? He never showed emotion. I sometimes wondered if he had any, apart from when we had intercourse.

Still, it was the right thing to do. Daddy should be with me at such a trying time. It was what husbands did. For instance, when a wife was delivering...I'd seen many men pace and pant while their wives were in labour. Daddy never went to the hospital when I had my babies, but there would be several brethren from the church waiting on me hand and foot. My husband did not believe he should go to the hospital except to heal people, and this had to be by God's direct instruction. Like when I had Chloe.

Daddy did not pick his phone, and I wasn't surprised. I had discovered in recent times that if I defied my husband, he kept malice. Funny as it ~~sounds~~ sounded, I was happy that at least, we were somewhat falling into a normal relationship where he responded to me in some way. Since this was not a time to keep malice, I sent him a message but also called Adam, and asked him to call his father.

"Call Minister Elijah," Adam said.

"Oh, thanks my dear."

I dialled Elijah's number, and he gave his phone to Daddy.

"Daddy!" Despite myself I burst into tears. "Daddy! Baami is sick and unconscious. We don't know what happened to him."

In a bland and cold voice, Daddy said, "Did I not tell you not to go home?"

What? Was that the issue now? "Daddy! Baami is unconscious..."

"I heard you the first time. If you are willing and obedient, you will eat the good of the land," Daddy said.

"Daddy, please, will you pray for him at least?"

"Are you going to apologize for disobeying me?" Daddy said. "You should learn your lesson, Mummy, don't be stubborn."

I sobbed. "Daddy, please..."

A doctor walked towards me. "Excuse me, ma. I'm sorry but we lost him."

Maami leaped up from the bench she sat on just behind me. "Yee! Mo gbe. My life has ended." She slumped.

I hurried to carry Maami, and she came to, sobbing. I didn't know what to do. Just like that, my father was dead. I checked my phone and noticed Daddy had dropped the call. My support would have to come from my sisters. I called Skola first. She lived the farthest away. After tearfully breaking the awful news, I called Alexa. It was close to midnight, and I told her she didn't need to come at all. Knowing my sister and in that state of health, she should not come to Oṣogbo.

From that moment on, it was unclear how I proceeded. I remember taking Maami back home from the hospital and calling on Baami's younger brother who lived in Ibadan. Skola arrived the following evening and a family meeting held to decide on the burial date. Maami sat mute through the meeting.

I wasn't too happy with the way my mother looked so I took her back to the hospital and had her checked. The doctor complained her blood pressure was extremely low. I got her admitted and she was placed on medication that would help improve her blood pressure.

That night, the worst thing ever happened to me.

The hospital called that my mother gave up too. In two days, I lost my parents. Baami was seventy-two, Maami was sixty-five. When Alexa heard, she went into labour and was delivered of a baby boy, premature.

Chapter 41

MEMORIES OF THIS PLACE held Calli's throat tight, and her chest constricted. She thought she couldn't breathe. Yet, there had to be some sort of resolution for her. She needed to come here to get closure. Bosa's family house in Benin. He had returned to his parent's shortly after Daddy came to pack all her stuff out, so he could have someone take care of him, since Calli was no longer there.

She loved Bosa. But it was different now. She was married and she loved her son more than anything else in the world. She would never leave her marriage if only for Victor's sake. However, she was getting to know Idong better too. When she married him, she had been under a certain threat by her father and Idong seemed to be her way of escape. She didn't know at the time that he had been planted in her life by Daddy but since they started "courting" in their marriage, as Idong put it, she had come to realise Daddy pushed him into her life so she could forget about Bosa.

"I thought he'd not let me marry you," Idong had said. "Many times, Daddy told me you were too good for me. I knew it anyway," he chuckled. "I was so much in love with you, I thought I'd kill myself if you finally got over Bosa and he didn't let me marry you."

"Daddy told you to woo me, so I'd be over Bosa?" Calli had asked. Idong nodded.

Calli turned now in her seat and stared at her husband. "Thank you for bringing me here."

He touched his index finger to her lips and traced the shape of it. "I'll wait in the car for you."

Calli half-smiled and came out of the car.

Bosa was not expecting her. She hadn't sent him a message because she no longer had his number, and she couldn't find him on social media. She thought of their mutual friends, but she lost touch with all of them too. These were people Daddy's IT guys had found on all her social media handles and unfollowed as long as they were mutual friends with Bosa. Calli couldn't believe close to eight years had gone by just like that.

"Good afternoon. I'm looking for Bosa," Calli told the young woman who opened the door.

"Bosa? Bosa doesn't live here," she said. "Who are you?"

Calli avoided eye contact. "My name is Calli Asukwo. Umm, sorry. I thought..."

"Calli? Bosa's Calli?" The woman smirked. "My name is Etse. I'm Bosa's cousin but I used to hear about you."

Calli didn't know if she would laugh or cry. She and Bosa had been so strong together. "I hope they were good things."

Etse shrugged. "Bosa doesn't live here anymore. In fact, he got married and..."

Calli gasped. "He got married?"

"Hmm uh. He did." Etse nodded. "Had a baby about two weeks ago. He's doing well." Etse looked behind her. "Do you want to come in?"

Calli shook her head. "I guess not. I thought I could...I felt it was..."

"We all know you moved on and he thought he should too." Etse smiled. "Don't tell anyone I said this. You're prettier than his wife. He'll never know, though. Good for him!"

Calli stepped back as though she had been hit in the face. For this lady to make a joke about Bosa's blindness was horrible. She turned without a word and hurried to Idong, who was parked a few metres away by the roadside.

"That was fast," Idong said.

Calli breathed through her mouth. "He doesn't live here. They said he got married and now has a baby."

"I'm sorry to hear that," Idong said.

"Sorry!" Calli exclaimed. "I'm relieved, baby! I am so relieved!"

Idong laughed. "You mean we're not going to go to his house?"

"Are you kidding me? I didn't even bother to ask where he lives. He has moved on. He's bound to a wheelchair for life. He has moved on." She smiled tremulously. "Baby, it's a long drive back home and our son needs to be put to bed by us."

Idong seemed to struggle to find the right words. "I remember the first time Daddy made it clear he wanted me to go after you. He sounded as though he would damn me if I failed. I had a huge crush on you, and I thought he could see it. I was terrified I would fail."

"I knew you had a crush on me. I noticed the way you looked at me in church. I just didn't know how you knew where I was," Calli said. "I didn't like you. I didn't like any man. Only Bosa. And Daddy had me locked up in my room. The only way I could get out was to be with you. I felt so helpless." She shuddered. "Daddy had never noticed me. He only cared about Chloe. The minute I choose something for myself, he turns all of his attention on me, to make me miserable."

Idong scoffed. "The day I proposed to you, I didn't plan to. When Daddy heard, he was furious. He said that wasn't what he sent me to do. Told me you would never accept my proposal."

"Really? I just said yes." Calli shrugged. "I felt stupid afterwards. But then I thought if I could get married, then I could leave the mansion! And if I could leave the mansion, I could find Bosa, and we'd run away where no one could find us." She laughed. "Stupid."

"Yeah. I lived in a small apartment on Mainland, and I just couldn't see how Daddy would allow you to move in with me." Idong smiled. "But I don't think your plan was stupid. I would think like that too!"

"Hmm. Only that Daddy gave us the east wing to choose any apartment in."

Idong laughed. "He was shocked when I told him you accepted my proposal. He gave me a condition for me. You can't marry Calli unless you stay in the mansion. I said yes, Daddy."

"I just wanted to be free to love who I wanted," Calli said softly.

"You had a right to love who you wanted. I hated being used like that, and yet I loved being with you. I thanked God for the opportunity," Idong said.

"Talk of conflict, right." Calli smiled. "Well, thank you for loving me, and for being my husband even through the circumstances. I was a horrible person to you."

"I didn't care, my love. Do you know how lucky I am to be with you? All my friends envied me." Idong laughed. "You are not only Daddy's daughter and a princess in this massive spiritual kingdom, and I a fatherless nobody, you are Daddy's best and most beautiful child."

"You flatter me," Calli said.

"Never, darling. I never flatter you, my love. God, thank you. I am so relieved we can go home now and build our future without ghosts," Idong said.

"Me too," Calli mumbled.

Idong leaned over and deep-kissed Calli. It was the first she let him kiss her on the mouth.

Chloe frowned for a full minute at the sound coming in from outside before she stood from lounging in her parlour and walked out to the porch on her first-floor apartment in the east wing. Below, she caught a glimpse of Calli as she giggled and ran around her Toyota jeep. Idong gave chase and caught her on the side of the chassis and pinning her to it, kissed her on the mouth.

"It's amazing how so much in love they are. Beautiful, best couple," Ms. Feyi, Chloe's housekeeper, but also a PAB, said from behind her.

"He's short and ugly." Chloe hissed. "Her old boyfriend, Bosa, was a hunk." She giggled. "Well, until mother nature visited and took his legs from him."

Ms. Feyi looked at the couple, who were now just making out. "Height or not, a woman's happiness is the most important thing."

"You think Calli is happy? This Idong was Daddy's choice. Calli hates him. Daddy forced her to marry him." Chloe laughed. "You should have seen them on their wedding day. Daddy said, you may kiss the bride. Idong moved closer and Calli turned her face in time for kiss to turn to peck." She looked at her sister and her husband, as both hurried into the building. "They are ridiculous, Feyi!"

Ms. Feyi crinkled her nose. Chloe knew she was the only one who called the middle-aged woman by her name. But who cared about giving any respect to a paid staff who fooled herself that she was "doing it all for God."

"They are in love as you can see," Ms. Feyi said.

Within minutes, Chloe imagined she could hear Calli and Idong smooching in their bedroom through the walls that separated their apartments. Whoever decided, Daddy, most likely or his advisors, that the offices, main kitchen, and garages be on the ground floor while the residences occupy the second and third floors of the building, didn't have community in mind. The walls, though thin, were thick bulwarks of defences for its occupants.

Chloe tipped her head back. "Since when? You were not here then, so you won't know." Chloe walked back inside and returned to her lounging. Ms. Feyi followed her. "So, Daddy pushes this Mr. Nobody to marry Calli. She was just twenty-two. I bet she was still a virgin." Chloe chuckled. "I don't know what their wedding night was like, Calli refused to tell me. Well, she didn't allow the guy to touch her and for three years, or so, she didn't get pregnant until Daddy threatened her." Chloe clasped her hand over her mouth, stifling her laughter. "Daddy gave them an ultimatum. Have a baby or you will regret what I will do to you!"

Ms. Feyi moaned. "We all know what Daddy's words are like. Especially when he's angry."

Chloe pressed her lips together. "He killed my Nat!" She hissed. "Once he sees these ones are happy, he will crush them too." She sniffed. "But it's all fake change. Whatever is making them happy will soon end."

"Don't talk like that, Ms. Chloe," Ms. Feyi said.

Chloe grunted. "Hmm. I'm just saying the fact."

"I think God has healed your sister's marriage. Don't you see things seem to have changed for her and her husband in the past few days?" Ms. Feyi folded her arms around her chest. "I know they were not very happy before, but things have changed."

Chloe sneered. "Fake change! I should take a picture of that nonsense they are doing and email to Daddy. See how fast he will dissolve the romance."

"Haba! Ms. Chloe, two happy couple sporting in their backyard?"

Chloe snickered. "Whose backyard? When did Jaja Mansion become Idong Asukwo's backyard? If Daddy wants, he can throw them out in a second."

"I am happy for them. I will be praying for them," Ms. Feyi said.

Chloe jumped to her feet. "Gosh, it's time I get a man! It's been too long." She marched towards her bedroom.

"Ms. Chloe!" Ms. Feyi called but Chloe entered her room and banged the door. "Lord, save her soul."

Chapter 42

PERHAPS TO MAKE UP for killing my parents, because I believe Daddy's refusal to pray for Baami caused his death, which caused Maami's death, Daddy made a big deal of my parents' burial. The whole church came down to Akwa Ibom state, where my parents were from. With so many Christian leaders in town, the governor of the state himself attended. It was a carnival.

Most important to my sisters and I though, was the emergency building Daddy put up in my father's village. Baami's family left their hometown for so long, none had a house to call their own, but Daddy changed all that. Within a month, a nice three-bedroom bungalow was erected. For several days before and after the burials, we fed the whole village. At the end, Daddy made up for his misbehaviour, if I could use such a word for the great man of God.

When I look back, I think my parents ended well. Baami's father was taken to Osun state as a boy and he worked for over twenty years doing odd jobs, and with no education until he met his wife who had also been taken to Lagos, and then Oṣogbo as a housemaid. Baami never got an education and neither did Maami. Together they raised me and my sisters, insisted we got university education, and marry decent men. Their end was good, as our people would always say.

One of our cousins, who worked as a labourer in Uyo, was given the key to the bungalow, and given the responsibility to use and care for the house. I knew in my heart he was going to make it his own, and I really couldn't care less. Who out of us three girls, married happily and living our lives in Lagos and Port Harcourt, would come to a village without power and internet to fight over a bungalow? None.

Skola's husband was doing well as an engineer and working for an oil company's contractor. They had their own house too. Alexa got married, just had her first baby, was the wife of a pastor of a big church, and they had their own house. I, Bettina Jaja, was a first lady of an international church. Coming to our village to bury our parents was the first time we would *be in the village, probably the next time would be next year for the first-year remembrance, and then every ten years. It was what it was.*

In hindsight, we should have buried our parents in Oṣogbo where we could easily visit their graves and change the flowers. Skola was the closest to Uyo and might have to travel there more often than once every ten years.

Returning from my parents' burial, the "romance" between Daddy and I returned, which meant I was once again submissive, doing anything he asked, which now included international travel. For some reason best known to him alone, Daddy had not subscribed to me leaving the country but now he wanted me to. I enjoyed travelling because of the way I was received in these countries. I was pampered, respected, and each time I went out, it was like vacation. Our churches were growing and the love these people had for Daddy and me, was exceptional.

On one trip to Britain, where we had more of our larger congregations, I got a call from Adam. He was weeping.

"What is the matter?" I raised my voice in panic, over his crying. "Adam!"

"I'm sorry, Mummy. I did not mean to do it, and now they said you or Daddy must come to the school," he said.

"Do what? Do what?" I screamed. "If you don't talk, I will hang up on you."

"We were drinking. At a party..."

I shouted. "Adam! Drinking? Child of God, drinking."

"Mummy, please." He sobbed.

"Well, I am in England. Call your father and tell him." I hung up.

I was furious. What was wrong with this boy? I couldn't understand. After all the powerful messages he had heard in his life. Why was he trying to self-destruct. First, that allegation by Mrs. Nedion, and now this. Why should he be having trouble with the school authorities? I couldn't believe this. As I fumed over the call, a soft nudge within told me my son needed me now, and all I could do to show him love was to go to his aid. It touched me to my bone. He really sounded broken. Daddy would not even listen to him if he called.

The first thing that came to my mind was to call Minister Elijah. At least, Adam had recommended him previously, so he must be close to the boy. I checked the time and knew he would likely be in church, so I left a message for him.

After service might have closed, Elijah called me. "Mummy, good evening, ma."

"Ah, Minister, good evening. Thanks for calling. Did you get my mes…"

"Yes ma. I have spoken to him. I will go there tomorrow morning," Elijah said.

"Thank you so much, Minister. Hmm, these children will not kill someone. Daddy must not hear," I said.

"Did Adam tell you what he did?"

"Hmm, he said they were drinking and partying!" I sighed. "Ehn, children of God. Child of a man of God."

"He led a group of them to scale the school fence, Mummy. They had alcohol, weed, and girls."

I moaned. "Oh my God. My God. Don't say it again, mo da'ran!"

Elijah never told me my son had been involved in several other escapades for which he had showed up to save face and rescue Adam, all without Daddy's knowledge and this was the last straw for the school.

Adam was expelled from the Christian university based on that incident.

Chapter 43

THE BEST THING TO *do to keep the scandal under wraps was to ship Adam out of the country. We had many churches in the UK and some members who had been with us in Lagos were there. Daddy travelled himself with Adam and got him into a high-paying private university. We could afford to have all our children in these schools. Why not? At this stage in ministry? It wasn't even an issue.*

The first year went well. But by the second year, Adam was indicted in a single crime – doing hard drugs. He was expelled and the school recommended rehabilitation because according to them, he was an addict.

Daddy first sent me to relocate to Britain to stay with him and monitor him. I decided to take Ben with me. The boy had turned twelve and with the Adam issue, it seemed I would be away for a long time. I had to do the recordings for our TV marriage program separately from Daddy, which somewhat added colour to the program. The whole world got to know I had moved to the UK "to oversee the branches there," and as usual, it was attributed to the growth in ministry.

As soon as we settled, I enrolled Ben into a private school, and they accepted him into year six though he was supposed to be in year eight. When Ben tested, it was advised that he stay two years lower. My son was not very smart as I would learn.

That year with Adam and Ben taught me a lot about being there, being home with my children. It left me wondering what damage I had done to them in their developmental years when, in the spirit of building ministry, I neglected my duty as a mother and left my responsibility to church people and PABs. I tried to make it up with Chloe and Calli, ensuring I called every day, but it made little difference.

After the first year, I asked for Calli to be sent to me, and Daddy refused, citing the fact that Chloe would feel neglected, and he wanted at least one of his children with him, so I couldn't take Chloe too.

I want to note here that Daddy had never taken any interest in any of the children except Chloe. In hindsight, I should have insisted on taking Calli. She never really had anyone's attention. When I was not attending to church and ministry matters, I was attending to Ben.

I was a failure as a mother, and I apologize to all my children here.

During the first year living in Britain, I tried to continue to stay connected with my PLL ladies, but it increasingly became difficult as I could only travel twice a year, and it was mainly for our church. Sharon closed her church, Chinwe left with her children, and Oluchi, bombarded by scandal after scandal of her husband's infidelity, went underground. The only leader who remained active was my Alexa, and I knew she still abused her husband. Our beautiful, lifesaving, female-pastor-cum-pastor's wife-saving group was in disarray.

There wasn't much I could do. The Chloe-Odami riddle remained unsolved. I wasn't even sure they were in a relationship or not, as Odami had a big wedding. The idea of getting close to Calli to get information did not work; Calli remained tied to her sister's apron. And now I had a major responsibility with Ben in school, and a crisis to attend with Adam in rehab. Perhaps my conscience was pricked, I poured all my attention on Ben. I prayed with him, cared for him, checked on his homework, talked about the things he liked. He took interest in football at his school, and I followed him to watch his games.

After six months of rehabilitation, Adam came home. I discussed his going back to school with him, and he got angry and violent. He threw plates and glass cups and stomped out of the house. The police returned him the following morning. He had gotten drunk and passed out by the side of the road.

The first year went by, and I tried to manage my life and my two sons. I did a lot of preaching around our churches and plunged into ministry while coping with my new-normal mothering my boys. Most of the time, it was just to protect me and Ben from Adam's tantrums. I started believing in my heart that the rehab made him worse than when he went in. For fear of returning him to confinement, I didn't tell Daddy any of the issues, just that Adam couldn't decide where to attend school. This went on until the school year ended.

One beautiful day in August, Elijah called me.

"Mummy, don't scream o!" He chuckled. "Daddy and I are at the airport."

I smirked. "Which airport?"

"Heathrow, Mummy. We're coming to the house."

I laughed. Our house on Willesden Green was five-bedroom, four-bathroom beautifully furnished in a nice neighbourhood. As with Jaja mansion, there were brethren who lived in the house on and off. We also had two church members who lived permanently. Daddy liked people in his house, and that never changed.

"Are you joking, Minister?"

"No, Mummy," he laughed.

Before I knew it, the chartered car arrived. Daddy landed with Elijah, another brother called Darlington, and our two daughters, Chloe and Calli.

Chapter 44

*C*HLOE *WANTED TO SCHOOL* in the UK and Daddy agreed, without discussing it with me.

"I have made all the arrangements," Daddy said. "We will leave Adam and Chloe here with Minister Darlington. Mummy and I will return home with Calli and Ben."

I snapped my eyes shut for a second. This was bedroom discussion, not seated in the parlour with all four children, Elijah, and Darlington, present.

Chloe clapped. "Yay! Thank you, Daddy." She went on her knees.

I blurted. "Are they not too young to stay alone, Daddy."

"Huh, Mummy!" Chloe gasped. "You always want to ruin everything!" She stood and started to stomp into her room.

"Chloe!" Daddy called. "Go and sit down."

Like a puppet on strings, Chloe did as she was ordered.

"Adam is twenty-one. Chloe is eighteen. For your information, Mummy, they are not too young. They are adults." Daddy turned to Elijah. "Ask the pastors outside to come in."

Like that, I was dismissed and all the talk about our children's future, ended. Some of the UK pastors entered the sitting room, and everyone except Elijah and Darlington left. I wanted to stay back but I could hear Chloe's excited chatter in the bedroom. The joy in her voice upset me so much, I went into my room, and locked the door behind me.

Daddy stayed in London for one week, and every single day, when we were alone in the bedroom, I reminded him of the danger in leaving Adam and Chloe in London.

"Adam has a drug problem you have not said a word about!" I cried. "And for Lord knows how long, Chloe was sleeping with your music minister!"

No matter how calm or rude I sounded, my husband simply stared at me, and when I ended my rant, he spoke about ministry, church or some other pastor or church.

Or he pulled me into himself and made love to me.

Daddy took the children out shopping, sightseeing, enjoying themselves, while I sulked at home most of the days, or attended a church function or the other, for which he asked me to represent him.

On the last day of Daddy's stay, after breakfast, he told me, Calli and Ben to pack all our stuff for an evening flight with British Airways. The one popularly called "goodnight, London, good morning, Lagos."

"I'm not leaving. Either we all return, or I stay with all my children," I said.

Daddy turned to Calli and Ben. "Go and pack all your things."

The children turned to go and do their father's bidding.

"Nobody is packing or going anywhere," I said. "Daddy can return to Lagos if he wants."

I knew I had started speaking up for myself, but it was the first time I would counter Daddy's instruction to someone else. Calli ignored me and continued to the room to do Daddy's bidding. Ben stood there, and his lips trembling, tears slid down his cheeks. I became depressed. I walked to him, took his hand, and walked out of the sitting room.

At about four o'clock, Daddy summoned everyone into the sitting room. Elijah and Darlington joined us.

"We will pray, and leave. Adam and Chloe, Minister Darlington is going to be your guardian, as I told you before. Focus." Daddy gesticulated by pointing his hands straight at his eyes. "Focus."

Chloe curtseyed. "Yes, Daddy."

Adam bowed. "Yes, Daddy."

"Calli, Ben, Mummy, get your bags," Daddy said.

My bags? I had been living in London for over two years. I didn't have bags. I had a truckload of belongings neatly folded in my wardrobe.

I snickered. "I'm staying with the children, Daddy."

Without being told, Darlington stomped past me and into the corridor that led into the rooms. Within minutes, he came out with two suitcases supposedly for Callie and Ben.

Ben started to cry.

"Mummy, if you don't pack your things, and return to Lagos with us. You will never see your children again in your life," Daddy said.

I stood my ground. I held Calli and Ben's hands. Daddy walked out to the car. Calli snatched her hand out of mine and followed Daddy. Darlington took the two suitcases and followed them. For the life of me, I wanted to defy Daddy. Let him take Calli. She'd be fine. I couldn't let Adam and Chloe live in London alone. With me there, Adam still wasn't well.

I had to wake him up on some days to take his bath, and he wasn't doing anything, didn't want to do anything! And I knew he didn't sleep at home every night, though he always made sure he was back in his room in the morning.

Elijah came to me. "Mummy, you don't want to fight this battle."

"Hmm, let me fight it, Minister." I lowered my voice. "You know...you know Adam needs me here."

Elijah took a step back and glanced at Chloe. It was a strange way to look at my daughter, as though accusing her of something. I couldn't place my mind on it because Ben was crying so hard, and my heart was thudding. Elijah shrugged and left the house.

Ben sobbed. "Mummy, let us follow them."

Chapter 45

I shouldn't have.

I shouldn't have followed Daddy back to Nigeria, leaving Adam and Chloe in London.

Chloe got into a university, and I was pleased but Adam continued to refuse to return to school. I made sure I spoke to him every day at first, then he stopped picking all my calls. Carefully, my calls fell into twice a week, and then once, and then once every two weeks. Chloe never picked my calls, and I only got to know of her progress from Adam or the loyalist, Darlington, who interestingly, always picked my calls, and answered my questions.

At the end of the autumn semester, Chloe and Adam refused to come home for Christmas, and Daddy forbade me from travelling. I was resentful of him. Sometimes I did what he asked, sometimes I didn't. I could not understand why he didn't want me to visit the children since they were not going to be home.

My story ~~gets~~ got very depressing from here.

A downward slope I never envisaged. The same question in my heart pumping…why did I let Love Jaja marry me? I didn't love him, and I wasn't sure he loved me. Why did I allow him to dictate to me all these years? It made no sense. Was I hypnotized? No. I didn't think so. Quite frankly, in hindsight, maybe I just felt flattered that he fancied me. I was my own mistake.

I bought a return ticket and flew to London. December was always a busy time for the church with the annual camp meeting convention coming up, Christmas, and New Year services. The only time I could travel would be before these programs, or after. If I went before, I'd not have enough time to spend with the children, but going after was too far coming, and so I travelled before. I intended to stay only one week, and I did.

How would I rate the visit? Depressing though I was happy to see my children. Adam was happy to see me. Chloe even warmed up a little.

We went shopping together and she introduced me to some of her friends. Chloe also had a boyfriend who she happily wanted me to meet. His name was Prince. If I would estimate his *age, he'd be in his forties, probably even a little older than me. He was a Nigerian politician who had a potbelly, a lot of money, and a family of his own back home, though he travelled a lot.*

Prince came to visit Chloe while I was there and wanted to take me out. I politely declined. Chloe entertained him in the parlour, and I should have just walked him out but out of shock and curiosity, I sat down on a single chair. Chloe sat with him on the couch.

"I told you Mummy will not want to take anything from you," Chloe laughed. "She's very conservative."

"I will leave something for shopping, anyway," Prince said. He took out an ATM card from his wallet and placed it on the centre table. "For Mummy."

How could my beautiful daughter be interested in this...this fat, ugly, smelly man?

Chloe screeched. "Oh, my goodness! How much is in it?"

Prince laughed. "It's a credit card with no limit for Mummy."

I folded my arms in my laps and listened with the trained patience being married to Daddy had taught me. I didn't smile because that would misrepresent me.

Chloe hugged his neck. "Thank you. I'll return it back when Mummy leaves." Then she stood. "Prince wants to go now."

I nodded. I didn't think I could say anything to them. The audacity Chloe had, bringing such a man to visit me, and the man, what a sinful fellow! Would he pretend not to know who we were? If Daddy heard of this man, he would curse him out. The man would get on a plane and die in a crash.

Chloe walked back in with a big smile on her face. "You don't want to spend a sinner's money, Mummy, shey?" She picked the ATM card. "How many sinners like him pay tithe to Daddy and we are able to live large like this."

"Don't you dare talk about God's money in that way," I said. "Chloe! Out of all the men in this world, why are you with an old man, a married man?"

Chloe folded her arms across her chest. "I like him."

"Chloe!" I walked to her. "Please, you are a child of God. This man is not...not a believer. You have no business with him." I reckoned it was no use fighting her over this. I could appeal to her faith.

"Hmm, Mummy." Chloe patted my cheeks. "What do you want? I was dating Dami who is a minister, you didn't like it, now I'm dating Prince, you still don't like it!"

I exclaimed. "Ah, Chloe, but you were a child then, and Dami was double your age, and you didn't tell me, Chloe!"

"Now I'm telling you, Mummy. I can't be you, sorry!" She walked into the room and came out a second later while I was still trying to coordinate my thoughts. "I'm spending the evening with friends. Bye."

Chloe didn't come home that evening.

Adam was almost never in the house, and so, the day before I returned home, I knocked on his bedroom door, when I was sure he was in.

"Who is it?"

"Me. Mummy," I said.

He grunted. "Huh, not now, Mummy, I'm naked."

"Put on clothes." Simultaneously I tried the door, it was locked.

"What do you want, Mummy, I can't stand up from my bed." He snapped. "I'll see you tomorrow."

It was just afternoon. "I'm leaving tomorrow. Open this door, Adam."

"I want to sleep, Mummy, please!"

"Adam, is this how you want to waste your life?"

"Ohhh! Mummy, please. Please."

The next thing, he turned on his music so loud, I was sure the neighbours could hear. I left him alone and went in search of Darlington, who I realized never went out to work. His job was caretaking the house and my grown children, and I could see how horrible a job he was doing. I made an important point to have a serious meeting with Daddy when I got back home. Chloe was dating a married man, and making no issue out of it, and Adam did nothing but go out all day, and perhaps all night, and nothing more.

Darlington was in the kitchen, tidying up, and preparing dinner.

"Minister Darlington, good afternoon."

"Good afternoon, Mummy," he said without turning to look at me.

"I want to talk to you," I said.

He turned and wiped his hands off a napkin. "Okay, ma."

"What is happening with these children? Adam is not doing anything, and Chloe is going out with a man more than double her age," I said.

He gasped. "Huh, I didn't know he was that old. She told me he is thirty."

I exclaimed. "Is thirty not too old for an eighteen or nineteen-year-old girl? A married man!"

He shrugged. "Some girls like mature men. Mummy, especially in this London, none of those young boys are of any good." His eyes darted towards the kitchen door. "And he's not married o."

I knew he wanted to infer Adam. Yes, younger men may not be of any good, but Chloe was too young, and this Prince of a man was too old.

"Hmm, she didn't tell you he's a politician? Okay, no problem."

"Mummy, you have nothing to worry about. These children have the mind of Christ, and they will do well," Darlington said. "Just be praying for them as a mother."

For a moment, it was as though I was hearing Daddy's voice saying that. It dawned on me that this man was just a décor. He was cleaning and cooking for my children since I had missed out on that important part of their upbringing and living in London on an allowance. Darlington was living the best days of his life. He had no worries about bills, a wife and children, or a corrupt government. He probably didn't care if Adam became something or not. This was just a job to him.

I returned home more resolved I had to save my children.

Chapter 46

I HAD BEEN AWAY for just one week, but things had changed drastically in my absence. The most horrid of the changes was that Daddy had renovated our huge bedroom. The bedroom had two walk-in wardrobes for Daddy and me, two bathrooms, and an adjoining prayer room. With the renovation, a wall was erected with a connecting door that did not have a knob or opening on my side of the room. I found all my things ~~were~~ neatly arranged in my room, ~~and~~ along with a set of furniture, very much like the one in my old master bedroom.

To make matters worse, I couldn't get access into the old bedroom. I arrived in the morning and made this discovery, but when I went in search of Daddy, he was busy, according to his secretary. No one had ever told me to my face that my husband was "busy." I didn't want to cause any drama in his office, and so waited until evening. When he came home, I could hear him moving around his room. I knocked on the connecting door, and after a few hard knocks, Daddy opened the door.

"Daddy! Ah, huh, why am I on one side of the room?"

He smirked. "Because I believe you want to be married to yourself."

"Haba, Daddy. I don't understand. I needed to go and see those children, and..."

"Good night, Mummy. Welcome back." He closed the door, and I just stood looking and feeling foolish.

What was this?

Everything else had changed too. I couldn't get access into Daddy's private parlour. It was always locked and at least two PABs stood at attention every time of the day. It was as though they had a shift. I called my husband's number and got voicemail. It was like a dream.

Over the years, our extended families had never been too relevant. Anyone who wanted to see us had to come to our house, and later the mansion strictly by Daddy's invitation, and so my parents chose never to visit, and Skola did only a few times. Baami in a rare moment of sharing his opinion said if he couldn't come to his daughter's house without invitation, then he couldn't come at all. Daddy's family, however, were all members of the church and leaders too. But no one ever referred to us as family. We were Daddy and Mummy. If you didn't see and address us as such, you didn't count. My husband's favourite scripture was of Jesus saying only those who did God's will were his father and mother. And brother and sister. In essence, you had to be a serious member of our church. My family structure was such that I didn't have in-laws. Now that my husband shut me out of his activities, there was no option of going to his parents or mine to intervene.

We didn't have spiritual mentors either or a father-in-ministry. We were Daddy and Mummy. We reported to only God, people reported to us.

It left me confused on what to do.

At first, I was angry. In my heart, I thought Daddy would come knocking on my door for sex. He didn't. A week, two, then three. I decided to ignore, then I panicked a little. Was he sleeping with someone else? With my orientation and faith background, it was my duty to keep my home, and fight for my marriage. Was I allowing someone else to do my duty? It would be adultery on Daddy's part and much as I could never imagine it of him, I didn't want to be the reason, like they say, the one who pushed him out.

Late one evening, I took my bath, and stood by our connecting door. When I heard movement in the other room, I started knocking. It took a while before Daddy opened the door.

I went on my knees. "I am sorry, Daddy. My love, my lord, my master. Please forgive me." I looked up at him. He stared down at me. "Please my darling husband. I will never do this again." I rose and kissed him on the mouth.

He did not respond at first, but he let me into his room. We made fiery love that night.

In the morning, he told me the sleeping arrangement would remain the same until he decided when the time was right for me to move back. Suddenly, I was at his beck and call again. I did not like my life, and even more so, now.

Subsequently, Daddy would let me into his room only when I knocked, though I didn't need to knock or wait long. Each time I knocked on that door, I felt my dignity diminish. It was as though I was begging to be loved by my husband. If I thought our relationship was strange in the beginning, it was worse now. I tried a few times to talk about the children and Daddy made it clear their future was in God's hands.

I was back to square one in my life; unsure of how to help my children, myself. The things I did to occupy myself, mainly PLL, besides my duties as Mummy, lost savour. So, when Alexa gave birth to her second child and requested my help, I was happy to oblige. When she had her first child three years earlier, we were both mourning our parents and Pastor Femi's mother had been there to help. Being able to help this time made me both happy and sad. Maami should have been the one to do the duty.

I took it to Daddy as a request. Thank goodness, he approved a month for me. Alexa lived on Lagos Island, in a beautiful four-bedroom duplex in Lekki. As school was in session, I couldn't take Calli and Ben with me, much as I wished, and they could only visit on weekends.

The new baby arrived on a bright, sunny morning at a private hospital, and I visited Alexa with Calli and Ben. She'd had a caesarean section and would be in the hospital for a few days. Daddy allowed me to visit daily, but I didn't move to the house until Alexa was discharged. After dropping their son, Delight at his school, Fẹmi came to the hospital and took us to the house and returned to his office at their church.

I laid the sleeping baby in her court, and then Alexa walked me to the room across from hers. Inside, the queen-size bed was arranged in a room decorated in baby pink and peach tones. It was adjoining Delight's room.

What I loved most about the room was the cross ventilation. Being in Alexa's house, was truly a blessing to me. The atmosphere for me was calm, and I felt welcome. Alexa had a maid, Lola, who helped with her chores, and caring for Delight.

"This is actually Baby's room," Alexa said. "The guest room is downstairs. But that's too far for me to come to you, climbing up and down the stairs."

"Yes, of course. I won't even let you do it. Rather, I will be doing the climbing." I sighed. "Is that where Lola sleeps?"

"We have a one-room BQ at the back. She sleeps there." Alexa sat on the queen bed. "Huh." My face shot to hers. "Are you in pain?"

"No, Sister. I'm just so exhausted. My body just feels weak," Alexa said.

"Pẹlẹ, at least now, you can rest. I advise that you sleep when baby is sleeping, like now." Alexa yawned. "To stand up now is a problem."

I laughed. "You need to be strong. Come on."

I helped her up and we returned to her room. She went straight to the cot and stared at her baby. "She's pretty. I think this one will have my face."

I laughed again. "I think so too."

It felt so good to laugh so freely. It dawned on me that I hardly smiled, talk less of laugh. The atmosphere in my mansion did not warrant a lot of joy. I was always with church members, or my children. Everything we did seemed to be under precision, no spontaneity like I felt with Alexa.

Alexa went to lay on her king-size bed. "Ahh."

"Will you eat before you sleep?"

"I asked Lola to make pepper soup before we arrive so I can have some," she said.

"Good, let me bring it for you." I turned.

"Sister, Lola will bring it when I'm ready. Don't worry." She smiled. "Come and sit down. What has been happening with you?"

I arched an eyebrow. "Happening, how? Nothing. Everything is fine."

"Sister!" Alexa grunted. "You think I don't know you? When last were you this happy, laughing freely? Even in church, you are stiff like iroko tree." She giggled.

I wanted to laugh it off, but she was right. It was quite embarrassing for me, and I turned away, unable to admit it or lie about it.

"See, Sister, Femi and I agreed to ask you, instead of his mum, to come and do this ọmụgwọ just to get you out of that mansion." She kissed her teeth. "It's so obvious you are not happy."

I gasped. "Really? How?"

"You never smile!" She lowered her voice. "I want us to talk, Sister. What is happening? Everyone pretends as though all is well, but we know. Is Daddy in trouble?"

I sighed. "Daddy! Ah, no o. Not at all."

I really needed to unburden, talk, rant and vent, so I offloaded all my problem on my newly discharged new mother little-sister. From Daddy, to Adam, to Chloe, to Calli who as the typical middle child was often neglected and forgotten, to Ben. Not that I expected Alexa to solve my problems, but it felt great to finally open up about them. Who else could I cry out to? Who would listen and understand? Did I even have a right to complain seeing how blessed and privileged I was?

"Hmm, Sister! You are carrying all this, and you didn't tell anybody?"

I didn't know I had tears in my eyes until Alexa wiped them with her bare hands. "Who will I tell?"

"Listen, Sister, do you have money?"

I nodded.

"As in, your own money that you can spend without a trace?"

I shrugged. "A little."

"Enough to buy like a ticket, book logistics and things like that?"

I didn't know where Alexa was going with this, but after the way she controlled her "powerful" and "anointed" husband with a dirty slap the other time, I couldn't put anything past her.

"Yes, not a lot but I have access to a decent amount."

"Good. Go to London." Alexa patted my hand. "Go and stay there permanently with your children, the ones there. God will take care of the ones here! I have said my own o, Sister."

"I can't, Alexa! Daddy will never let me."

Chapter 47

ALEXA AND I PLANNED *that in the last week of my approved stay helping her care for her new baby, Destiny, I will take a quick trip to London. There was no way anyone would know except me, her, and Pastor Fẹmi, at least until I get there, and Daddy will be told by his loyalists. Dealing with that would be a major issue, but we planned a good "peace offering" afterwards. The worst sin would be to tell him, he refuses and then I go. Better to do it without informing him and then do damage control...as though I was a five-year-old. Even Lola was told I was going into a retreat in the house and would not want to be disturbed.*

To stay permanently as Alexa suggested was impossible. But a week at least would relieve me of my worry. Pastor Fẹmi bought my return ticket and, on the day scheduled, I flew to London.

I took a cab from Heathrow to the house in the morning hours. By all plans, I should not meet anyone except Darlington, unless he had errands to run. I was ready to sit at the bus stop close by until someone returned if by chance, the house was empty and locked. However, that would be strange. People always lived in our house.

As expected, Darlington opened the door to me. His mouth dropped open, and he went pale. It went beyond surprise. He looked horrified to see me. He leaned forward a little and glared.

"Is Daddy here too?"

"Minister Darlington." I smiled. "Surprise!" I followed his gaze.

Well, probably Darlington may be able to keep this visit secret from Daddy! But why would he look so terrified.

After confirming Daddy wasn't behind me, Darlington just stood there, glaring.

"Will you let me in?"

He stepped back and I walked in, my heart thudding, wondering why Darlington hesitated.

The sitting room looked neat and normal. I dropped my hand luggage, which was the only thing I packed since much of my clothes still hung in my wardrobe here. In his shock, Darlington had not even offered to help with my bag.

"I said I should give you all a surprise visit. How has everything been?"

Darlington stood stuck to the same spot, but he turned to face me. "Mummy, everything is okay."

I knew everything was not. "Chloe and Adam?"

"They are fine, in school," he said.

"Adam is in school?" I folded my arms across my chest. "That is great. No one told us. Which school?"

Darlington visibly relaxed. "Yes, Mummy." He smiled. "We were going to surprise you at the end of the semester."

"Well, that is amazing surprise. Please, can you make breakfast for me, I'm hungry. I'd like to take a bath and sleep. Thank you."

"Of course, Mummy. Huh, welcome, ma." He hurried off into the kitchen.

I checked the girls' room, and then boys' room. I least expected to see either Chloe or Adam with the news they were in school, but I just wanted to sniff things, see if I could pick Darlington's unease. Nothing in the two rooms showed anything unusual. I got into my room, had a bath, and placed a call to Adam. His number did not go through, which was not a surprise. Since the last time I saw Adam on the last day of my stay in London, his number had connected maybe once in twenty calls. It was usually always switched off. I called Chloe.

"Hey. Mummy, I have a class, I can't talk now," Chloe said.

Not a surprise, either, but when she didn't want to talk, she would not pick up.

"I'm in London. When can I visit you in school, or can you come home?"

Chloe heaved a heavy sigh. "I knew you'd come immediately you heard."

"Heard what?"

"Huh! You didn't hear? Oh, Mum, umm, I can't talk now. I'm…"

I screamed. "Heard what?" My body shuddered. "Chloe?"

"Adam. He's in jail. I have to go."

The line went dead. My heart sank. A strong headache hit the side of my face. "Yee!" Jail? For what? Did Daddy know?

"Darlington!" I ran to the kitchen.

He must have heard my voice on the phone, realized the news was broken to me from the shriek in my voice. When I stepped into the kitchen, Darlington went on his knees. Without knowing why or what I was doing, I hit him several times, sobbing and screeching.

"Where is my son? What did you do to my son?"

"He was always locked up in his room. I did not know he was doing drugs," Darlington said. He swiped off tears from his eyes. "It was just in the middle of the night. The police came. They said it was a drug burst." He sniffed. "I was terrified. I told them this was a mission house. They just started entering everywhere. Thank God, Chloe was in school. They broke down Adam's door. He had run out through the window. They caught him."

I sat on the kitchen floor, my arms folded across my chest, my voice hoarse from screaming and crying. I leaned my head down. Only one thing came to my mind. I wanted to see Adam. That was all. I couldn't be mad with Darlington. What could he have done under the circumstances? A mere hired hand. Well, he could have called Daddy or me, and then what? My son had become the product of my negligence. This was all my fault.

I sniffed. "When can I see him?"

That was all that mattered. I wanted to see Adam. Talk to him. I wanted him to see me, look into my eyes and know I loved him no matter where he was. I raised him.

"He is awaiting trial, so his lawyer gets to see him at least three times a week. I will ask the lawyer to arrange for you to see him," Darlington said.

It took everything within me to not have an outburst when Adam, in prison garb, and handcuffed, walked out on the other side of a thick glass partition, and sat down opposite me. He had been clean-shaven, his head had no hair either, and in my mother-eyes, he had lost half of his weight and beauty. He started crying.

"It's okay," I said.

I know the strength that flowed through those words could only be God's. In my wildest dreams, I never imagined my own son, my first blood, would be a criminal, behind bars.

"I'm sorry, Mummy." Adam sobbed. "Daddy should just curse me, and I die. I have brought disgrace to the family. Mummy, please, forgive me."

I just sat there as he cried and sobbed and begged. Something inside me snapped that day. I stopped feeling remorse. It was the strangest feeling. Adam seemed to have been removed from my life. I had thought I would cry and break down completely. I had thought I would never be able to live again but instead, a spirit of nonchalance overwhelmed me...so difficult to describe. It was as though I had gotten to a cliff and didn't care anymore. If I perish, I perish.

"I told Minister Darlington not to tell you and Daddy. But Chloe was very helpful. She and Prince."

Hmm. Prince, Chloe's sugar-daddy.

Adam sniffed. "If not for them, it would have been worse. They helped me get this lawyer. He's a very good lawyer. Expensive but Prince is paying him. Ah, Mummy, I have suffered. I want to go home. Please take me away from here, Mummy. Please." He sobbed hard.

"It is well," I said stiffly.

Chapter 48

DADDY VISITED ALEXA THE evening of the day I returned from London. There was no way he'd have known I travelled. The people in London had more problems to hide from him than my visit so, it was all good for them to keep silent. I pitied Darlington, though, and I told him so. If Daddy got to know Adam was in jail, and all the mess around it, and that he was kept a secret, it would not be funny.

"Daddy will curse you, Darlington, you know that," I'd said.

The whole world knew the fear of Daddy's curse was next to the fear of God.

Why was he visiting on this day when I just arrived in the morning and had not gotten time to unwind and unpack from the short but devastating trip? I'd not even given Alexa the full story. This was Love Jaja! The man full of discernments and a unique spirit of judgement. If he didn't know for sure where I'd been, he knew something was not right. He had come to confirm, and I knew he would. I wasn't a good liar.

Alexa, on the other hand, was perfected in the art of camouflage. She came into my room and smiled.

"Daddy is in the parlour downstairs. I gave him Destiny to play with and Delight is asking him questions as though he's on trial," she said.

The irony of the joke. Our whole family ~~has have been~~ are placed on trial by Adam!

I gasped. "Did he come while I was away?"

"No, Sister. Fẹmi said he asked after you in one of their meetings, and that's all," Alexa said.

"Hmm, okay, I'm coming," I said.

"Act very spiritual. The story is that you decided to do a retreat up here." Alexa winked. "Quote scriptures." She laughed.

I smirked. "Yes, Mrs. Liar Pastor."

"Huh, Sister. Be there doing holy holy. You need to be smart in dealing with these our husbands o. You're too slow." She laughed again. "Let me go downstairs before Daddy starts wondering."

After she left, I took in several deep breaths. Daddy was the last person I wanted to see but I had no choice. I stole a glance in the mirror, and though inside I was a tangled mess, my face looked calm, and I could even muster a small smile. Thank goodness, my husband wasn't an enthusiastic type. His general façade remained cool and calm. I would not need to be lively to cover up anything.

Maybe I would never know what that visit was about. Daddy was not unusual. He ate dinner with the family, chit-chatted a little, carried Destiny all through except for when he was eating and prayed over her, and left. Nothing strange but everything was. Daddy never did anything spontaneously. He visited that night for a reason, and it hurt that I may never know it.

We put baby Destiny to bed, and Alexa came to my room afterwards.

"Why do you think Daddy came?" Alexa toyed with her wedding band. "He hasn't seen Destiny since after her naming ceremony. But I doubt that is the reason."

"He has premonition, Alexa." I sighed. "Sometimes I want to doubt it but how do you think the church grew so fast. The man at the head hears from God. He is the oracle of God."

"Okay, I hear, but I can't let him intimidate me, Sister." She crossed her arms so tightly, her fingers dug into her biceps. "Just don't tell him anything about this your London trip, please. I don't want to be doomed o!" She laughed.

We both knew it was as true as night and day, Daddy cursed people and though it wasn't frequent, when he did, it came to pass, just as much as when he blessed people. He just had to say it, and it came to pass. Many people came to our church just to receive the blessing that would carry them through the week. Our monthly prophetic meetings were the most attended in the whole country because people from other churches came just to receive their prophecy for the month. Literally, my husband had the whole world in his hands.

Politicians begged to be recognized by him, but he never did. We received more cars and houses as gifts than we could count; more clothes and shoes than we could wear, but Daddy gave them away as soon as he received them. People came to give him their children, and in the same vein, he handed these children to those waiting on God for their own. In nine out of ten cases, such women conceived in the same year they received a baby from Daddy. "None shall be sick" was a scripture that lived in us and lived through us. No one came to Daddy sick. Once they got close, they received their healing. What did we want that we could not have? Nothing.

Except Adam in jail, Chloe in an ungodly relationship, Calli in her own shell, and Ben tied to my skirts. I didn't think it was automatic to have good children, but at the same time, I never thought children born and raised in a Christian home needed as much work as every other child. It was a hard truth that hit me square in the face when it was too late. Pastors' children probably needed more work than ordinary children, but no one ever told me. I never knew! It continued to baffle me...why could Daddy not simply speak the blessing over his children, and they would turn alright? Was Daddy's word not potent when it came to his children?

"Alexa," I whispered. "There is trouble."

I proceeded to tell her everything I saw in London. Alexa screamed, and Pastor Fẹmi hurried over to the room. He met me staring into space, while Alexa cried.

"What happened?"

I calmly related the story. He broke out speaking in tongues. It just dawned on me that I still felt nothing. My only concern now was that Daddy had to know. But who would break the story to him?

Or did Daddy already know? Did he know I travelled to London? Did he come to see if I would own up to my deceit?

Chapter 49

"I WAS READING UP some stuff on the internet," Calli said. "About sexes."

Idong grunted. "Sexes?"

"Hmm huh." Calli snuggled closer into the crook of his arm. "How to get a baby girl and how to get a baby boy."

Idong yawned around a chuckle. "Nice. What did you find?"

"We'll probably be having a baby girl." Calli giggled. "With all the non-stop lovemak i..."

Idong covered her mouth with his before she could finish her statement. She leaned into the kiss until it became a full round of lovemaking.

When they were spent, Calli moaned. "Don't be so aggressive, baby. I don't want you to make me lose the baby. I mean, I don't have a lot of experien..."

Before she could finish, Idong yelled. "You're pregnant."

Calli scoffed. "What did you think I was trying to say before you bombarded me?" She giggled. "For the third time in one evening!"

If they were on their feet, Idong would have probably carried her. But they were on their back in their bed. Still Idong lifted her on top of him.

"Oh, my love, thank you! Thank God." He leaned in and placed a kiss on her still-flat stomach. "Yes!" He screeched. "Yes, yes! How far gone are you?"

"Three weeks." Calli laughed. "Victor is going to be so happy to have a baby to play with."

"We'll have to move out of the mansion. We need a bigger space." Idong groaned. "Daddy won't like it."

"He won't but I don't care. If you want us to move, we move."

"I'll give him the good news and make my request," Idong shrugged.

Calli sighed. "You do know the space argument won't fly, though. There are at least thirty rooms in this mansion and apartments have been merged or divided in the past.

And there's expansion still going on. It's like Daddy is taking this mansion to hundred rooms one day. As for us, he will just have his team come in and tear down a wall or two and boom, we'll have a five-bedroom house if we want."

Idong threw back his head. "You're right."

Calli traced her fingers over his throat. "You hate it here, don't you?"

"Not hate. I like being where you are. I feel you don't want to be here." He shrugged. "But honestly, sometimes, I think about how comfortable we are. This is paradise compared to what obtains. We have great security, constant power, constant water, constant Wi-Fi. Office is right here. Roads are great, no traffic. We have family and friends on the camp..." He chuckled. "We are living in the UK in Nigeria. So, unless you want to leave, I'm fine."

"I've thought about that, you know." Calli smiled. "Regardless of what I think about my father, Jaja Mansion is a dream accommodation. And I'm grateful for it." She sighed. "We don't even pay any utility bills. Aunty Alexa has to run her generator twenty hours a day, yet her electricity bills are five figures monthly, and her internet flips, huh, even when it is loaded o. Huh, I like the comfort here."

"We can ask for more space. Daddy will not object to breaking down walls so our three-bed can be joined to a two-bed," Idong said.

"Yeah. I'm all for that." She kissed his mouth. "Thank you."

He kissed her back. "Thank you! What are you thanking me for?"

"For loving me, all these years," Calli said softly.

"I can't say it was easy, but I'm grateful for it." He laughed. "Considering three months of funny dating without talking, seven years of marriage, we pecked once, had sex once, which produced Victor, and never had a conversation unless others were there or it was necessary. Hmm." He pressed his lips into a fine line. "I think I want to accept your thanks. You're welcome. I endured."

Calli laughed. "I never knew my husband was a drama king." She rolled off him and resumed the cuddle with her head in the crook of his arm. "Sometimes I wanted so badly to kill myself. I just didn't have the courage."

"Thank God for lack of courage. I was just praying that God would touch you. Help me love you despite all. I never stopped praying, believing God to heal our marriage and give us peace," Idong said.

"He answered." Calli looked up at him. "I love you so much. I never thought that would be possible."

"I love you more." He sealed her mouth with a kiss. "You know, seven years of marriage. I didn't know when God would answer me, and let you see me...because you looked through me. You never saw me."

"It's true. I didn't want to acknowledge you. I just was there like a zombie," she chuckled. "After Victor was born, I devoted my life to raising him."

"That day I walked into the room..."

"I wasn't expecting you. You were supposed to be in a meeting with Daddy, I thought I'd be alone, have enough time to cry," she said.

"I knew it could only be God." Idong snickered. "I never saw you cry. Never. I was terrified. I thought you got some news, maybe you had cancer or something."

"I never wanted anyone to see me cry. But for seven years married to you, I probably cried every other day." Calli shuddered. "I was really miserable."

"Huh, sorry, baby." He caressed her back. "I knew God wanted to do something that day. I was in the meeting with Daddy and felt a pressing need to use the restroom. I went straight to the toilet, and it was jammed. The lock was bad, which you know is strange. Toilet door jams in Daddy's office and no one fixed it? I just ran here without thinking, only to hear you in the room. Crying. No, wailing."

"I thought I was alone." Calli chuckled. "I was fully expressing myself."

"Ah, my baby. You cannot imagine how frightened I was." Idong pressed his face into her hair and dragged in a long breath. "You smell sweet."

"You smell sweet," Calli repeated and giggled.

"Meanwhile, can I say something?"

Calli smiled. "Shock me, if you haven't yet."

"Daddy asked me if you were a virgin... you know, if I found you," he swallowed. "Whole."

Calli gulped. "No. That's so wrong and inappropriate of him."

"He did. At first, you know, we didn't do." He shrugged. "I didn't know so I said so. Then after we did, he asked again."

Calli closed her eyes. "I feel so violated."

"He asked if I was too." Calli's mouth and eyes opened at the same time, and Idong placed a gentle kiss on her eyelid. "So, since I lied for myself, I lied for you too," he said softly.

Calli huffed. "He would have cursed me. Huh." She stared at him. "I... you know, Bosa taught me everything. How to cook, how to kiss...he was the only one. Before you..."

"I don't need an explanation, my baby. God's saving grace is sufficient. I have made many mistakes too, but God forgave me, and I have moved on. Sinning no more," Idong said.

For several moments, they just cuddled.

Then Calli murmured, "Thank God you came that day. But you didn't even use the toilet oh if I remember."

"That's why I said it was God. I didn't feel like it anymore after we spoke. I was on cloud nine! It was just like that day when I asked you to marry me, and you said yes." He slid his hand over her stomach. "Like the day you told me you were going to have Victor." He kissed her forehead. "Like the day you let me kiss you on the mouth." He kissed her hungrily. "Like today."

Chapter 50

IF MY FIRST TRIP to London raised hell, this second trip brought it home. I realized Daddy knew exactly what I did when I got back to the mansion the following week, from doing ọmụgwọ for Alexa. My room was locked. None of the PABs had an idea who locked it or where I could get the key. I ordered one of them to get a carpenter to break the door, and this was how Daddy's secretary called and informed me my new room was in the east wing of the mansion.

Prior to this time, the east wing was luxurious and designed for visitors. Many of the guests who came to the mansion from outside the country were lodged in the east wing. My family, and most of the PABs who lived in the mansion, stayed in the west wing, which had many more rooms.

"Why?" I asked Daddy's secretary.

"This was the instruction we have, ma," the secretary said.

I didn't want to argue with Daddy's staff, so I went to the east wing. A PAB there took me to an apartment that had one bedroom, a sitting area, kitchen, and a bathroom. It was one of the newly created apartments as Daddy added a new three-story structure to the east wing, while maintaining the design. The mansion was beginning to look like a huge square and I wondered if one day there would be north and south wings, as there was enough land to build this.

Again, like the last time Daddy threw me out of my matrimonial bedroom, all my belongings were in this new space. I suddenly felt violated. How dare strangers touched my personal belongings...my underwear, my jewellery, my stuff! Such disrespect! Disrespect ordered by Daddy. It was obvious I was expected. I looked at the PAB, a beautiful young lady I had never seen before.

"What's your name?"

She fell on her knees. "Ṣiju, ma."

"Stand up, Ṣiju. Please." I smiled. "You are very pretty. I've not seen you before."

She smiled shyly. "I just joined the church, ma. Like three months ago."

"Oh, no wonder." I chuckled. "Don't mind me, I see so many people I get easily confused."

"I understand, ma," she said.

"See Ṣiju, I want you to help me tell Calli and Ben, I am here, and they should come and see me when they come back from school."

"No problem, ma."

"Thank you, my dear."

I could never have imagined the deep mess I was in. That day ended without me seeing my children. Calli was in the Christian university Adam was expelled from, but she commuted from home; a PAB and a car had been assigned to her. Ben was in his final class in one of the four secondary schools in Lagos owned by our church, being to my surprise that, when we returned from London, Daddy put him in the same class with his old classmates, hence he skipped two classes; a PAB attended to him too. I called their numbers and didn't get through. I didn't get through to Daddy too. I tried to be calm and spent the rest of the day praying and gathering my thoughts, and next course of action. Ṣiju had no luck reaching my children too.

The following day, I went in search of my family early in the morning and discovered the security door on the corridor that linked the west wing to the east had a new code for the lock, and none of the PABs were awake or around to open for me. I spent the whole of that day asking questions no one had an answer to. My family had been shut away from me.

I called Alexa.

"Pastor Fẹmi and I will come late in the evening when the traffic has gone down," Alexa said.

True to her word, they arrived in my apartment at about ten o'clock.

"I came with the children so we can all spend the night," she said. It made sense.

"Hmm, Alexa, Pastor Fẹmi. This is strange." I waved towards the bedroom door. "I found all my things in the room. They even stocked the kitchen for me. I don't remember the last time I cooked a meal."

"Huh, this is nonsense." Alexa snapped. "Why is Daddy doing like this? Do you want me to prepare something?"

"Haba, I know how to cook. Hmm. The story of my life." I sighed. "The way things are going now, I don't know how to see him. And the children. I can go to their schools, but I don't know if I will have access to a car or I don't even know what is going on."

"Daddy is in the parlour now. Let's go and see him together," Pastor Fẹmi said.

I exhaled. "And I have to tell him about Adam..."

"You don't have to, Sister!" Alexa cried. "Let's solve this problem of you being here all alone first. How do you even know he doesn't know about Adam. Shey he is the holy spirit!"

Pastor Fẹmi retorted. "Alexa!"

"Let's go and see him in the parlour." I rose. "Are the children alright?"

"Yes, Lola is with them in my old room," Alexa said. "We will sleep in one of the guest rooms there."

Daddy had a few of the pastors with him when we arrived. Pastor Fẹmi and Alexa went to kneel before him. I noticed the couch closest to him, which I normally sat on was not there. It was the most awkward moment for me. Elijah, who stood at attention beside Daddy, walked over to me as I contemplated what to do, whether to wait to be given a seat, or just go over and take any empty seat available.

"Mummy, please let me see you outside for a second," Elijah whispered.

"Okay, Minister." I followed him out.

"Mummy, this is very difficult for me, and I know you have been a wonderful mother to all of us, but I have to follow the orders Daddy gave me." Elijah held my gaze. "Daddy does not want to see you just yet."

I exclaimed. "Ehn? I mean, what does that mean?"

"Listen, Mummy, and calm down. I am on your side," Elijah said. "He has not told anyone why, but he does not want to see you. I will just advise that you pray and wait..."

"Pray and wait to see my own husband? Huh! Are you joking or what?"

"Let's go for a walk, Mummy," Elijah said.

"I'm not going for any walk, Elijah. Please excuse me." I pushed him aside and walked back to the door.

"He'll embarrass you, Mummy. You don't want that," Elijah said softly. "Please. Go back to your room and wait until he calls you."

His words halted me. As though I was a paid servant? I swung around, and Elijah went on his knees. He clasped his hands in supplication. Who was he, anyway, and what can he do? Like all of us, he was just a messenger at Daddy's beck and call. He lived somewhere in the mansion, in the west wing, with his wife and twin toddling boys. He had a house, given as a gift by Daddy in the heart of Lagos and he collected rent from his tenants there. And who was he before he got close to Daddy? What did he have? This one saw serving Daddy as serving God. He had a lot to lose if he fell out of Daddy's favour.

I marched past him and to my room, thinking about that. What I had to lose if I fell out of Daddy's favour. He could, as he threatened once, to not let me see my children again. That was the worst he could do. And could he? So far, he was succeeding but Ben would soon be on his way to university. Once my children were out of the mansion, they could decide if they wanted to see me or not. Angry beyond words, I sent a text message to Alexa to tell her what happened.

She replied much later that Daddy engaged her and Pastor Fẹmi in a very long discussion about their church and by the time they were done, she had to go and breastfeed Destiny, and that she would see me the following day.

Chapter 51

Exile from my family stretched. On service days, I sat beside my husband and anyone seeing us thought things were normal. The first one week was super weird. I did not see Calli and Ben. Not once. Everything had been put in place in such a way that it was not possible. That was when I realized how huge the mansion was, how the cameras everywhere meant something, how powerful my husband was. How stupid I was to let all this ride by me in my nonchalance and ignorance.

No one still knew what my offense was, at least, going by what Elijah said, so it seemed. I was going crazy, and so I reached out to Sharon. Since she shut down her church, all had been silent around her and her family. We spoke on the phone, and she sent the address of her mother's house, where she lived to me.

I still had access to transportation, so a PAB drove me to Sharon's house. To my pleasant surprise, Chinwe was there visiting as well. We all hugged and laughed at how we were not even different from the last time we met. It had been three years since Chinwe left and a year and some since Sharon closed church. None of us had been active in PLL for at least one year.

Over soft drinks, we each caught up on what was going on. Chinwe had the best story to tell. Her three children were all in boarding school, which was partly why she was in Lagos, and she now ran her own NGO for empowering small-scale female entrepreneurs. She wasn't doing ministry anymore.

"Of course, I am still a Christian. I am not married but I am not divorced," Chinwe said. "But God has been good. My life is smooth, busy, fulfilling, I have more than enough to take care of my children."

"Hmm, even a blind man can see that," Sharon said. "Three children in boarding school. A good private school. God has been good to you."

I sighed. "What about your husband?"

Chinwe shrugged. "We are co-parenting. He's running his church. He visits the children in their school, I do too. And during holidays, they spend part with him, and part with me."

I moaned. "That can be devastating on the mental and emotional health of those children."

"What will I do, now? It is more devastating for them to see their father caning and flogging me and kicking me," Chinwe said. "Strangling me."

I gasped knowing Chinwe's decision was right, the best for the children under the circumstances.

"My husband has my children." Sharon shook her head. "They all refused to follow me. It's sickening. They blame me for destroying their lives."

"That's how much they know," Chinwe said. "They just don't understand now. When they grow up, they will."

"When? The youngest is ten. The oldest is fifteen. They understand everything. I'm sad. I'm depressed. They don't want to see me," Sharon said. "Some days I just cry from morning to night."

I clasped my hands under my chin. "Is he preventing you from visiting them?"

Sharon stretched. "I haven't tried. My mother thinks I should go and beg him to take me back. She sings it like a mantra to me every day. But how? If this man wants the marriage, won't he come and look for me? He's the one who broke our vows for crying out loud."

"Our parents sometimes don't understand what we go through with these men, especially since he is a pastor." Chinwe shook her head. "My parents nearly disowned me when I left."

I pressed a hand against my ear. "What?"

"Yes o. They walked me out of their house. They didn't give me a kobo," Chinwe said. "But I just thank God for everything. I have my children."

"Mine are a mess," I whispered. "And now Daddy won't let me see Calli and Ben, though we live in the same house."

"Why?" Sharon and Chinwe chorused.

I told them everything. "I don't know what to do."

"You can use that Minister Elijah, he seems empathetic, and he is close to your husband," Chinwe said.

"No," Sharon said. "Those ministers are too loyal. They will be feeding back information. Use Alexa and her husband instead."

I moaned. "I don't want Alexa to get into trouble."

"I agree with Pastor Sharon. Use Alexa at least to see Calli and Ben," Chinwe said. "You can also go and see the pastor your husband submits to, though those Babas sef, they really don't care a lot. I know how they added to my problem when I reported my husband. Once you give them fat honorarium, they start speaking from two sides of the mouth."

"Shey, my sister!" Sharon exclaimed. "I reported my husband to his mentor. You won't believe that he told me the Holy Spirit told him not to intervene in our matter!"

"Ewoo! These Babas lie against the Holy Spirit the same way members lie against the devil. So sad," Chinwe said. "Now, if you don't give them fat offering, you won't even have access to them at all!"

"Shey?!" Sharon clapped. "I remember when our church was small, and we were still struggling. We went to submit to one Baba with a fat offering, all our money in this life o! He prayed for us. Do you know after three months and we couldn't give anything, he stopped picking our call!"

Chinwe grunted. "Na wa!"

"My husband submits to only the Holy Spirit." I shook my head. "I thought that was so spiritual of him until now."

"It's simple. Ask the Holy Spirit to speak to him," Chinwe said. "It's even the fastest way." She hissed. "As if this Holy Spirit is a monopoly to only some people."

Sharon crooked her neck. "Will he listen?"

Having a new baby did not help the Alexa plan too well. I didn't think it was proper for her to take her baby out with the horrible traffic jams in the heat of the day, and coming at night wasn't ideal either, and I wasn't allowed to go to the west wing to see my children. I wrote letters to them and had Ṣiju deliver to Calli and Ben. I wrote to Daddy too, asking to have conference with him, but got no responses. Chloe didn't pick my calls anymore either. I had Adam's lawyer's number, and he could give me updates on the case. Nothing much happened with my first son, and eventually, he was sentenced to three years in prison, which the lawyer called a miracle.

Three months went by before I knew it, and Alexa dedicated Destiny at their church. They invited Daddy and me to do the blessing and dedication of the baby. During the service, while Daddy preached, a male usher tapped me on my shoulder, and asked me to follow *him. Unsure of the situation, I did. The usher led me to Pastor Femi's office, and there seated, were Calli and Ben.*

I burst into tears. Ben jumped up and ran into my arms. Calli held back a little, and eventually hugged me too.

"Mummy, I'm not doing this again. I can't be in this town, at home, and not be allowed to see you," Ben said. His lips trembled and I could see how hard he tried to hold back tears. "Whatever the problem is with you and Daddy, please settle it."

Calli, to my surprise had tears streaming down her eyes unbidden. She was such a beautiful young woman, and I wondered where I was when she was growing up.

"Daddy gave orders that we should not have anything to do with you. He put an app on our phones that tracked our calls and text messages," Calli said softly. "I just want to see you around me, Mummy."

I couldn't believe my ears. What sort of app tracked someone's phone like that?

I wiped her tears with my bare hands. "I know your Daddy is very angry with me, but we will sort things out. I will soon be back in the west wing. Meanwhile, I am going to get a new number. I will give Pastor Femi, and Alexa. You can call me on the new number. And we can say it is Alexa's second number. Save it as Aunty Alexa 2 or something."

Calli nodded. "I will use my friend's phone anytime I'm in school."

I thought that was horrible. Why couldn't these children be allowed to have a normal life? Why did Daddy bring our children into the tangled mess of our marriage? This was so depressing and so unfair to them.

"I will run away, Mummy." Ben cried. "I am tired."

"Call me when you get my new number." I hugged them both. "I miss you, but we have to get back into church."

We did.

Subsequently, I spoke with Calli every day of the week, and Ben, every other day. Talking to Calli this way made us become closer than I ever realized we could be. It was beautiful, and I was grateful to God for giving me this chance even in the middle of a family disconnection.

One day as we chatted over the phone in between Calli's classes, she asked when next I was going to London.

"I don't know, my dear. Why do you ask?"

She seemed to catch her breath. "I haven't seen Adam in so long. And Chloe too. I miss them. I want to go with you if you are visiting them."

It nudged my heart to tell her the truth. But how could I? With the issues between me and Daddy, I decided it was conversation better left for when we could sit face to face.

"I'll keep that in mind, dear."

She screeched. "Thank you, Mummy!"

Chapter 52

DARA HAD NEVER MADE herself conspicuous to the Pedros. She was like a house slave on a large plantation – the masters trusted her enough to keep their children with her, but she wasn't any more important than any of the field slaves. The servant seemed to understand the dynamics of the family she worked for more than they understood her. On Sundays, she went to church as part of her half-day off, only that this Sunday, she didn't visit her family church. She went in search of Calli Asukwo at her church.

When Chloe was still Mrs. Pedro, she religiously attended her father's church with her daughters, and Dara as the girls' nanny, went with them, and so Dara knew where exactly to find Calli. The best time was in between services, especially as she had to time her return to the Pedro villa perfectly.

Calli, as Idong's wife, had to choose between the women's ministry or the children's ministry, and she chose to work with children. She was helping other teachers to clean the nursery two class in preparation for the second service kids, when Dara knocked on the door, and walked in.

"Ah, Dara! Good to see you." Calli walked over to her.

"Good morning, ma." Dara curtseyed. "I will not stay long. Chief Pedro has eyes here." She pressed a piece of paper into Calli's hand. "Bye." She marched off quickly.

Calli smiled and turned. It was such a small piece of paper, and she thought it would be a phone number or something.

Calli paced the spacious space of their bedroom. "I want to kill someone right now."

She could hear Victor in the sitting room jumping and screeching at a freeze-dance video, glad he wouldn't interrupt for now, while she and Idong unravelled Dara's mysterious visit to their church today.

"You should be grateful to Dara, first." Idong sat at his writing desk and held a flat file with several sheets of paper in it. "She apparently is much smarter than I ever thought."

Calli giggled. "I didn't even know she could read and write." She sighed. "First, how do we proceed."

Idong waved the file. "We follow her plan."

"Except that her plan includes Chloe, and Chloe is loath." Calli massaged her temple.

"I have a feeling Dara doesn't know…" Idong shook his head. "She must know Mummy doesn't live here anymore."

"She knows. Everyone knows." Calli clenched her jaw. "But in the note, why would she ask me to find this file under a flowerpot outside Mummy's old office, and not elsewhere?"

"Because no one goes around there especially during church service. She's afraid," Idong said. "Those people are horrible. She's smart too."

Calli cried. "Chloe will kill him. She'll kill OPJ if she finds out he's been touching the girls."

"I want to kill him. Goodness!" Idong gasped. "Anyway, right now, do we follow Dara's plan or make ours?"

"Ours? I mean, besides improvising Chloe's part…"

"Dara suggests Daddy involves the Commissioner of Police on this one. You want to work so closely with Daddy? You want Daddy to know we've been going to see people?" Idong arched an eyebrow. "That you read Mummy's book?"

Calli slouched.

"My thoughts exactly," Idong said. "Sometimes Daddy glares at me and I look away because I can't bear to hold his gaze. He will know I'm doing something behind his back."

"Why are we living as though we are in a prison?"

Idong sneered. "Aren't we?"

Calli gazed at him, and her heart swelled with joy and pride. She knew from the beginning her husband was smart. But she thought he was too short, though he was just an inch shorter than her five-foot-six; pale and ugly. She couldn't see any of that anymore. His crooked smile melted her heart faster than butter in a hot oven, his simple yet classy fashion style made him look sharp always, and the older Victor got, the more her handsome son looked like Idong. He was genuine, and kind, and funny…

Idong picked out one of the sheets of paper in the file and started to speak but stopped when he looked up from it and caught Calli's gaze. "Why are you eyeing me like that?"

Calli shrugged. "I'm just wondering about all the years we were married, and our lives only rotated around Daddy and his whims."

Chapter 53

SCHOOLS CLOSED FOR THE year and Ben finished secondary school. He didn't do well. In fact, he barely passed, and I took the blame on myself. The relationship between Daddy and I continued to be the same. Perhaps people had started realizing something was not okay with us, but no one really spoke about it. During public meetings, my place beside my husband remained. My duties in church remained. Our family in public remained solid, pacesetters to everyone spiritual and temporal!

I continued calling my children secretly until they came home for the holidays, and we had to devise another way because it was too risky to know who to trust in the mansion, or in church. Alexa became our main middle person. The small circle of friends the children had were still church people, and I didn't want to risk anything or anyone.

The Sunday after the school year ended, Daddy did a prayer for all the students who were commencing on the long holidays. Some were going to travel, some would be moving on to the next level of their schooling, some their jobs. It was usually a beautiful annual meeting with the Holy Spirit moving in the lives of these young people.

A young man came to the altar to give a testimony of how God helped him after Daddy prayed for him the year before when he graduated from the university. His name was Idong Asukwo, whose parents were from my part of the country, South-South. He had graduated from the Lagos State University and applied for a scholarship, which he received, gone to do his masters, and was about to complete it. I liked Idong for some reason I couldn't explain. He had a slight accent, and really reminded me of my father.

Before Idong finished his testimony, Daddy stood, which was unusual, and walked to the altar.

"Watch this man, says the spirit of God," Daddy spoke into his microphone. "He is going to be very great in the kingdom of God."

The crowd roared. Idong fell flat on his face.

Later that evening, I got a surprise summon to see Daddy in his private parlour. It would be the first time in four months. I quickly showered and made up my face. Daddy loved the colour white, and so I wore one of my best white flowing dresses. Perhaps this would be the day the almighty daddy would have mercy on my horrible soul. As I dressed up, I prayed in tongues, asking God to intervene in my marriage. I was tired of the malice between my husband and I, and wary of what to do.

Inside the parlour, I saw Calli on her knees in front of Daddy. I stood just inside of the door because my seat was still not there. Elijah once again came to me, and this time, led me to a couch by the side of the room, just a random couch. Daddy asked Calli to stand, and she did. She walked towards the entrance, and it was then I noticed a young man who stood by the door. He couldn't be more than in his early twenties, and I reckoned he was a PAB. There were so many of these men and women around all the time. Besides us, no one else was in the room. My heart thudded in apprehension. Had Calli done something wrong? Why was she here?

Calli spoke briefly to the young man and took his hand. Both walked back to Daddy, ignoring me totally, and knelt.

"Ẹ dide," Daddy said.

"Thank you, sir," the young man said.

"Daddy, this is Bosa Osagie. He's my boyfriend," Calli said.

My heart throbbed. Child! Why didn't she tell me about this? In the last month before school closed, we had become so close. My face shot to Daddy's, and my heart sank. It did not look good. Daddy glared at Bosa, and the young man bowed his head when he couldn't hold the gaze anymore.

For several stretched seconds, Daddy just stared at the boy then he shook his head. "Boyfriend, Calli?"

"Yes, Daddy," Calli said softly.

Daddy snapped. "And how many boyfriends will you bring to me before you get married?"

"Only Bosa, Daddy."

"Only Bosa. A boy with no future?"

I gasped and stood. "No, Daddy, please. Don't say anymore."

Contrary to my expectations, Calli and Bosa remained on their feet. I had thought they would kneel and plead for acceptance. Instead, Calli just looked past Daddy, and Bosa's head remained bent.

"Stay out of this, Mummy!" Daddy glowered at Calli. "You have the nerve to come here."

"*I have a future with him,*" *Calli said.* "*I love Bosa, and I'm going to marry him.*"

Daddy clicked his tongue. "*You are going to marry him. Here on earth or in heaven?*" *He stood, puffing, then marched out of the sitting room. Elijah followed him out.*

I hurried over to Calli and Bosa. "*Don't let Daddy intimidate you.*"

Bosa prostrated before me. "*Thank you, Mummy. Calli speaks so highly of you.*"

My head swelled at those words, and I hugged him. "*You have a future and a hope, and I am happy you stood your ground.*" *I smiled at Calli.* "*You didn't tell me you have such a fine young man.*"

Calli half-smiled. "*I just pray Daddy doesn't mess it up.*" *She sighed.* "*Bosa needs to leave. He has a long commute.*"

"*It is well, my dear.*" *I hugged Calli, and then Bosa.*

"*Thank you, Mummy,*" *Bosa said.*

I was happy in my heart for Calli. Despite everything, she seemed to be doing so well. She was no longer tied to her sister's tail, well with Chloe in the UK. But Calli was coming into a beautiful smart woman, and she made me so proud.

Days went into weeks, and weeks into months, and Calli stood her ground. Bosa was a final year student of electrical engineering and Calli brought him to church. He joined the hospitality department and served God to the best of his ability. Calli introduced him to everybody. People in our families, and in our circles knew Calli and Bosa were together, in courtship to be married.

Daddy acted as though he didn't see them, though the two young lovers went everywhere together.

Months turned to years. Calli graduated in her business administration degree. By this time, Bosa was working at a computer firm in Lagos and earning a decent income. He had a studio apartment he was living in. Everything looked good for the two.

"*Bosa and I want to get married, Mummy,*" *Calli said to me one day.*

"*Congratulations. You two are blessed.*" *I clasped my hands together.* "*What about Daddy?*"

"*We're going ahead without him,*" *Calli said.*

"*Ah, Calli. Listen, let's call a meeting to talk to him...*"

"*No, Mummy. Bosa and I are going to do a small registry wedding. And that is it. I will move into his apartment in Lagos after our marriage...*"

"*Daddy will not be happy,*" *I said.*

"Mummy, look at you, are you happy? I don't want my life to look like yours, I'm sorry. I want to marry a man who loves me," Calli said. "I'm sorry to say that but it's just the truth. I've watched Daddy treat you like nothing for too long. I don't plan to end up like that."

Shame enveloped me, but she was right. It had been over two years since I was moved to the east wing, and my relationship with Daddy had gone totally down, and it was no longer a secret. People knew I was estranged from my husband even though we lived in the same house and worked our ministry together, even the marriage program. What hypocrisy. What irony. What "grace" as Daddy would qualify it. I couldn't blame Calli for thinking and talking like this.

"I will support you, Calli my darling. Completely."

She hugged my neck, and I noticed tears in her eyes. "That's all I need to hear, Mummy. Thank you."

She told me she was going to meet Bosa's parents in Benin the following week. I prayed with her and encouraged her I would continue to do so.

The following week as planned, Bosa and Calli took a public transportation to Benin. Calli later told me the trip went well. Bosa's parents were happy to officially know the young lovers wanted to get married. She was twenty-one, he was twenty-four.

Bosa made it clear Daddy was not in support, and so they would have a registry marriage and the traditional rites would be fulfilled when Daddy ~~comes~~ came around. Bosa's parents were not happy about it, but they agreed.

I could never forget that day on their return to Lagos, along Benin-Ore express road, Calli called me, sobbing so hard she could hardly talk.

"Mummy," Calli said. "Our bus had an accident. Bosa is not talking. He's not talking!"

Chapter 54

BETWEEN THAT DAY CALLI introduced Bosa to Daddy and the day they had an accident, two years precisely, many things happened in my life. Six months after Daddy had me incarcerated, as that was what it was, I decided I needed to get help somehow. I could no longer bear the pain of living on my own, cooking my own food, speaking on the phone to my children through a private line, and though I tried not to reckon with this too much, not having sex with my husband. It rankled that Daddy had not even bothered to call me once...he was a very active man, did he have someone else, though that was adultery, but did he?

Since I still had access to a car, one of the PABs drove me to Oṣogbo. From the time when my parents died, I had not been there as the house they lived in was rented. My plan was to visit my old pastor, Apostle Akande. He had been the pastor who raised me after I gave my life to Christ as a teenager. He was the pastor my parents knew as our family clergy. It was in his church I met John. Though it was well over twenty years since I moved to Lagos and married Love Jaja, I still saw this man of God as my father-in-the-Lord, and though I had not maintained such a relationship in all those years, my heart was drawn to him for help at this point in my life.

Apostle Akande started his church in Oṣogbo when I was sixteen years old, and I was one of the first three members of the choir. We later grew the choir to a formidable twenty-member strong before I left. In all those years, Apostle's lifestyle did not change much. He lived in a bungalow he built with his wife long after I left Oṣogbo. His two children had grown up and left home. It wasn't difficult for me to find his number, call and book an appointment for a Tuesday morning.

I got to Oṣogbo the day before and lodged in a hotel. The PAB who brought me returned to Lagos with instructions to be on standby for when he would come back for me.

When Apostle Akande walked into his parlour that Tuesday morning, I wanted to cry. In twenty-four years, he had not changed much, and he had a smile on his face. He was supposed to be angry with me for not being a good "daughter-in-the-Lord" but this was not my Apostle. His humility and love humbled me.

"Mummy! This is your face," he said. "I can't believe I'm seeing you without getting a visa."

I smiled shyly and went on my knees. "Apostle, good morning, sir. Please don't call me mummy."

"Ah, please take a seat. I must give honour to whom it is due. I am so proud of you." He sat on one of five single chairs, and I sat on another. "Daddy and you are doing such a great work in Lagos, and the world as a whole."

"Thank you, sir. What about Mummy?" I asked after his wife.

"Oh, she went for a women's meeting. She's fine," he said. "But she cooked yam and stew and insisted I must give you food."

I laughed. His wife was such a simple and dear woman too. "Ah, thank you, sir but I am on a fast. Hmm. And when you hear what I have to say, sir, you will understand why I cannot even eat."

Apostle shifted in his chair. "There is nothing too big for God."

I related my life's story to Apostle Akande. As I talked, the reality of my truth dawned on me. It scared me a lot to see clearly on hindsight many things I could have done differently. One was that I never sought counsel about Love Jaja. I never prayed about him either. It was like a whirlwind with him. I was like a leaf in the breeze. Not until I landed in a puddle did I begin to realize how complacent I had been in writing my own story. I left Love to write it, and he wrote only from his point of view.

"Did he ever cheat on you, or show any signs?" Apostle said.

"No, sir." I shook my head. "Love Jaja has never had eyes for any girls. I have never seen him look or speak inappropriately to a woman."

"No rumours or reports?"

"No, sir."

Apostle leaned back. "What about money? Does he give you money on a monthly basis?"

"Sir, I have cards that I use. I don't have a personal account. Love is not into money. He doesn't care about money." I shrugged. "We both have access to money when we need it. Any amount. Money has never been a problem between us."

"You see, Mummy, the Bible talks of three things that are in the world, that if we are not careful, will destroy us." Apostle counted on his fingers. "The lust of the flesh, the lust of the *eyes, and the pride of life. Talking about physical pleasure, ojukokuro greed wanting more gold money possessions and pride, believing nothing can shake you and no one can best you."*

I lifted my eyes heavenward.

"Let me ask this. Do you know the one thing your husband hates most?"

I picked at my cuticles. I couldn't think of anything. Love Jaja had no feelings of attachment to anything. I shook my head. "Nothing, sir."

"I hear he has a reputation of cursing people, and it comes to pass," Apostle said. "Is it true?"

I nodded. "Very true, sir."

"What warrants cursing. Do you know?"

I took only a moment to think. The few times Daddy cursed anyone in my presence, it was because they either defied or disobeyed him.

"He hates someone disobeying him or doubting him," I said. "He hates sin too."

"Hmm. If they disobey him or disobey God?"

"Most of the time he speaks the mind of God, God's will. Sometimes it's difficult to know if what he was saying was God or him," I said.

As I tried to explain this, I saw clearly my husband must have the pride of life. Love detested someone confronting him. Measuring all that he had and achieved, people thought he was humble because he never boasted. In truth, he loved being worshipped. It was why you dared not come into his presence and not kneel until he asked you to stand. It was why he had to approve every single thing I or the children or his leaders did. Every one of the uncountable churches he oversaw must submit to his leadership. While it was necessary to run a great organization with diverse people like ours, Love ran it not out of love and empathy but out of the need to control. It suddenly dawned on me that he must have seen me as insubordinate. I was supposed to be his number one worshipper. And things were fine as long as I behaved myself.

"What is on your mind, Mummy?" Apostle said.

"I am just pondering on what you are saying, sir. My husband thrives on worship. And he is the oracle, I know for sure, he has the word of the king in his mouth." I shut my eyes, battling bitterness with comprehension. "Everything he does, sir, is with one purpose. To establish his authority over me. The children. The people he serves. He is quiet but subtly boastful. He talks down at everyone. Everyone. His parents, my parents..." the reality weakened me. "Love forgives everything except insubordination."

Apostle sighed. "Does he have anyone he submits to in ministry?"

My heart beat harder, and tears engulfed me. "No, sir."

"Don't cry. God will help us find a way out. You will be reconciled to your husband," Apostle said softly. "Does he have contemporaries that he respects, friends in ministry?"

I sniffed. "They all look up to him."

"God will still help us. When are you returning to Lagos?"

"I am here for as long as you wish, sir. My husband doesn't ask after me. I don't think he cares about me. Not once has he even tried to make conversation about what we are going through. We go to church as if everything is normal but the people in the mansion know we don't technically live together. My son is in jail in the UK, and my husband doesn't want to talk about it. My older daughter has affairs with older married men. My family has fallen apart," I cried.

"And God who is the mender, will mend it back again! Don't say negative things, Mummy. Call the things that are not as though they are," Apostle said.

"Sir, is it even possible to have a happy marriage as a pastor? From what I see in my own life, and Sharon, and Chinwe, and Oluchi. Even Sunbo, our marriages are all a big mess." I sobbed. "See Alexa that I thought was in a great relationship. She is in an abusive relationship. She beats and insults her husband!"

Apostle smiled. "The marriages of pastors, and servants of God is God's priority. But we pastors are all flawed, and with our wives, and our children. Only a marriage submitted to the Holy Spirit can thrive," Apostle said. "If there is lust of the flesh, or of the eyes, the marriage will be a mess. Pride of life either in the pastor or in his wife? Messy." He sighed. "We need to allow God to be the head of our marriage and our home. And I am a living testimony. I have been married for forty-two years. Did we have problems? Of course. We are human but we always ask God to help us. We refuse to abuse ourselves because abuse is not of God."

On and on and on, Apostle Akande showed me the things Love and Bettina Jaja did that were not in consonance with the word of God. This had nothing to do with the gifts and calling of God, which the whole world saw and celebrated. It was not the "working" for God my husband and I displayed in public that mattered, but the "walking" with God.

"What I see is that you two live by the spirit, but you are not walking in the spirit," Apostle said. "Living a life laced by the manifestation of God's existence but behind closed doors, you have nothing to show for it." He stood. "I will give you an assignment. Continue your prayer and fasting but begin to do deliberate acts of tenderness and kindness. What is your husband's love language?"

I shrugged. "I don't know, sir. Maybe touch."

"Let's start by you doing everything. Are you allowed to hold meetings? Do programs, speak in church?"

"Yes, sir."

"Good," Apostle said. "I think word of affirmation may also be your husband's love language, but whatever, you now have to practice all. Service, buy gifts for him, any opportunity you have to hold the microphone, bless him with your sweet and praise words, hang around his office when you know he is there. Send messages to him telling him you miss him in your bed," Apostle said.

"Huh, he will think I have gone mad, sir."

"You don't know what he is thinking, Mummy. So, we will not assume."

I nodded. "Yes sir. Thank you, sir."

"Do this for two weeks, and report back to me."

Chapter 55

Six months later, Apostle Akande decided we would change tactic. He asked me to pray and fast with him for three days, and then fix an appointment to see Daddy.

In the six months of doing his assignment, I reduced to sending pictures of myself in lingerie to my husband. I felt ashamed of myself but thought this would catch his attention. I printed out the provocative pictures from my laptop and printer and had Calli slide them under his bedroom door. There was no way he didn't see them.

Years ago, as the sisters' coordinator in my fellowship, I would have condemned such an act of indecency. And here I was, doing the unbelievable. Sister Bettina Silas, vibrant, spiritual sister, and leader. How art the mighty fallen!

Every opportunity I had, I praised Daddy, and thanked him for being such a blessing. I hugged him in front of the whole church on his birthday. Soft-sell magazines put the picture on their cover and tagged us the best couple in Christendom. I bought gifts every week, perfumes, ties, different outfits in his favourite colour white, though Daddy had no interest in material things.

Meanwhile, as I battled with my marriage, Adam continued to serve his time, Chloe graduated and came home. To my relief, she was no longer in a relationship with Prince, but a young pastor who was one of the ministers in one of our churches back in the UK. He was finishing his doctoral program in research methodologies and was coming back home to a job in the new university our church built. I was so happy for Chloe. She was happy to be back home in the mansion. She had a degree in French, and Daddy gave her a job in his office translating and ~~transcriptioning~~ transcripting his messages. My beautiful daughter was in tune with the word of God. I was glad she was calm and ready to settle down and have a family of her own.

With Chloe's return home, she wanted to live in the east wing where I was still detained. Her main reason was that the west wing was too busy, and she planned to get married and *live in the mansion with her husband. She disagreed sharply with Calli about Bosa, and this put a firm wedge between the sisters.*

Being in the east wing with me though gave me easier access to Chloe, and I started getting close to her. I visited her in her apartment at least every other night and we had small talk. At the back of my mind, I hoped she could help with reconciling me with Daddy, though she showed no such interest.

At the start of the long holidays that year, Dr. Christian Joseph, Chloe's fiancé, graduated and returned to Nigeria. Daddy was so proud of him, and glad to have him join the host of ministers at our main church in the camp. He was at the mansion every day, and in the east wing.

I liked him from the moment I saw him. The mere fact that he was young, in his early thirties, single, and a minister of God, endeared him to me. However, he was a handsome man too, tall, dark, and muscular. He was everything a young woman like Chloe should have. She was twenty-two, going on twenty-three, had a great job and prospect at the church, and engaged to such a wonderful man. I felt blessed.

The blessing was short-lived.

Dr. Chris, as we fondly called him, knocked on my door one evening with scratches on his face, his white shirt torn at the neck. He wanted me to come and speak with Chloe. I hurried behind him, as he refused to say anymore.

Inside Chloe's apartment, I found my daughter curled up into a ball on the couch.

Dr. Chris snapped. "I'm going to bring Daddy."

"Ah, wait, what happened. Let's talk about this before you call Daddy," I said.

"No, Mummy. Talk to your daughter. I'm getting Daddy," he said and left.

I sat close to Chloe's waist and tapped her. "Chloe, talk to me, what happened?"

"I'm pregnant," Chloe said.

"Ehn, yeepa. But, ah, that means you have to marry quickly before it starts showing." I clasped my hand over my mouth. Oh, dear God!

"Chris is not the father," Chloe said.

"Yee!" I pulled her shoulder in order to see her face.

She resisted and remained in her ball. Ah, abortion was a sin. Dear Lord, no wonder that man was so angry. Did Chloe scratch his face? Why did he have bruises? I paced, unsure of what to do?

Daddy walked in with Dr. Chris. Apparently, he had no idea what was going on too. He spared me a quick glance; much the same way he did in the last one year anytime we were in the same space at the mansion. Just one glance and none else. It hurt deeply each time.

"There, I have your father and your mother," Dr. Chris said. "Goodbye." He stomped out of the room.

I never saw Dr. Christian Joseph again.

Daddy moved closer to the couch. "Chloe."

Chloe jumped up from the couch and hugged Daddy's neck and he held her as she sobbed. There were bruises on her arms and the parts of her thighs and legs exposed by her short dress.

Daddy stepped back and looked at her face. It was swollen like someone who just endured a boxing match.

"Oh my God!" I cried. "He beat you up."

"Yes," Chloe said. "He just kept going."

"What did you do, Chloe?" Daddy said calmly.

"She is pregnant," I said, when Chloe remained quiet. "Dr. Chris is not the father."

Daddy arched an eyebrow. "Who is the father?"

"You will hate me, Daddy," Chloe returned to the couch.

Daddy snapped. "Tell me!"

My heart broke. When everything was going on so well, why, God? Why?

"Chief Pedro." Chloe whimpered. "It was just one night. It meant nothing." She clasped her hand over her mouth.

Daddy stood rigidly for several minutes. No one said anything.

Chief Ọlayọde Pedro of all the useless rich men in Lagos! Where did Chloe come in contact with such an irresponsible public rascal. He was notorious for sleeping around. He had more children than he cared to know, and how he made his money continued to remain shrouded. Above all, if Chief Pedro worshipped or believed in anything, it was in himself and his wealth. Such a pagan. Oh Chloe!

"Then you will be married to him immediately," Daddy said.

"God forbid!" I shrieked. "Ah, Daddy, please. Chloe cannot marry..."

"Let him know I said so if both of you don't want to face the consequences," Daddy said, and walked out of the room.

I slumped on the couch beside Chloe and wept.

Apostle Akande finally got an appointment to see Daddy.

It wasn't the best of seasons for Daddy. Chloe had just gotten married to Chief Pedro in a "sitting room" ceremony where me, Daddy, Chief Pedro, Chloe and the chief's son, OPJ, witnessed the taking of the vows, signing the register, and exchange of rings. Daddy refused to take any dowry. Within minutes, we were done, and Chief Pedro left with his bride. For the following several months, the tabloids ran crazy with the news.

Daddy hosted Apostle Akande in his office, and for several hours behind closed doors, both men talked. When I later spoke with Apostle later on the phone, he had quite a short summary.

"Daddy is not happy, Mummy," Apostle Akande said. "And that is not a good thing at all. We will continue to pray, and fast until we have victory. Good news is that we were able to talk about your marriage and he is willing to invite me back again. For now, keep doing what you have been doing. Daddy's ego has been bruised."

"How, sir? What did I do? Is this all because I travelled to London to see my children or something else?"

"That is the start of it all. He used the words disrespect, insubordination, noncompliance, sabotage. He said you are trying to rub shoulders with him."

I couldn't believe my ears. Sabotage!

"But I have apologized. Done everything you told me to," I said.

"We will continue to pray, Mummy."

Chapter 56

CONTINUE TO PRAY I did, and one full year rolled by. Chloe gave birth to a set of twin girls, and I went to visit and help her out for about a month. I would later hear from Apostle Akande that Daddy was offended I didn't ask his permission before going to Chloe's house. When we still did not converse. He never picked my calls, respond to messages, or acknowledge any of the five love languages I was speaking to him. Most of anything he had to say that affected me either came from Apostle Akande or the pulpit. People like Darlington, and Elijah never had any discussions with me anymore. If I need to hear about Adam, I had to call his lawyer who saw the case as done and didn't always oblige me. I didn't want to go to London to visit Adam, without "permission" and so, I only relied on prayers for my son. Maybe, I didn't want to visit at all!

Daddy was now estranged from me, Chloe, and Calli, who was still courting Bosa at this time. I knew he was in touch with Adam, at least, which was good. I hoped he was praying for his son!

Shortly afterwards, the accident happened and Bosa was unconscious for several days. Calli had suffered only a minor scratch. She believed Bosa covered her with his body and took the impact of the accident. The doctors discovered he had a spinal injury and there were shards of glass in his eyes. They knew that even with surgery, he was never going to see again. Bosa came out of the accident without his sight or the ability to walk. Calli stuck beside him all through.

Several things were happening in my life at this time.

Calli was in and out of the hospital with Bosa for the next year and a half. Chloe had her twins. Towards the end of this turbulent pain-joy season, Adam was released from prison. Daddy refused to allow him to come home. Within six months of being out of prison, he got arrested again, and based on a guilty plea due to insanity, his stay in the UK was revoked, and he was deported. But at the time of Adam's deportation, I was battling something else entirely.

Reconciling with Daddy during this period became tough for me. I wanted to be there for Chloe. I wanted to be there for Calli. I wanted to be there for Adam. I didn't want Ben to feel insignificant, even though his life seemed to be the only one on course in our family. Apostle Akande arranged one meeting with me and Daddy. He was meant to be there with his wife too. This was supposed to be the meeting *that restored normalcy to my marriage. Apostle Akande hinted on the possibility of my return to my matrimonial bedroom.*

I totally forgot to attend the meeting.

On the day of this all-important reconciliation meeting, I was at the teaching hospital offering emotional support to Calli. My phone was dead, and I couldn't be reached. It was just such a day. One more operation on Bosa's spine. It came out unsuccessful. Calli was devastated. This operation was the one we prayed would succeed and Bosa could have a slim chance of walking again. Calli cried her eyes out, and I was the only one there for her.

When I got back to the mansion and charged my phone, I saw several messages from Apostle Akande. He understood my plight but doubted Daddy could.

In all this turmoil, I didn't quickly notice Ben. My son was in the university Calli graduated from, studying computer science. He chose to live on campus, although his father was against this, giving how Adam was expelled. Daddy's first choice was our university, but Ben didn't want to go, and this caused some friction. However, reluctantly, Daddy let Ben do what he wanted. I know I was too distracted and didn't give Ben the attention he needed. Growing up, he had tied himself to me, and I was attached to him. However, he seemed to need less attention when he was away in school, and this was a relief to me and my unhappy life.

The year Chloe gave birth to her twins, Ben finished his second year in the university, and came home with a request.

"I have thought about this, and prayed," he said. "I want to go to the mission field. In Asia."

It sounded like a great idea, but we didn't have any churches in Asia, save one in Singapore, and one in Beijing. He wanted to tell me first before telling his father. I just started crying. I was overwhelmed by everything going on, and sad that my life had gone onto a mudslide.

I exclaimed. "What about your study? At least finish. Get a degree!"

"I can't concentrate, Mummy," Ben said. "I'm failing my courses. Better to follow my heart than disgrace you and Daddy."

I knew this wasn't the reason though. He was unhappy with the way things were at home. I couldn't stop him. I couldn't give the stability and peace he wanted. I couldn't control anything. Sometimes when I prayed, I asked for death. Maybe it was the best thing.

"You will not disgrace us, Ben! Asia is so far."

"It's okay, Mummy. You will still see me," Ben said.

He was wrong, though. The mission organization he signed up for took their missionaries into remote hinterlands with no network and very little connection with the outside world. The missionaries spent at least the first four months without talking to their family while they learned the culture and language of their community.

It did not surprise me that Daddy gave his blessing. He never really liked Ben because he was my boy. Mummy's baby. The one closest to my heart. My favourite child without apology. I believe everything happening was too much for Ben. Being on campus was not enough. He needed to get as far away from home as possible, and it hurt my soul.

I missed the reconciliation meeting, and Daddy refused to give another date. Ben dropped out of university and travelled to Asia. Calli moved in with Bosa to take care of him. Chloe nursed her twin baby girls. Adam was deported.

Without my knowledge, Daddy went to Bosa's house. It was long after it was done that I got to know. He had some ministers with him. They packed up Calli and took her out of the apartment while Bosa lay on his back, helpless and in tears, with black patches over his eyes, begging Calli not to go, Daddy to help him, forgive him. Calli didn't contact me after she was forcefully returned to Jaja mansion. She locked herself in her room and cried day and night. I usually spoke with her every day, and after two days and I'd not heard from her, because she didn't pick my calls or answer my messages, I called Bosa who told me everything that happened.

I was furious.

Since Apostle Akande started speaking with Daddy, my "imprisonment" rules had slackened, and I could visit Calli freely. I went to her room, and my daughter looked twenty years older. A PAB called Evelyn waited on her and told me she had not eaten for the three days since she was returned. Calli refused to talk to me. She just lay on her side and stared at nothing. It was too much for me to bear to see her in that way. I decided to take the matter up with Daddy.

I didn't think it was proper to go to his private parlour. This was a close family matter. I marched to Daddy's room at a time I assumed he must be rounding up whatever he was doing outside and waited in front of his door until he returned.

Fortunately, or unfortunately, it wasn't a long wait. Daddy saw me at his door and acted as though I was part of the wall paint. He unlocked his door, and stepped in, and I put myself in the doorway before he closed it.

"If you don't remove yourself from here, Mummy, I will curse you," Daddy said.

"It's about time you do it, Love Jaja!" I shouted. "What is wrong with you? If this is how the God you serve behaves, will you be saved?"

"Bettina!"

My husband had not called me by my name in at least twenty-four years! Not even by mistake. For some reason, hearing my name from his lips took me back to my beginning. Not breezy and sensuous like the first time, but harsh. It drained the fight out of me. I went on my knees, and tears streamed from my eyes.

"Daddy, please. For God's sake, for heaven's love, please, let Calli return to Bosa. He needs her help. I know it is not right what she did, but you can just join them secretly or something and..."

"L'ẹnu ẹ!" Daddy snapped. "How dare you? After supporting all these children to misbehave and desecrate the faith! You dare come to me with such a request? I close my eyes now and give you five seconds to get out of here!"

In hindsight, I should not have stepped back. Let him curse me, and I die! I should have entered the room and established my presence, push him out of the way if I had to. This was my husband, wasn't he? Regardless of what our marriage was like, we were married, and we had to work on getting back together.

That night, I felt defeated and dejected. Was I moving forward or backwards? I had failed all my children but what right did Daddy have putting all the blame on me? This was really how he saw me? "Supporting all these children to misbehave and desecrate the faith!" Wow!

I returned to Calli's room, and assured her, I would take up her fight. She didn't say a word to me. I believe she blamed me too.

The following day, I called Apostle Akande and spoke at length with him about Calli, and what happened. He promised to bring it up with Daddy. When I got to the west wing, to visit Calli, the door code had been changed, and I could not access my daughter. I was suddenly back to the shocking day years back, when I needed trusted PABs to move around my own house.

I am not sure which of the recent events triggered it, or perhaps all the events combined to do the trick, but one week later, I got an envelope in the mail.

It contained divorce papers.

Chapter 57

OPJ STARED AT SERENA, while he handled Irene. Both twins had the lost and frightened look of abused children. Serena sat on the floor in the girls' playroom, which OPJ designed and built in the garden behind the mansion after Chloe left, waiting for her turn, while Irene was on her back on the huge Peppa Pig branded bean bag.

OPJ winked and blew a kiss in Serena's direction. Her gaze remained transfixed at nothing in the garden. Irene let out a soft cry and OPJ groaned, a moment before a mortar hit him on the back of his neck. He freed Irene, turned in the direction of the assaulter and screamed at the same time.

Dara took a startling step back holding a mortar, trembling and crying. OPJ lunged at her, but two policemen came out from hiding in the garden, their guns corked.

"Raise your hands up!" One of the policemen shouted. "Or I shoot!"

OPJ succumbed quickly. "Calm down officers." His gaze shot to Dara. "After all we did for you, you silly b*tch." He snapped. "You don't have a job anymore."

Calli and Idong came out of their hiding too, where they had been kept by Dara at least one full hour before OPJ came into the playroom with the girls.

"She still has a good job. In fact, now she has her job and with a hundred percent raise, you wicked fool," Calli said.

Dara lowered the mortar, which had been frozen up in the air, and shakily curtsied. "Thank you, ma."

The policemen closed in on OPJ and pressed his hands behind his back. One of them put the hands in handcuffs.

OPJ resisted. "What is my offense? What is this?"

"Your offense is that you are sexually assaulting children," Calli said.

OPJ yelled. "You have no proof. I bring the girls out here to play so Dara can go to her church!"

"No proof because video recordings lie?" Calli planted herself in front of OPJ and raised her phone so he could see it. "You will rot in jail. For raping minors. And incest."

"Incest? What incest? My father is not the father of these little b*tches!" OPJ culled up phlegm and before Calli could step away, he spat in her face.

Calli screeched in disgust and staggered back.

Idong stepped forward and punched OPJ twice in the stomach. OPJ grunted and doubled over. One of the policemen patted Idong's arm and he moved aside. The policemen took OPJ away.

Idong went to stand by Calli who cleaned her face with a handkerchief. "Sorry about that, baby," he said.

Calli moaned. "I will never get that out of my mind."

"Sorry ma. Is how he always do. Spitting like a child," Dara said. She dropped the mortar and rushed to Irene. She pulled both girls into her arms.

"Don't mind him, Calli. He won't be able to hurt anyone from now," Idong said.

They started to walk out of the garden. "What next? Chloe or Aunty Alexa?" Calli said.

Idong shrugged. "I still think we should keep Chloe out of this until we know she's ready to cooperate. If Daddy knows..."

"Oh yeah, but I'm just worried that getting Aunty Alexa involved will annoy Daddy more." Calli sighed. "I'm tired."

Idong pulled her closer and rubbed her shoulder. "We have two options, and we can keep our secrets and manage our issues. Aunty Alexa and Sister Bolu." He pressed a kiss on her forehead. "Trust me."

They got to their jeep and Idong helped everyone to settle in, then he got into the driver's seat and drove out of the Pedro mansion. The plan with the arrest had gone well. Dara's and the twins' belongings were already in the jeep. Chief Ọlayọde Pedro would not learn about the whole occurrence until later in the evening when OPJ was finally allowed to make a call from police custody.

Alexa opened the door to Calli and Idong, her eyes wild, and her weave in a disarray. "Ah Callista! Idong. God brought you. Ẹ gba mi!" She cried. "It's Ọ̀fẹmi."

Calli and Idong rushed inside and saw Pastor Fẹmi sprawled on the floor in the big sitting room, face down. The couple hurried over and Idong knelt beside him, feeling his pulse and temperature. He rolled Pastor Fẹmi over with much effort.

Calli looked at Alexa. "Aunty! Ki lo ṣẹlẹ? What happened?"

Alexa stomped her feet and cried like a child. "Please help me. Is he alright?"

"Get me a bottle of water," Idong said.

Alexa ran out of the room.

Calli knelt beside Idong. "Will he be okay?"

"He will be. I speak life into him." Idong looked at Calli with a frown. "Pray. Pray."

Calli started to pray softly. Alexa returned with a half-litre bottle of water.

Idong collected it from her hand and raised it up. "Water of Life. Turn this chemistry into a mystery. Restore life into your son's body. Forgive every weakness. Shame the devil, do what only you can do."

"In Jesus' name. Amen," Calli said.

Alexa sobbed. "Amen."

Idong opened the bottle, took a long drink, and then put the mouth of the bottle on Pastor Fẹmi's mouth and poured the water in his mouth as he prayed in the language of the spirit. The water filled Pastor Fẹmi's mouth and poured out. Shortly before the bottle emptied, Pastor Fẹmi coughed.

Alexa screamed. "Thank you, Jesus!"

"Hallelujah! Glory to God," Calli said.

"Thank you, Jesus!" Idong said. "Thank you, Father." He stood. "We need to get him into his bed. Let him rest."

"Yes, Pastor Idong," Alexa said. "Oh, thank God! Thank you, God."

Calli and Alexa helped Pastor Fẹmi into the bedroom. He opened his eyes but said nothing. A small fresh wound on his temple trickled blood. Alexa got a wet towel and cleaned it quickly.

Calli watched her aunt with suspicion. Back in the day, she had heard her mother scold Alexa about her anger and violence, but she refused to assume Alexa was physically abusive. Pastor Fẹmi was much taller and heftier, so how could Alexa overpower him physically.

They returned to the parlour where Idong paced and worshipped. They joined him and when it was over, Alexa sighed.

"What can I offer you?" Alexa said. "Are you just coming from church?"

"Aunty Alexa," Idong said. "Please sit down. What happened?"

Alexa touched her throat but did not sit. "I need help. God knows." She sobbed. The couple remained on their feet and watched her. Alexa exhaled. "I know it is my weakness and God will help me." She clasped her hand and after several minutes of silence, said. "We came back from church. The children followed one of the members to their house for birthday party." She stole a glance at Calli and Idong. "I can't even remember what the argument was, and I slapped him."

Calli gasped but Idong remained mute.

Alexa shook her head. "When we got inside, the quarrel continued. I lost control and started...hitting him. He tried to hold me still, so I pushed him hard." She sobbed. "He hit his head on the centre table and didn't talk again."

Idong looked at Calli. "Well, thank God we came on time. Calli, let's go." He headed for the door.

Alexa ran after Idong and knelt in front of him. "You raised him. He was like that for more than ten minutes and he wasn't breathing before you came."

"Jesus raised him, Aunty," Calli said softly. "We have to leave, please. Please stand up."

Idong side-stepped Alexa and Calli followed him out.

Back in the jeep, Calli stole a glance at Dara, and the twins, who were asleep, probably due to the air conditioner that was left on while Calli and Idong went inside.

Idong sighed. "Well, we move to plan B, Bolu."

Calli slouched. "What if Bolu can't?"

"Then we go to plan C. Sister Imabong," Idong said.

Calli shook her head. "She lives on the camp...no."

"We just have to be discreet, and she's my sister." Idong shrugged. "I brought her to this church, got her the land and the house on the camp. She's more loyal to me than anyone else. She'll do anything I ask."

"Okay, baby."

"Thank you," Idong said and drove out of the beautiful compound that was home to the toxic couple they called family.

Calli couldn't sleep. Curled up in the crook of Idong's arms, in the darkness of their bedroom, she closed her eyes, but it was to no avail.

Chloe's twins were safely with Bolu and her family, and they had Dara there to look after them until she and Idong could decide on when to discuss the issue and involve Chloe and Daddy. Their decision to take matters into their own hands was based on Dara's desperate call for help for the girls, clearly outlined in the file she left for Calli when she visited their church a week earlier.

However, Calli's sleeplessness was not about Chloe and her girls, but because of what happened in Alexa's house. She still couldn't believe her aunt was abusive. The couple seemed so sweet in public, and Pastor Fẹmi openly showed his wife affection. How could she be so violent with him?

And...

Did Pastor Fẹmi actually die? And did Idong raise him? They had been back home for at least five hours and neither discussed these issues causing her insomnia. Calli shuddered.

"Are you alright?" Idong mumbled.

"Can't sleep," Calli said.

"Me neither," Idong whispered.

Calli raised her head and though it was too dark to see the expression on his face, she looked at him. "Why?"

Idong sighed. "Did Pastor Fẹmi really die? Or he just fainted."

"Just what I was thinking. Aunty Alexa said ten minutes. It could be more or less." Calli exhaled. "He was probably in a coma."

"I don't even know where the boldness came from. Or the water thing," Idong said slowly. "It's terrifying."

"Maybe you have the gift of the working of miracles," Calli whispered.

"Maybe," Idong whispered.

Calli rested her head on his chest. "We just give all the glory to God for saving Pastor Fẹmi. And Aunty Alexa."

"Yeah." He sighed. "Aunty Alexa. May God continue to save her and her marriage."

Chapter 58

MY FIRST REACTION TO the divorce papers was sheer, brutal anger. Thoughtless of me, I called Chloe and ranted my frustrations and anger to her.

Chloe's response was simple. "Please go and do all that shouting to your husband," she said.

What else did I expect? Empathy? Or I hoped she would talk to her father for me, since, as I came to realize, she still had her father's ears.

I took one of the PABs and went to Ọṣogbo with the divorce papers.

"Apostle sir, Daddy wants to divorce me," I said. "Look!"

The strange words out of my mouth overwhelmed my heart and I burst into tears.

"It's okay," Apostle Akande said.

He let me cry, and when I calmed a little, he took the papers from me, and read through.

Apostle Akande shook his head. "Your husband was upset you didn't show up at that reconciliation meeting quite alright, but that does not warrant this?"

"After all the way he has been treating me all these years," I sobbed. "What have I gained in this marriage? What have I gained?"

"Calm down. We are not going to rush this matter. Let's pray about this for a day or two, then we will go and see him," Apostle Akande said.

A day or two, turned to many days.

Many days. I stayed in a hotel and fasted. Apostle Akande made it clear he did not want to go and see Daddy without an appointment, and so we waited. At the end of the week, I decided to return to Jaja Mansion. I hoped to be in church on Sunday and speak to Daddy. Apostle Akande offered to come to Lagos on Sunday too.

When I got home, I couldn't gain entrance into my house. The door code to the east wing had changed. And no one was available to help with it. I called Daddy's office, but they had no idea what happened to the code. I fell back to my sister, Alexa. I'd not had the guts to tell her about the divorce, but there was nothing I could do now.

Alexa had only one answer for me. "About time, and this divorce sin is not on you."

I exclaimed. "Alexa! How can you say that?"

"What can I say, Sister? You should never have married him. If he says he's done, what can the righteous do?" Alexa shrugged. "The Bible says if the unbelieving depart, a sister is not under any bondage..."

"But God has called us to peace! Alexa, is it Daddy you are referring to as the unbelieving?"

"Does he still believe in your marriage?" Alexa clapped and jeered. "Did he even ever believe? My thoughts o. Anyway, while we wait for him to give us appointment to see him, you can stay here."

No matter how much disrespect Alexa had for Daddy, I knew she genuinely wanted my happiness, and it seemed in her home, she had the final say, so I had accommodation at least.

For how long? I could not say.

I attended church on Sunday and noticed Daddy had moved his seat in the church to the altar, and there was only one seat. It would be awkward to go and sit with the pastors and ministers, so I went to the children's church. Afterwards, I tried to see Daddy in his office, but there were too many people waiting to see him. I went to the mansion, but I could not gain access. All the PABs I saw were not familiar. I returned to Alexa's house. Subsequently, Daddy changed our marriage program to feature only himself. The program's name changed to "Reconciling Differences with Daddy."

The days turned to weeks, and I could not see my husband. Alexa advised me to sign the divorce papers and send to Daddy, but I could not find it in my heart to do so. More than anything, I wanted to be with Calli. She didn't pick her calls, and I could not reach her.

As time passed, people started to talk. First, Alexa came back from her church on a Sunday afternoon with a soft sell magazine. My picture was on the cover with the caption, "Pastor Bettina Jaja aka Mummy, booted out of the Mansion." The story read that I had lost favour with Daddy, and it no longer made sense for me to live in the same house with him. The reporter said no one knew where I was as my family were not able to locate me.

I cried. "What family?"

Alexa pointed at the end of the article. "Chloe. They spoke with Chloe."

"I have spoken with Chloe. She knows I'm here with you," I said.

Alexa shrugged. "Well, maybe she's trying to protect you."

"Alexa, I need to go and see Adam. And I want to visit Ben in Asia. He left a number to call to locate him. I don't know why Daddy is doing this to me, to our marriage but..."

"There are rumours there's another woman in his life," Alexa said.

"I can't listen to rumours. I can't live my life like this. Maybe the children can talk to him," I said.

"Chloe won't. Calli can't. Adam, maybe. Ben is too far away," Alexa said.

A summary of my life in one line. So depressing.

With the way I was locked out of my house, all my belongings were still at the mansion, including my documents, particularly my passport. Alexa volunteered to go there with me and get whatever she could. Once again, I was at the mercy of other people in my own house. I got access and taking my sister's advice, packed everything I could. I was not able to see Calli that day.

I sent a message to Apostle Akande that I needed to visit my sons. Thankfully, I still had access to the two bank accounts I used for my personal expenses. Alexa again advised that I open an account in my name and start moving money out of the church accounts I had access to.

I bought a ticket to the UK, and another to Singapore, from where I would be taken to the mission field where Ben was. It gave me tremendous joy I would see my boys again.

My trip to London was not as happy as I had wanted. It had been just a few months since Adam was released, but he wasn't home. Apparently, he had continued taking drugs while incarcerated and he was a full cocaine addict. Darlington had him admitted into a small private rehabilitation centre. He looked stoned when I visited.

"I want to take him to Nigeria," I told Darlington afterwards. "I'm taking him back home with me."

"Daddy may not like that, Mummy," Darlington said.

This was how I knew Daddy was in fact in charge of Adam's welfare. Like that, the subject of doing anything for Adam closed. I didn't even have my own accommodation. He would later be deported, and I never got to see my son after he was brought home. Daddy made sure.

I called Alexa and asked her to get me accommodation in Lagos.

"I think you should buy a house instead of renting," Alexa said.

"That is more money than I can get," I said.

"See, Sister, there are some estates now that are doing mortgage. If you drop like thirty percent, you can spread the rest over five years," Alexa said.

It made sense, but what would I be doing in five years? I never thought of the future, never had reason to plan for one. How would I have income if Daddy ordered the cards in my possession blocked? I had nothing. I was nothing without my husband and our ministry. It reminded me of the financial abuse Sharon spoke of, and Sunbọ's warning to build a house without Daddy's interference. Come to think of it, Sunbọ didn't take her own advice. She didn't build behind her husband, but I guess Pastor Jide wasn't like Daddy in many ways.

"Okay, dear, please help me do that," I said.

With a house of my own, I could find Adam and take him home and care for him. People like Darlington only obeyed Daddy; they had no interest in me or my children. For the first time in my married life, I started planning for my future. Hopeful I could have my marriage back, but what if I didn't?

What if Daddy did the unthinkable and remarried? I'd heard of some big names in the kingdom getting divorced and remarried, and I thought they had fallen in the faith. I never imagined I would be in this situation. Like Sharon and Chinwe. All on my own. Buying my own flight tickets, planning my own itinerary...brainstorming how to steal from our ministry account into my personal account so I could have something to depend on. Unbelievable.

Ah! Sister Bettina Silas. How art the mighty fallen.

The mission Ben served gave me two options – to wait for Ben in Singapore, or travel to him on the Island where he lived and served amongst an ethnic group. I chose the latter. Definitely, I wanted to see where my son was. Each time I remembered how young he was, I punched myself for letting him go. But what alternative did I have. He saw what was going on with his siblings, and how my life was spiralled out of control. He didn't want any of it.

We took a short ferry ride to St. John's Island from mainland Singapore and joined a mid-day service at a church. It was a small gathering, and Ben was in attendance, but I couldn't speak with him until the service ended about an hour after I arrived. I was so happy to see my boy. He seemed to have matured so much in the last few months that I saw him. He even spotted a small hopeful beard. He smiled across the hall at me and hurried to give me a bear hug as soon as service was over.

I had never been to Asia, though Daddy had travelled to every continent of the world, preaching. We didn't have many churches in Asia, but I thought Singapore was the most beautiful country or island in the world.

"How are you?" Ben cried.

"I should be asking you." I had tears in my eyes too.

We had to ride bicycles to the church camp where all the missionaries lived. I never rode a bicycle in my life, and Ben laughed at my several attempts. Afterwards, we just decided to *walk. It took over an hour to get to the camp and I was tired, but glad to have the elongated time I got to catch up with Ben.*

"I have to learn how to ride that bicycle," I said, breathing hard as we got to the camp.

Ben laughed. "It's good exercise for you."

The camp had three bungalows, and Ben explained this was where they all lived. In his bungalow, there were three rooms, and he shared a room with two other young men. A second bungalow housed the women, and the third was for offices and storage. From the camp, they travelled to interior communities for days, and sometimes weeks for evangelism.

He took me to a small room with bare furnishing, a single bed, and a table and chair in the bungalow meant for offices and storage. I would have to use the bathroom in the women's housing, though.

"This is the only guest room that we have." Ben sat on the chair. "How are you, Mummy?"

"I miss you." I swallowed. It was so good to see him.

"I heard you are going through a divorce," Ben said.

For a moment I lost the mental ability to know where I was, with who and what I should say. I had not planned to tell him. Who could have delivered such horrid news knowing he was so far away? How cruel people could be.

"Don't be surprised, Mummy. I asked Bimbo. She told me," Ben said.

Bimbo was Daddy's niece from his sister. I could understand that Ben wanted information about home, and Bimbo was his agemate, a year younger, but what surprised me was that Ben had a speaking relationship with this cousin of his. The families interacted only in church, and on special occasions. I was always kept as "Mummy" sacred wife of Daddy. It baffled me.

"Bimbo? Aunty Monica's daughter?"

"Yes. I talk with her. She's my friend. I know Daddy wanted us to be in that holy bubble all the time, but I make friends and I like to interact with people in my family." Ben shrugged. "Like every normal human."

"You don't need to be defensive, darling. Yes, you are very right," I said. What did we do to these children, dear Lord!

"So, what's going on with the divorce?"

"It's true but I don't want you to worry about it..."

Ben jumped to his feet. "I'm not worried about it. I just want to know how you are. Where do you live now? Bimbo said no one knew, and that makes me worried." Ben paced. "Why would you not be allowed to live in the mansion. It's your house. You worked hard to build that church as much as Daddy."

I stood. "I am fine." I pulled him into my arms. He was so much taller. I cupped his face and wiped the tears rolling down his cheeks. "I am here, visiting you. I am very fine. Okay? Daddy has made provisions for my welfare," I lied. "I have money to spend. I am okay. Our marriage didn't work out doesn't mean we are not the same people we are. I am coping well. You must never think otherwise. Mummy is a big girl, and she can take care of herself."

When he later left to his room, I cried myself to sleep.

The mission organization allowed me to visit with Ben for a week, and then I returned home, fulfilled. My boy was on course. He could cook his own food, wash his own clothes, and care for himself, things Daddy forbade the children in their growing up years because PABs were available to do all that as service to God.

My Ben had matured into a strong, spiritually balanced, self-sufficient, and equipped man. I could take no credit for any of it.

Chapter 59

"I DIDN'T WANT TO discuss this on the phone since you were on your way back," Alexa said on my return to her house. "The houses in this Lagos are very expensive and the ones that accept mortgage are in the bush and still so expensive, so I told my agent to look at other places like Ibadan and Oṣogbo."

I shrugged. "Oh, okay. I mean those are not far from here."

"She also checked Ota, Ẹpẹ, Abeokuta," Alexa said.

"I will rather go to Oṣogbo than Ota," I said.

Jaja Mansion and our camp was ten minutes away from Ota. Too close for my comfort. I didn't want to have to pass by the camp if I was leaving my house to go to other places.

"I found one I really like in Oṣogbo. And you should be able to pay for it. Still under construction." Alexa opened her smart phone.

She showed me pictures of a bungalow with all the blockwork and roofing completed. It was situated in the outskirts of the city but not too far away. I liked it.

"It's only five million naira. The owner is desperate to get money and selling cheap." Alexa said. "With another five, you should be able to finish it to your taste,"

"I can't take ten million out of those church accounts. Whoever manages it will make a lot of noise," I said.

"Let's go to the bank whenever you're ready. There has to be a way around this," Alexa said.

There was a way around it that bordered on ignorance. I got tokens for the accounts, which were both in Daddy's name, but I was a signatory to the account. Prior to this, I had not shown any interest in what was what about the account. I had initially had access to one for my personal upkeep and then the other to support with PLL.

Both accounts had more than I needed for a house. I had cheque books for both too. On the banker's advice, I made out four cheques for eight million naira each. Two of these I paid into my personal account, and the other two into Alexa's.

It wasn't a surprise that a week later, on Daddy's orders, both accounts were closed. At least, I made away with thirty-two million naira, irrespective of the fact that our ministry was worth several billions. The amount was enough to buy my house, finish it to my taste and have a little change.

In order to supervise my house, and find something to occupy my time with, I moved to Oṣogbo and stayed in a cheap motel. Since I had the money I needed, the building project moved fast and a month afterwards, my house was ready.

Alexa and Pastor Fẹmi came with all my stuff and helped me to move into my four-bedroom bungalow. I knew I couldn't live in it alone and after some deliberation, I contracted the builder again to redesign the house to be a twin three-bedroom bungalow. I thought it would not only serve as income for me, I'd at least have neighbours inside the compound.

The minute I moved into my house, the news burst wide. It was on all the tabloids that the divorce was actually true, and I had moved back to my hometown. A few news agents came to my house, and asked me questions, which I politely declined. Apostle Akande said people came around him as well, and Alexa complained of the same. My sister, Skola, who wasn't even close by told me journalists asked her about us too.

It was the biggest trending news. Daddy and Mummy – Divorced!

My greatest surprise was how people quickly dissociated with me. People I least expected cut me off. Groups I was in such as the classy pastors' wives' prayer meeting where I met Sharon, told me I was no longer welcome. Mutual ministry friends, though few, made it clear I was out of line. Anonymous people sent me messages that I was Jezebel, and my plan to destroy the servant of God would never be successful.

Elder Elizabeth, the one who was there at the very beginning when we held night vigils, told a newspaper I had tried to seduce Daddy from the times when I would insist on sleeping in his house. In the interview, she said she tried to warn Daddy that I was there only for what I could get.

Another tabloid leaked my bank transactions and I suspected this would have been through the person Daddy sent to close the accounts I had access to. The news item reported that I stole more than a hundred million naira from missions' accounts, but Daddy magnanimously forgave me and just blocked the accounts.

People started to take sides based on what the tabloids had to say. The social media broke with sentimental topics. I suddenly realized the different ways people saw me. I was called different names from cold, snobbish, usurper, evil, childish, greedy. People blessed God for saving Daddy from a woman like me. They sympathised with him, wondering what he might have been through all these years.

One opinion page analysed pastors' wives and named the names of the ones doing well, and the ones not doing well. Sharon's name, along with mine, came up as part of the destroyers. Oluchi, shown in a picture she took with Bishop Oye on their church's anniversary, got accolades for being a model pastor's wife.

Daily I got calls, text messages, and when I went out, people pointed at me. It did not help that we had a very big church in Oṣogbo, and since I moved back, did not feel inclined to attend the services. People wrote anonymous letters asking me to leave my town, and my country, and I considered this at a point. But I liked living here and I decided I was not going to allow anyone to intimidate or chase me out of my homeland.

At first, I thought I could bear the pressure. It got bad, and as an excuse to get away, and also allow the work being done on my house to progress faster, I returned to Alexa's house in Lagos.

On the day I arrived, all the pastors had a meeting at the mansion with Daddy, and I babysat Delight and Destiny. Being with the children was refreshing for me. I enjoyed the company of children and Delight especially had the funniest questions for me.

Alexa and Pastor Fẹmi stayed so late, I thought they would spend the night at the mansion, but then they returned. I stayed up to open the door for them, as they no longer had Lola or any other house maid.

Pastor Fẹmi had a small swell on his face, and faint scratches, and Alexa's eyes were wild and angry. I knew they had gotten into a fight, and as much as I wanted to help my sister, I feared from my experience, things would get worse if I took sides with her husband. Instead, I pretended I didn't notice the way they looked. It was after midnight and past all our bedtime.

"Odarọ o," I said.

"Sister, please wait," Alexa said. "I just want you to warn this man. He is looking for a mad woman and I will show him madness today."

"Calm down, Alexa, jọ!"

Pastor Fẹmi sighed. "Mummy, tonight at the meeting, Daddy told all the pastors that you have divorced him, and the divorce is official, and he would not be expecting you to come to any of our churches because he had settled you. He said we were not to associate with..."

Alexa cut in. "You better say it exactly the way he said it. You all were to be aggressive in resisting any interactions from Sister."

Pastor Fẹmi arched an eyebrow. "Will you let me talk?"

"No, unless you say the right thing," Alexa shouted.

Pastor Fẹmi inhaled. "Daddy in essence said we should not offer any help to you for any reason..."

"Even if she's dying and you are the one who can save her!" Alexa screamed. "Is that the man you have been killing yourself with worry, Sister. He saw me sitting in that room and he could say that! Anyway, I am done. I have no business in that church anymore."

"So, the best way is to start shouting in front of everybody?" Pastor Fẹmi said.

"Yes, and you should have supported me." Alexa lunged at her husband and dealt him a hard slap. "Support your wife, useless man."

Pastor Fẹmi clutched his face. I jumped in between them, upset at Alexa for humiliating her husband in this way.

"Stop it, Alexa! Will you stop it?"

Alexa staggered back and started crying. "I'm not doing this anymore, Sister. If he wants to continue being a pastor in that church, I am leaving him. I am tired."

"I am not continuing in the church. I have written my resignation letter," Pastor Fẹmi said. "But behaving the way she did tonight will only bring a curse on our heads."

"He cannot do anything to us!" Alexa screeched. "I pray too, and God hears me. His curse cannot touch me."

"Mummy, ma, Alexa stood up in that meeting accusing Daddy of being a miserable, jealous and annoying husband to you." Pastor Fẹmi groaned. "Screaming and pointing at him. Ushers had to carry her out..."

Alexa screeched. "Did you follow me out as a good, supporting husband?"

"No! I..."

"Instead, you fell on your knees and started begging Daddy! Traitor," Alexa said.

"Oh dear," I spread my fingers out against my breastbone. "Dear, Lord."

"Coward!" Alexa breathed hard. "You have written resignation..."

"You shouldn't resign because of me, Pastor Fẹmi," I said. "You have worked so hard in the ministry and..."

Alexa shouted. "He must resign..."

"Shut up, Alexa." I raised my voice above hers. "What is wrong with you? When did you become this wild uncontrollable animal?"

Alexa folded her arms and looked away.

"I'm so sorry, Pastor Fẹmi. I will leave in the morning..."

"I'm coming with you," Alexa said.

I snapped. "Shut up. I said shut up! You will stay here and build your home! Is this how Maami taught us?"

"Please Mummy, you are welcome here. I am sending in my resignation in the morning and Daddy knows how I served for all these years, but it is over." He sighed. "I will not treat my wife the way he treated you, ma. And I cannot support him doing it either. I cannot serve under such a man again."

I ordered Alexa to apologise to her husband. "Kun'lẹ!"

Looking her husband up and down with a disgusted expression, Alexa knelt.

Pastor Fẹmi pulled her up. "It's okay. Thank you, Mummy. Good night, ma." He walked quickly into the house.

"What is wrong with you, Alexa? Why are you so disrespectful and violent?" I shook Alexa after her husband left. "He is such a gentleman, why are you treating him like this?"

"Oh, you want me to wait until he treats me the way Daddy treated you? I watched you while growing up in your house. You didn't have a say in anything. You allowed Daddy to ride over you..." Alexa sniffed.

"Come on, stop that. Is Daddy the same as Pastor Fẹmi? If you lose this man, you will have yourself alone to blame. Is it because he doesn't hit you in return? You better get sense." I retorted. "I will still return tomorrow, and it is because I want to give two of you space to sort your issues."

"Sister, I am sorry."

"Go and give it to your husband, not me." I marched out of the room.

Pastor Fẹmi resigned from the church, and Daddy in his usual munificence, allowed him to take the property and everything in the church. They simply changed the name on the signboard. This singular action went viral, and people praised Daddy the more for being such a great man of God.

It further tainted me as evil and stupid. Sister Bettina Silas who led young women on campus for one year, praying weekly, leading Bible studies, singing for God, loving on God with my whole heart. Pastor Bettina Jaja, who became Mummy to hundreds of thousands of people worldwide. To think I had not even signed the divorce papers at this time. And I never did.

Me. Evil and stupid.

Chapter 60

PASTOR FẸMI STARTED HIS TV program with a testimony of his resurrection. It was as detailed as anything one would expect. He did leave out details of the incident that led to him hitting his head but explained in detail his beautiful wife's fear as she tried to resuscitate him, and then search for her phone to call for help. When her niece and her husband pressed the doorbell, it was a sure deliverance.

Idong received a copy of the recording the evening it was premiered, just as he was about to leave his office and go home. He called Calli.

"Baby, are you at home?"

The tremor in his voice worried Calli. "Yes, what happened?"

"Pastor Fẹmi has started a TV program. Hour of the Miraculous. My God!" Idong grunted. "He shared his testimony. He mentioned our names."

"Come home," Calli said.

She couldn't think of anything else to say or think or do. People loved miracles and went crazy about it. And if Daddy heard...that was a whole different issue.

"I'm on my way," Idong said.

Calli hung up. She didn't know what they would do especially with the way social media trended everything. Such a testimony would go viral within minutes. She had just finished preparing dinner and so served a little for Victor, rather than wait for Idong so they could all eat together as usual. Tonight, she'd rather watch the video before eating and if it was really implicating, she was sure she'd not have appetite for food. And neither would Idong.

She wished she knew which channel and when the program would air but just as she helped Victor settle on the dining table with his food, her phone rang again. This time it was Alexa.

"Hello Aunty."

"My darling Calli! Wife of a powerful man. Mbọk, tune in to watch your Uncle Fẹmi's program. On cable channel 10, it starts in about five minutes," Alexa laughed. "Oh, this God is too good."

For a moment, Calli wanted to reprimand her. It wasn't even a month since the miracle, and they had run to TV? Well, she knew they had been planning to start a program but still, Calli didn't feel comfortable with this at all.

Calli moaned. "Umm, okay Aunty. How's Uncle?"

"He's fine, thank God, and thank you! Just be praying for us," Alexa said.

"Yes ma." Victor put two spoonsful of rice and stew into his mouth in quick succession, and nearly choked. Calli exclaimed. "Victor, slow down. Huh, Aunty, please I have to go. I'm feeding Victor and..."

"No problem, dear. Even I want to tune in now." Alexa blew a noisy kiss over the phone. "I just spoke to your mum, and she's tuning in too."

Calli gagged. "You...what did Mummy say?"

"That God is faithful! You sound so depressed." Alexa laughed. "Believe me, God is up to something with you and that fervent man of God, Idong. Tune in. I have to go."

Calli hung up and breathed through her mouth. "Dear Lord... Victor! Stop putting so much in your mouth."

She took the spoon from Victor and made him drink a little water, and then walked to the sitting room and turned on the TV. The program was just starting.

"Mummy! Look, Mummy. I almost finished my food," Victor said around a mouthful of food. "Mummy!"

"*I was dead but now I live!*" Pastor Fẹmi said at the end of the opening montage.

Calli closed her eyes. She couldn't hear this. She turned off the TV and focused her attention on Victor. When he was done with his meal, she took him to the bathroom to have his bath, and straight to bed. She thought Idong should be home by now. His office was a ten-minute walk from the mansion. He should have been home before the program started or thereabout. To take her mind off her stressful thoughts, she read a Bible story to Victor until he slept and then returned to the sitting room to wait for Idong. It was only nine o'clock, but he should have been home at least two hours earlier since there were no evening meetings on Mondays.

She picked up her phone to call and saw his text message.

I'm just leaving now, sorry, love. I'll tell you why, he wrote.

She knew Daddy had heard; this was the only explanation that came to her. She dreaded what it meant. Daddy could not be angry Idong prayed for Pastor Fẹmi. That would be ludicrous but when he warned them never to talk to Mummy again, he included members of her family who left the church because of her. This was Aunty Alexa on top of the list. It was a wonder Daddy did not curse her after her hysterical outburst all those years ago.

Idong walked in and Calli hurried to hug him. He pressed a kiss to her temple, and then her mouth.

"Daddy?"

Idong nodded. "He called as soon as I finished talking to you the first time." He led her to the couch, and they sat. "I thought he would be angry."

Calli rubbed her small bump. "What did he say?"

"He's giving us a church." Idong groaned. "Calli, I can't lead a church, God knows. I can't preach every Sunday. I'm a teacher. I'm just a teacher of the word. I can't pastor a church."

Calli cupped his face. "Calm down. What did Daddy say? Was he angry with you about the miracle?"

"You know Daddy. He's more diplomatic than that." Idong swallowed. "He said he had a leading it was time for me to move on and follow God's calling for my life. He said he believed you were not ordinary..."

Calli snickered. "Really!"

"Yeah. He said you were called to support me to lead a large congregation and it was time," Idong said.

"Such a time, such a coincidence." Her chest hurt just hearing her father's words. "So, are we starting fresh or he's moving someone out for us?"

Idong breathed hard. "Yes and no. He said they found a building, and we will start fresh, but get all the support we want. He wants to send at least five ministers and thirty workers. And if we want more..."

"What on earth is so special about this? You being a pastor, leading a congregation..."

"He's giving us seven million cash too, and providing all the equipment," Idong said.

Calli stood. "I don't get this. For what? Why?"

"Maybe he thinks I want to start doing miracles all over the place." Idong stood too. "As a pastor of a church, I definitely can't go out to any other church without his permission." He shrugged. "I don't know. I'm confused too. He knows I can't preach. I can't even teach without an outline." He threw his head back. "God, I just want to teach only Sunday School."

Calli walked into his arms. "What does Daddy want from us?"

"The venue, I think. I'm not sure but it can't just be chance," Idong said. "Our church venue is right across the road from Pastor Fẹmi's church."

Calli cried. "Are you joking?"

Idong moaned. "No. Daddy acquired a huge property on Pastor Fẹmi's street for our new church. He did so just yesterday." He scoffed. "And he wants us to be pastors."

"If we have a big church, the traffic from our church with what already obtains is going to destroy sanity on that street." Calli sighed. "Daddy doesn't just act without a reason. He's practically pitting us against Uncle Fẹmi."

"We'll have to move to Lagos, you know," Idong said. "The mansion is too far out."

Calli bit her lip. "I don't want to live outside this place. At least not Lagos."

Idong grunted. Calli tucked in her head, taking comfort from his warmth.

"Calli," Idong said so softly, fear gripped Calli's heart at the quietness of it.

"Yes?" she whispered.

"There's something you should know."

No, she nearly cried. She couldn't handle anything more tonight. She wanted to die just from the fear of what this is.

Idong lowered his voice even more. "Daddy gets Adam a supply of cocaine to keep him addicted. That's why he's not getting better."

Chapter 61

WHEN I RETURNED TO Ọsọgbo, I got two surprising visitors. The first was Minister Elijah.

Since everything started on a downward turn, Elijah had been on Daddy's side, doing his bidding and obeying his every whim. He remained polite through most of the time, but at times, his messages from Daddy to me could not be nice no matter how he delivered them. With time, Daddy stopped sending him to me, and he blocked my number. Considering this was over a period of a few years, I was really surprised to see Elijah at my door in Ọsọgbo. I thought perhaps Daddy had died, but that would be in the news, anyway, unless Elijah was being respectful.

"I feel guilty," Elijah said. "You were so very kind to me, and my family. And I know you did nothing to deserve what happened."

My mouth dropped open. What was he saying? Why was he here? "Please, come in."

I led him into my simple sitting room, and he sat on the sofa.

"Thank you, Mummy," Elijah said.

I sat on one of the chairs. "Well, I did not think you had much of a choice, working for Daddy. Can I offer you something to eat? Drink?"

"No, Mummy, thank you. I will soon leave. But please can I have your number?"

I gasped, then shrugged. I gave him my number because with all of the calls and harassment, I changed my phone number and email address. A small voice cautioned me and warned that he was sent by Daddy and all the people who wanted to continue to disturb me. But on second thoughts, I knew my ex-husband better. If he needed my contact detail, he would get it without my help.

"I know how worried you were about Adam and then Calli. And I know when you went to Singapore," Elijah said.

"Thank you," I murmured.

"Adam is really very sick. Mentally," Elijah said. "But Daddy is looking to it. They will get him the best treatment, I promise."

I sighed. "Thank you, Elijah. I haven't seen him or heard anything since."

"Just be praying. I don't know if you remember this new minister, Idong Asukwo," Elijah said.

"Huh, I do. I didn't know he is now a minister."

"He is. I think Daddy wants him to marry Calli…"

"Ehn! How? Why would Daddy do this? What of that poor boy, Bosa?"

Elijah shrugged. "You know how Daddy behaves. We were in a meeting. He just turned to Idong and asked him if he didn't want to get married and was he waiting for Angel Michael to carry him to Calli."

"My God! Poor Calli. Do you know what she said?"

"I don't know, Mummy because she wasn't in the meeting. It was a ministers' meeting. But Idong is going after Calli for sure. He has been visiting her every day since Daddy said that thing like two months ago."

"Thank you for telling me all this. I would never have known," I said. But what good was this information to me?

I didn't want to ask for people's numbers from him, but I really wished I could get more news about my children. Elijah chatted a bit about other things happening at the mansion and then left.

I was grateful to him that he came, and told me about my children, but apprehensive of the aftermath of his visit. But I would realise I had no need to worry. He was just feeling guilty as he had said, and nothing more.

As things turned out, Calli did get married to Minister Idong, the man who reminded me so much of my father. I didn't hear about the wedding until a few days before it. I went to our church on the camp, hopeful I could be a part of this joyous occasion, but I was not allowed past the main entrance. My husband had left a standing order about this.

The second surprising visitor I had was John. For a moment, we both stood and just stared at each other. What did he want? After one and a half years of living in the same town!

Since Sunbọ's death, I had not seen him. To my utter shock, I liked the way he looked with a full beard that was almost all grey, and his hair cut low to the scalp. He was the same age as Daddy, but I think he had aged better. He maintained his slender figure and unlike men his age, including Pastor Jide and Daddy, he did not have a budding potbelly.

Seeing John at my doorstep sent me back to the future I could have had. The inner sensations his presence evoked probably would never go away. This should have been my husband, the father of my children.

"Good evening, Bettina," he said softly.

He hadn't called me by my name in over twenty-five years.

"Good evening. John."

He glanced at something behind me, and I took it as the sign I should let him in. For the past several months that I lived alone, Alexa had tried to convince me to get a maid, and Skola offered to let her teenage daughter, Princess, come and live with me, but I declined both offers. I needed my own space. I could wake up in the morning and cry all day without any interference. That was what I wanted.

I stepped back. "Please, come in."

It was early evening on a Saturday I decided I wanted to just lay on my bed and do nothing until sleep took me. I hadn't cooked anything and had only water to offer a guest.

"Thank you," John said, and entered my sitting room. "You have a lovely place here."

"Thank you." I motioned to a chair, and he took it. I sat on another chair. "Sorry I only have water. I don't normally have guests..."

"That's okay," John said. "Thank you." He sighed. "It's good to see you."

"Good to see you too." And I meant it. "It's been...since Sunbo."

"I've wanted to come since I heard you were back in town." He leaned forward. "But one thing or the other just kept me away."

"I guess you've been busy with work, and then elections, new governor, new demands and so on," I said.

He smirked. "Well, not quite, but thanks for pointing out some credible excuses. And leaving out the fact that I just lacked the courage to come here."

It reminded me of so much about us. "You never were one to give excuses."

"No." He sighed. "And sorry about Sunbo. I...I never consoled you and I know how much you two loved each other."

"Yes. Sad."

"I think she was quite happy at the end, though, regardless of what happened," he said. "The house was her dream come true."

I wanted to ask if he knew how she died, but suddenly, talking about Sunbo lost savour.

"You never married, did you?" The words flew out of my mouth before I could stop them. I itched to know. I never asked these questions from Sunbo or anyone who knew him because I felt they were not appropriate.

"Never," he said.

"That must be difficult. No children?"

"None." He scoffed. "My wife was in another man's house."

We were both quiet after that. What could I say? He blamed me for not waiting for him. I blamed me for not waiting for him.

"I'm sorry," I whispered.

"Don't apologize. I guess...we both didn't imagine...such a thing could happen."

I searched his face to see if he meant this and I knew he was lying. "I was careless." It hurt me to my teeth to say this.

"I don't believe so," John said as a matter of fact. "You see, I have not been busy outside office hours, so I've had many hours in many years to think about it. Why I am alone, and you are not."

"And what did you conclude?"

He blinked rapidly. "Unbelievably nothing."

I saw years of pain and agony etched on the wrinkles around his eyes, and through his eyes I could see the depth of his loneliness. He had lived his life holding a grudge and he couldn't hide it anymore. See how his aspiration to one day become a pastor washed down the gutters of disappointment!

"It's okay to blame me. I left..."

John cleared his throat. "You know, I decided to join a very small church just on the street behind yours," he said. "And I thought you may be looking for a congregation to worship with." He chuckled. "Maybe you would even want to join the choir. You must miss singing."

How swiftly he changed the subject when he didn't want to talk about something.

Same old John.

John. How did he know Bettina ~~was not~~ hadn't joined any church and needed one. It seemed like yesterday when we could predict each other. Long ago when our love was pure, innocent, anticipated. Except that I failed us. We both never saw my betrayal coming. We took each other for granted and paid the ultimate price. Loss. John never moved on from it, and here we were... John.

I tried to hold it, but it was impossible. Tears dropped down my cheeks. I was too overwhelmed to clean them. I just sat there crying softly at first, and then sobbing, and weeping. John did nothing about it. He clasped his hands and stared at me. What a ridiculous sight to behold. The forty-nine-year-old woman and her fifty-four-year-old ex-lover, sitting in her parlour, crying.

Crying!

My gaze shot to John, and I realized the wailing was not from me alone.

The following Sunday, John came by my house, and we went to his church together. It wasn't actually his church. It was a new church. We were both first-time visitors.

Chapter 62

OLIVE NEDION'S FATHER HAD a lot of money and big friends, though many of them knew Daddy and revered him. Still, Olive could go on a major national talk show with Hermon and answer candid questions about her main thoughts on the church.

"Do you go to church?" The show's presenter asked.

"I do. God is a good God with animals who try to impersonate him," Olive said. "I am not here to try God but to make it clear that my son has a father, and we know him even if he denies it from now until kingdom come."

Olive raised two pictures, one of Adam at age seventeen and one of Hermon. No one could argue the resemblance.

"How do you feel about this, Hermon?" the presenter turned from Olive's pictures to Hermon.

"I am relieved. My mum suffered many years trying to get this family to acknowledge me. I don't care about it. My mum and grandparents are more than enough," Hermon said. "But it means something to my mum, so I will support her through and through."

"We have Calli Jaja Asukwo's audio-visual recording, pleading for her brother's mistake," Olive said. "But a rape happened. There was a crime, and it must be punished."

Calli sat on the couch in Chloe's apartment and watched the interview Olive and Hermon granted, with her attention on her phone most of the time.

Chloe hissed. "She will get nothing. The media will eat her up. How dare she challenge Daddy's family? Hian!"

Calli grabbed the TV remote control and muted the show. "How are you doing?" She turned to Chloe.

Chloe snickered. "Fine, thank you, Aunty." She mimicked a child's voice and then snapped. "Why did you mute the show?"

It was over a year since Nat died, since Chloe broke everything breakable in Daddy's office, since she cursed out loud at her father in the presence of church and mansion staff, since Daddy decided to lock her up in this apartment until she came to her senses. Whatever coming to her senses meant.

Nothing mattered.

Only Calli came to see her, like a ritual, every single day unless she was out of town, and Calli didn't go out of town a lot. And when Calli visited, she watched a movie, or a TV show, tried to make small talk, which never worked, and left after a few minutes. So much like Mummy did in those days when she returned from the UK.

"You know, Chloe, a lot is going on, and I know I have never spoken to you a great deal, but it's time we do something for ourselves." Calli heaved. "Why are you locked up like this under watch for days, weeks, months, years soon. Only allowed to go to church."

Chloe threw back her head. "I don't care. And guess what, I met Feyi's son. Oh. My. God. What a bloke. I've asked Daddy to transfer him here. He's a PAB. He's resuming on my floor next week."

"Daddy agreed?"

"Of course. Why won't he? He knows what it's like to burn!"

Calli gasped. "Chloe! Don't be rude."

"Yes?! I am a human for goodness' sake. I need a man. You and your Idong move around the mansion kissing and making out. Yeah, I see you every day!"

"Chai, every day, Chloe. That's not true."

Chloe hissed. "Huh huh. And you have a little bump. Even though you didn't tell me."

"I'm sorry I didn't tell you. There has just been a lot going on..."

Chloe clapped. "Yeah, the baby bump says it all."

"If I didn't know you better, Chloe..."

"It's alright darling sis. You live your life anyway you want. Right now, I don't care. I have a really handsome guy in my radar, and he is a Christian, at least, though that may be a little problem if he is stiff like you," Chloe said.

"Would you care if I told you I have been here before? When Bosa became paralyzed, and Daddy came to take me out of his house." Calli shook her head. "I was so angry, so miserable. I was so helpless. And I was just in my room. Daddy forbade anyone from seeing me. I couldn't go out except to church. For two weeks, under watch two-four-seven. In prison. Then he sent Idong my way."

"Why are you telling me this? I don't even want to go out anyway," Chloe said. "My sunshine has set for life. Although, really, I must confess, you and Idong really really got my blood pumping again."

Calli's chest rose and fell as her breaths came quicker with the excitement to tell all. "Do you know how I got out of it? Idong. He was my passport to my…" she wrote inverted commas in the air. "Freedom. I hated Idong more than the devil, but he was the solution Daddy brought. I could live my life again if I forgot Bosa. Daddy made me swear never to go near Bosa again or Bosa would disappear."

Chloe arched an eyebrow. "Daddy stoop that low to threaten you?"

"He sent his footmen. Minister Elijah particularly. Daddy's Angel Gabriel."

Chloe burst into laughter. "That's a good name for him, though. You are a clown."

Calli exclaimed. "You laughed, Chloe!"

"Of course, I laugh." Chloe snickered. "It doesn't mean I have joy."

"For all these years, I never smile or laugh with Idong." Calli sighed. "Until after I read Mummy's book."

Chloe's eyes widened. "You told me you threw it away."

"Because that was the only way I could keep it from Daddy."

"Isn't Mummy going to publish? She'll make a lot of money from all the juicy tales of how I got pregnant!" Chloe smirked. "Nonsense."

"You read it too!" Calli shouted. "You told Daddy you didn't."

"I wasn't reading it at the time. Until they locked me here like a prisoner. Going only for church meetings and with escorts. I got bored."

Calli shook her head. "You're lying. You read it before coming here. Or did you go back to pack your clothes and decided to take it with you?"

Chloe smirked. "I finished that book the first three days after I got it. Full of nonsense grammar errors, she mixed up our ages, and dates of events, but I give it to your mother, she has words. But what did I care? She wrote her story, not mine."

"You have to care. Daddy used this tactic on Mummy, and she ended up divorced. He used it on me, and I married a man I knew nothing about, at least thank God now, he seems interested in pleasing me." Calli moaned. "You have to care, Chloe, you don't know what Daddy is going to shove down your neck after he's done locking you up here."

Chloe rested back on her chair. "It worked on you and Mummy because you hated what Daddy was doing to you. I. Don't. Care." She stood and went to pour a glass of juice for herself from the fridge. "Care for some? You've been talking a lot tonight."

Calli grunted. "No, thanks." She sighed. "Anyway, if you don't care about leaving Daddy's imprisonment, it's your business. I need your help. And I need to ask Daddy a favour."

Chloe shook her head. "I don't need Daddy's favour."

So much for talking about important issues with Chloe. Calli had hoped she could bring up what happened with the twins and get them to come to live in the mansion with Chloe and under Daddy's protection. But the request had to come from Chloe. The girls were her children. Calli planned to bring Mummy back too. But again, it was better Chloe asked. Chloe played a vital role in this Jaja family redemption plan.

"Dara came to church. OPJ has been sexually molesting your twins." Calli watched Chloe for reaction, there was none. "Dara wants us to either get Daddy on the matter or kidnap the girls. And I'm all in but I need you, Chloe. And we need Daddy. And Mummy. There is a clear plan and Mummy needs to be in it too. Mummy, we need to find her. We need to reconcile. We need to get our family back together." Calli fought tears.

Without Calli seeing it coming, Chloe threw her glass cup with the juice at the security door and it crashed with a loud noise. Calli screamed.

Ms. Feyi ran in from outside. "Blood of Jesus!"

Chloe followed her action with a hair-raising shriek. "I will kill OPJ."

Calli slumped and chuckled and swiped tears from her eyes. "At least now, I have your attention."

Epilogue

IF OLIVE NEDION KNEW her talk show edition would go viral the way it did, perhaps she would have not done it. A national television news station invited her to their most-watched show, and without Olive's knowledge, Daddy came on the show too. Olive as usual brought Hermon and in Daddy's usual calm, and unassuming way, he asked Hermon if he would be a guest at Jaja Mansion.

The poor boy stammered, "Yes, Daddy!"

The presenter clapped. "God be praised."

Olive was not invited, and I knew what that meant. Olive may not see her son again in a very long time. Daddy had stepped in!

I watched the show with John, who had become my regular visitor after our teary reunion. Were we dating? We couldn't. But we were not too far from each other. John did not like the way I lived alone, so I got a housekeeper, a middle-aged mother of five called Mama Ibeji.

At first, Mama Ibeji came in the morning and left in the evening. I later discovered her five children lived with her aged mother after her husband dumped her for a younger woman and threw her and the children out of the house. It was no longer an option for me, and I invited her to move in. Mama Ibeji became my closest ally after John.

Dear John, who had excelled in his career and risen to become a director in the ministry of finance, and later a commissioner before he retired early to run his own business consulting firm. He came by my house every evening and we chatted till late. We resumed our weekly prayer and fasting. He prayed with me and helped me untangle some of my emotions. We discussed my children at length and prayed about them. This man was my soulmate and how could I have lost him?

Since I got married shortly after I graduated, I had never worked in my life. John thought it was important for me to get a job. One, it helped to pay my bills. News blew it wide open that Daddy paid me several hundreds of millions of naira in divorce settlement, but it must have gone to a wrong bank account because I didn't get any of it. A newspaper went as far as printing documents with my signature and Daddy's, evidence of the monies I received. But I got nothing. It reminded me of how Chloe forged my signature to get into the choir. Was she contacted to do this too? I decided not to make a big deal out of all this. So, I got a job as an after-care coordinator at a nursery and primary school. At first, it was awkward for some of the teachers who knew my history, but everyone soon got used to having me around.

Eventually, with some funding from a grant John helped to apply for, I started a day care centre of my own. He bought a car for me and taught me how to drive at the age of fifty.

Elijah kept me updated on everything happening with my children. Chloe continued to be married to the old man, and seemed to settle down, and remained close to Daddy. Calli married Idong, and I watched the ceremony on YouTube after I was disgraced away from the gate of the camp. Elijah had warned me not to come because Daddy had some people on standby to throw me out if I showed up, but who would take such a silly advice. Adam was indicted on rape charges but was too mentally sick to stand trial. Daddy and Idong travelled to escort him home because he was deported and banned from the UK.

Only Ben remained in direct contact with me. My sweet son, however, was not interested in getting married to anyone. He just wanted to dedicate his whole life to God's service. He didn't want to come home either, but we at least tried to speak any week he was in a location he could get good network connection. He answered all my emails promptly, though.

Elijah stopped calling. I saw in the news a church was opening in Asia, and Elijah had been ordained to be the Bishop of Asia. My last insider to my church was gone. I knew I had to find a way to get back in but how? How was I to contact my children without an inside person? How did I hope to get my book to them when I was done writing?

Maybe Chloe and Calli ~~will~~ would come around when they read this book. I ~~can~~ could only pray. I have no idea on how to get Adam's copy to him but if any of my girls could get theirs, I could trust them to give Adam. Ben confirmed receipt of his, but I doubt he will read it. Then, John got a friend in Festac who agreed to send them out with DHL and use his address for possible return. I was sure Chloe and Calli would get their copies, but would they read? And if they read, respond?

John thought it is too revealing to make it public, and he thinks all the gossip ghosts will rise again and descend on me. So, I will just wait to hear from my children. Adam should be healed by now. Elijah had made it clear he didn't know where Adam was, and I could only pray.

"Adam is hiding from God," Elijah said. "But be praying. There's a call on his life."

I chose to start writing this story five years after my divorce because the silence is killing me. John encouraged me and helped with the editing, though I know I will still need a professional editor to read through but not before my children see and read.

I want my children to read and decide for themselves. Do I deserve to be left out of their lives after all these years?

Did they receive their copies? And did they read? How would I ever know? I want to reconcile back with them. I haven't heard from Adam since I saw him in London. Chloe is still married, I hope. I know Calli had a son, and I would love to be a part of his life. Ben...Ben will never return home, but I pray he doesn't forget it.

I have been praying for all these years, but now I just need to tell my story.

The End.

Thank you for purchasing my book. If you enjoyed this novel, *I'll Tell My Story*, please leave a review.

Thanks again!

Acknowledgments

For the first time in my twenty years of writing, I acknowledge myself in the writing of this book. I acknowledge my courage in bringing it from nothing to what it is today, a book of hard truths. It is a book God put in my heart to write for a long time, but my fear of rejection and criticism made me hold back. So, I say thank you God for keeping this story livid in Sinmi and thank you Sinmi for finally writing it.

Oh, psst! I must acknowledge my sister, Kike Kuponiyi, for saving me from professional disgrace with her advice on legal matters, and my dear friend of over twenty years, Onose Callima Inino MD, for taking time out of her crazy-busy schedule to read and feedback. God bless you both.

ARE YOU SAVED?

All that is written in this book may not be of much use to you if you haven't yet given your life to Christ. We cannot take difficult decisions unless we have the Righteous and Wise One who is greater than the devil to help and choose for us. The Bible says that "greater is he that is in you, than he that is in the world." (1 John 4:4 King James Version) And "we wrestle not against flesh and blood, but against principalities, against powers, against the rulers of the darkness of this world, against spiritual wickedness in high places." (Ephesians 6:12).

This is why I want to encourage you to take this important decision if you haven't yet given your life to Christ. I took this decision over twenty-five years ago, and I haven't regretted it even for one day. Please pray this prayer of faith if you are willing to surrender your life to God:

Lord Jesus, I honour you. I praise you, and I acknowledge you that you are Lord. I know I am a sinner, and I ask that you forgive me all my sins. I want you to be my lord and personal saviour. Wash me clean and give me grace to serve you wholly from now on. Come into my heart to reign supreme. In Jesus' name, I pray. Amen.

PRAISE GOD, YOU ARE BORN AGAIN.

Now that you have prayed this prayer of faith, I admonish you to

•Get a Bible and read it every day. (Start from the first four books of the New Testament to familiarize yourself more with your new commander in chief, Jesus Christ.)

•Pray every day.

•Attend a Living Church.

•Introduce yourself to the pastor and seek further teaching. (You can join the foundation class and activity group in church. You are, hence, making yourself available to work for God.)

•Tell others about your salvation.

May God help you in Jesus' name? Amen.

The Nigerian Child: My Vision

Then the LORD answered me and said: "Write the vision and make it plain on tablets, that he may run who reads it." —Hab. 2:2

More than before, it's time for the well-to-do to cater for the less privileged. Over the past few years, the Lord has laid this burden for The Nigerian Child on my heart, and I believe it's time to spread the vision. I have a desire to help and to instigate help for The Nigerian Child. There are currently five areas of help I have been able to identify.

1. The Market-school Project: This vision is aimed at eradicating street and market hawking in the long run. The strategy is to erect schools in marketplaces where children hawking can take a few hours out to learn and then go back to their jobs. It is a long-term project and a highly capital intensive one.

2. The Bread and Milk Project: Bread and milk will be given in the morning to children trekking to school just before school resumes. It can be done once a month, once a week, or every day or as rampantly as the provision is available. It is not very capital intensive, and as little as N50 or $0.35 USD can feed a child with bread and warm milk.

3. The Umbrella Project: This will help alleviate the suffering of children who hawk on the streets (while we work toward eradicating hawking on our streets) by providing umbrellas, especially during the rainy season. The umbrellas can also be useful during the scorching hot weathers. Umbrellas of different sizes will be given depending on the size of the child. Prices of umbrellas range from N1400.00 to N2100.00 or $2.00 to $3.00 USD.

4. The Sort-a-child Project: This is aimed at helping at least a child in whatever capacity you can. It can be by paying a sick child's hospital bills, buying food and clothing for a child, or paying a child's school fees. It can be as long as a lifetime commitment or a onetime affair.

5. The Student Care Project: This is for secondary and tertiary students who can't afford their school fees. The idea is to help through the bob-a-job initiative.

The Nigerian Child vision is not another nongovernmental, money-spinning organisation. It is service to God and provision for The Nigerian Child. It can be done privately or corporately. The important thing is to help a Nigerian child.

I beg to challenge every church in Nigeria to adopt the sort-a-child project or as the Lord lay it on our hearts.

HELP! Signed

- THE NIGERIAN CHILD

Also By Sinmisọla Ogúnyinka

Blue Dawn

Frail Flesh

Scent of Water

Her Lover

Pepper

Foreverland

The Days after that Night

Tisha

Under a Red Delta Sun

Way of the Unfaithful